Halley's Casino

Written By

Mark JG Fahey

Library and Archives Canada Cataloguing in Publication

First Paperback Edition: January 2016

The characters and events portrayed in this book are fictitious. Any similarity to real persons, living or dead, is coincidental and not intended by the author.

Fahey, Mark, 2016 --
Halley's Casino: The Adventures of Nebula Yorker: a novel / by Mark Fahey. – 1st ed.

ISBN 978-0-9948918-0-8 (Paperback)
Copy write registration # 112506

I. Title.

PS8611.A43H35 2015 C813'.6 C2015-906621-2

Edited by Mary Taker Baskin and Helen Durrant

Jacket photo by Michael Gagnon. Cover design by Mark JG Fahey and Lili O'Reilly

Halley's Casino

For Rosemary

No one really knows the future.

Sometimes just living in the present is enough.

Thinking about the future is really just that, thinking.

In my case, the past is the future.

Nebula Yorker, Rome, 12 BCE

February 16, 1986, 1:16 AM
Woodside Hills, California

Nebula Yorker reclined on the cool grass and looked up through his telescope into the clear early morning sky. Stars, planets and faraway galaxies reached down to his searching eyes. After a few minutes of stargazing, he turned his lantern up a notch so he could unpack his knapsack and take out his notepad, pencil and thermos. Pulling the cup from the thermos, he slowly twisted the cap. The coffee aroma drifted up and out. Steaming, cosmic-like vapours of coffee danced around and reached his nostrils. He took it in with a smile and poured a cup. Drawing it up to his mouth, he could feel the heat as it began to burn his lips. He knew he should stop but he couldn't. His body instinctively straightened up and half the coffee flew from his mouth, shooting out over the top of the telescope lens and himself.

"Shit. Shit, shit!" Neb cried. Reaching back into the knapsack, he snatched out the lens cloth and, within seconds, was cleaning off the lens with cat-like quickness. "That's all I need right now," he said to himself. *Good thing there was no sugar in the coffee*, he thought. *That would have been a disaster.*

Satisfied that no damage had been done, Neb readjusted the telescope. He peered into it, adjusting the lens back to where it had been pointed.

"Hello, Mr. Big Dipper," he whispered, reclining back on the grass. Then, clutching the thermos, he poured another cup, this time gently blowing on the hot liquid before he took another sip. *Mmm, that's better*, he thought.

Leaning back on his elbows, cup in hand, looking up at the brilliant night sky, his thoughts turned to his Mom and Dad and how they had so longed for 1986 to arrive. To see it twice in their lifetime had been a dream and a goal. They had both been ten years old when they first saw it in 1910. Neb sighed sadly as he thought of them. He missed them terribly.

He was six years old when they had adopted him 20 years before. He never understood why, at the age of 66, they had decided to adopt. But he didn't object. He'd just been grateful to get out of that orphanage and begin a somewhat normal life. Being raised by older parents was an adventure for Neb as it had been for the Yorkers and something he would never trade for anything imaginable, not even to find out who his birth parents were and why they gave him away. Though, like anyone who was adopted, it did cross his mind now and then but never to the point of obsession. Perhaps there was a good reason for their decision; perhaps one day he would know, or maybe not. He didn't think it made a difference in how he turned out and how he was raised and loved by the Yorkers. He was Nebula Yorker – Neb to his friends.

He remembered that day so etched in his mind – Thursday, July 10, 1966, 11 AM. He was washing the dishes in the kitchen, standing on a footstool so he could reach the sink. He heard the footsteps behind him. His hearing had always been impeccable, even at an early age, making him imagine he had superpowers. Now if he could only fly away from this place. Before he heard her voice, he knew it was Miss Strummer, the matron of Saint Joseph's Orphanage.

"That's him, the small one on the stool." Her voice snarled as it always did. "Get your ass over here. These nice people want to get a look at you!"

A shiver ran down his spine as it always did when he heard or saw Miss Strummer. A portly five-feet-four inches of mean. Never had a good thing to say about anyone. Turning slowly around and thinking, *now what have I done?* Neb saw them standing like giants above and behind her. The plate in his hand slipped and crashed to the floor. He cringed, watching in slow motion as the plate dissected itself everywhere. His face reddened and he looked up and saw that Miss Strummer's face was about to explode into her regular fiery rage but, for some reason, it didn't.

"He's yours! Good riddance!" She faced the older couple and stomped out of the kitchen. Neb leaped off the stool, avoiding any shrapnel from the plate, and ran into the waiting arms of one Mrs. Victoria Yorker. It was just instinct. He did that without thinking. To her right stood her husband, Neb's new father, Mr. Bancroft Yorker. Bending down now, face to face, eye to eye, he gave Neb a hug and whispered in his ear.

"This is the first day of the beginning of your life, the one that you should have had at the start." With that, Neb walked out with his new Mom and Dad, holding tightly to their hands swinging him back and forth. He remembered walking out the front door of Saint Joseph's and seeing Miss Strummer, her eyes glaring down at him for the last time. He stuck out his tongue at her. It was picture perfect, as only a six-year old boy can do.

"Now that wasn't very nice," said Mrs. Yorker, with a grin. Mr. Yorker just winked and smiled.

Coming back to the present, Neb took out his notepad and pencil. Gazing back up at the night sky, he began to write.

1:35 AM - Feels like I am watching and waiting for a kettle to boil. Nothing as yet, though I remain optimistic that soon it will appear.

Placing his notepad and pencil down, he remembered something. He pulled out a photo from the back. It slipped from his hands onto the now dewy grass. He picked it up and gave it a quick shake. He beamed with pride looking at it. It was his favorite picture of his Mom and Dad. They were standing outside the Griffith Observatory in Los Angeles, California. He remembered the day he had taken it as if it were yesterday. How could he not? It was his sixteenth birthday. Below the photo was written:

> Nebula, when you reach for the stars, anything is possible.
>
> Let your star shine radiantly wherever you find yourself.
>
> Always remember, the goal is to move forward. The past, present and future lie above, which we strive to reach and understand.
>
> Happy 16th Birthday, May 10, 1976
>
> Love always, Mom & Dad

He kissed the photo and placed it on top of the scope so that they both could get a good look when it came into view. *Man! I wish they could be here, all three of us together*, he thought. He rubbed a few tears from his eyes and smiled.

For 18 years, they were stitched together for the most part. They would take him everywhere with them. London. Paris. Rome. Greece. Germany. You name it, they were there, except for two weeks every August from the 15th to the 30th .

Neb would then be left with some of their university colleagues while they went off to the Amazon. He did ask them once why they always went alone and why they did not take him. Downtime, you know, personal stuff, they would say. In the end, he really didn't mind. He kind of got to live like a kid and hang out with other kids his age during those two weeks – swimming, fishing, camping, and to enjoy his own downtime.

Both Victoria and Bancroft Yorker were professors who taught at the University of California, Berkeley. Bancroft's field was Astronomy and Earth and Planetary Science. Victoria's specialty was in Science and Quantum Physics Mathematics. As for Neb, he knew a little of just about everything there was to know. He chalked it up to the benefits of home schooling and never gave it a second thought. He never went to grade school or high school or any school, for that matter. Everything came naturally to him. You only needed to tell him something once and he retained it. He was a proverbial sponge, so to speak, and having the Yorkers as teachers wasn't a bad thing either.

He didn't miss out on the entire hijinks that kids go through. He had a few friends in the neighborhood and they could be somewhat mischievous. Like the first time they smoked pot. Pot was Neb's Kryptonite. His brain just didn't function as it should, not that anyone's does on pot. It was indeed a trip, an inner, outer, in and back out again adventure. Quite amusing at times. Its effect on him was slightly different. He got high and laughed, listened to rock 'n' roll like the rest, as they did back then. He would go into a state of flux where everything that he knew became tangled. He saw faces and places he had never been to, as though he had. Or perhaps he was just stoned, who knows? It was trippy to say the least. Once he started to mellow out, all became clear once again. Of course, the munchies would soon overtake logic and everything else.

Neb had worked part time since he was 17, and still did, at Free Bee's Record Shop. Not that he needed to. He had enough funds without working. After his Mom and Dad disappeared on their last trip to the Amazon and were declared missing and dead two years earlier, he inherited everything. He spent a year searching, retracing their every step, every movement. Every lead ended up empty, a cold trail in the Amazon. It was as though they had vanished from the face of the earth.

Victoria and Bancroft Yorker were quite the unique odd couple if ever there was one, but in a good way. They never seemed to have aged from the first day they rescued Neb. He remembered that they had never been sick, not once. Never saw a doctor. Never took pills of any kind. He realized that he had never been sick either. He liked to think that they were out there somewhere, perhaps doing what sneaky 86-year-olds do. And to believe that they were cuddling together somewhere under the stars. Perhaps sitting around a campfire with their own telescope set up, looking up at the same sky, waiting for that one magical moment to happen, as he was now doing. That's how he liked to think of them, retired and living happily. No one is really gone as long as you remember them, ever.

Neb stood up and gave his body a good stretch, bending fingers to toes, slowly breathing in and out. His eyes stared over to the brush. All this moving about had given his bladder pause. The coffee wanted out. He stood there looking, thinking. He had heard that Neil Young, the musician, lived nearby and hoped that he was not trespassing on his property, though it would have been cool to meet him. He was sure that if he did meet him, Mr. Young would appreciate what was taking place. Not the peeing of course. He zipped up, refreshed, ready to continue on with his task.

Heading back to his telescope, he tripped and fell face down. Grass and dirt stuck to the side of his mouth. *I didn't see that coming*, he thought. Slowly, he got up, dusting himself off and spitting out little bits of grime. He looked up. *I see it! I can really see it!* Dashing over to the telescope, he took a deep breath and peered in.

There it is,finally!

HALLEY'S COMET!

WOW! He gushed. He couldn't get over it. It's really there. It was named after the English astronomer Edmond Halley, who, in

1705, had determined the comet's periodicity, meaning its tendency to recur at regular intervals every 75-76 years.

Halley's prediction proved to be correct. The comet returned on December 25, 1758, though he did not live to see it again. Throughout history, the comet had made itself known, from 240 BCE onward. Chinese, Babylonian, Roman and Medieval European chroniclers had reported sightings, but they were not recognized as a reappearance of the same object at the time.

Halley's Comet is the only short-period comet that is clearly visible to the naked eye from Earth and the only such comet to appear twice in a lifetime, if you're fortunate enough to live that long. Edmond Halley's confirmation of the comet's return was the first time anything other than planets had been shown to orbit the Sun. It has probably been in its current orbit for 16,000–200,000 years, give or take a century or two or three. Halley's projected lifetime could be as long as ten million years, or less depending on past, present and future developments.

What's that saying?

"*What goes around usually comes around.*"

At last! Neb gasped looking up at the comet. Nervous enthusiasm rattled his whole body like a kid in a candy store waiting for that first bite of chocolate, cotton candy, a jawbreaker, a long stick of licorice, if you're prone to be into that sort of thing. High up above the atmosphere, Halley's Comet soared. Pulling his head away from the lens, Neb was as giddy as could be. Looking up again, he could see it; it was now visible to the naked eye.

AMAZING! BRILLANT! OUTSTANDING!

He danced a little jig around the telescope, enthused, jubilant and overflowing with joy. He stopped and looked around, hoping no one was watching. Then he didn't really care. He watched the comet through the lens, so beautiful, so far away. As he continued to gaze at it, it almost felt like it was moving closer to him. Drawing away again from the lens, he could see it moving towards him. He thought, *it can't be!*

Wait! That's not a comet. Peeking through the lens once more, he did a double take. It was unbelievable! It was definitely moving, and in his direction. He fell back on his ass. It was now hovering above him, a small glowing ball of light. It almost resembled a jellyfish floating on air; it made no sound whatsoever, just hovered. He lay motionless on the ground as the jellyfish-like object positioned itself about ten feet above him. He could have pissed his pants if he had not emptied his bladder 15 minutes earlier.

In what seemed like an eternity, but was probably about 10 seconds, the object the size of a football sat above him, and then zipped into the nearby brush. Staring up from the cool ground, Neb could see Halley's Comet, picture perfect, also looming over him, protecting him, as it were. *What the hell just happened?* Still lying on the ground, he turned his head to the left and looked straight into the woods where whatever it was had entered.

OK, he said to himself, *let's try and be methodical about this*. Standing still, though not overly frightened by this event, he could hear his father's voice as if he was teaching him one of his lessons.

Now, Neb, what do we do next?

MOVE FORWARD, he heard. *Always move forward*. Slowly, and without a second thought, he moved forward towards the trees and entered. Broken twigs crackled beneath his feet, a light breeze hit his face. He raised his hand to push away a branch in front of him. It flipped back, slapping him directly in the face. The swipe burned and the branch swung back, hitting him again. As if once weren't enough. It stung but he somehow held back from screaming out loud, not wanting to disturb whatever might be waiting.

His eyes darted from side to side, back and forth like he was in a Bugs Bunny cartoon. He could hear up ahead what sounded like water trickling, perhaps twenty to thirty feet away. It was so dark though that he was not sure; when he found this spot the week before, he really did not do much surveying except for the opening where his telescope now sat alone, waiting for his return.

Suddenly, a bright beaming light overshadowed the entire circumference of the brush where he stood, as if someone had switched on the lights at a ballpark. He held his hands to his face to shield his eyes from the light. Opening his fingers, he peeked through and could now make out the shadow of a figure standing next to a tree.

The figure began to move slowly towards him. His feet were like cement; he wanted to move, but couldn't or wouldn't. He was immobilized with fascination. Most of the light seemed to be emanating from the head of the figure, as if the moon was reflecting off it. Or was it the other way around?

The light now began to dissipate and, as it did, his eyes quickly adjusted back to his surroundings.

It was a man, a short stocky man, about five feet tall. The hair on his head was pure white, as though the light had absorbed itself back into his full head of hair. He wore a black tuxedo, a white shirt with a black bow tie, and on his feet were the most shocking, intense red shoes Neb had ever seen.

All he could do was say hello.

"Hello there!" an enthusiastic British accented voice answered. "Sorry about the glare. It usually takes a few minutes to die down."

"Of course it does," Neb said, as if everything was normal.

"I really had to drain the lizard." The little man zipped up his trousers.

“Excuse me?” Neb asked.

“I had to relieve my bladder, dear boy. People haven’t stopped peeing, have they?”

“Not as far as I know,” Neb answered, wondering who this guy was and how he had come out of the middle of nowhere. He thought maybe he was a stray from one of Neil Young’s parties or something. He looked harmless enough.

“What’s with the red shoes?” Neb blurted out. He felt as though he had to say it. The man looked down at his shoes and back up at Neb.

“They are kind of bright, aren’t they? Never really seemed to notice before, but they are so very comfortable and the anti-gravity hopper inserts really do cushion the feet. Forgive me. Archibald Tict at your service,” He bowed and held out his hand to shake Neb’s. Neb hesitated for a second, then held out his hand.

“Nebula Yorker,” he replied as they shook hands.

“You can call me Mr. Tict, which most do, or just plain ole Tict,” he smiled.

“Most of my friends call me Neb. Hmm, I don’t mean to be rude or anything, but where did you come from?” Neb asked, rubbing his chin. “I thought that I was all alone out here.”

“Where did I come from? London, England or, more precisely, I was born in London, England in the year 1707.”

Tict quickly changed the subject.

“Hey, did I spot a telescope out in the clearing?” Tict pointed and started to make his way out from the brush, walking past Neb.

What is happening here? Neb thought to himself. He wondered if there was an old folks' home or an insane asylum nearby.

"No, there isn't," Tict shouted back at him.

Neb hadn't said anything. He turned to see Tict exiting the bushes. By the time he reached him, he was sitting, pouring himself the last cup of coffee from Neb's thermos.

"Wow! Real coffee beans! Remind me to pick some up before we leave." Tict continued to drink the last cup of coffee as Neb looked on.

"I am glad you like it, Mr. Tict, but, more importantly, who are you and what is going on here?"

"My dear boy, you may drop the 'mister' part of the name. Tict will do fine."

"OK Tict, here's the question. Did you happen to see a hovering white mass flying around here?"

"What? Are you on drugs or something?" Tict took another sip. "Mmmm, good to the last drop." Tict finished the coffee, shook the cup and returned it to the thermos, twisting it back on. Now turning his attention back to Neb, he said, "Now, what was it you were saying? Oh yes, a hovering white mass of light. Did it look like a kind of jellyfish floating in midair?"

"Yes, yes." Neb finally thought he was getting somewhere.

"Sorry, can't say that I have."

Neb tilted his head down, shaking it in dismay, not knowing what to make of this tuxedo-clad hobbit-like man.

"Hey, is that Halley's Comet, Neb?" Tict sheepishly pointed up, changing the subject again.

"Yes, it is Halley's Comet." Neb looked down at his wristwatch. It was 2:05 AM. "Where's my notepad?" Neb asked, searching the ground.

"Looking for this?" Tict held up the notepad and pencil. "Give me that!" Neb grabbed for it and missed.

"Now, now, don't be rude." Tict handed it to Neb.

"I am sorry. It's late and I am getting tired and you drank my last cup of coffee." Neb sighed heavily. "I'm sorry, Mr. Tict. I mean Tict." If his parents had taught him anything, it was to be polite to strangers and this Mr. Tict was strange indeed. He kind of reminded Neb of a tic.

"That's OK, Neb. I can understand." Tict patted Neb on the back.

"Now, where were we? Oh, yes, a white hovering mass of light."

"So you did see it? I thought I was going crazy. No offence, Tict."

"None taken, my dear boy." Tict moved towards the telescope. "Yes, I did see it. Or rather, that white glowing mass was me," Tict said, looking into the scopes lens.

"What do you mean, it was you?" Neb sarcastically quipped. "And I'm a giant ball of belly button fuzz."

"Well, you asked." Tict gestured Neb over. "Come here and take a peek." He moved away while Neb peered into the telescope lens.

"I don't see anything." Neb pulled back and looked at Tict. "Wait! I don't see anything!" Neb straightened up and looked to the sky. "Where did it go?"

"Where did what go? You mean Halley's Comet?" Tict grinned.

"Yes, crazy man! Halley's Comet! Where did it go?"

"Do you know this is the first time in 75 years that I have taken in real fresh air, not that any kind of air isn't real. Recycled air just doesn't have the same freshness that makes it real fresh air. Thus, fresh air. My lungs are getting a high out of this." As Tict breathed in, his nostrils flared open, taking in deep snorts of air. "Man, this is good stuff." He stood there with his eyes closed.

"Don't change the subject. What do you mean you haven't breathed in fresh air for over 75 years? Have you been locked up somewhere?" Neb asked, thinking, *Yeah, I think you might be high on something. I don't think it's the air. Are you one of Neil Young's friends or something? He's having a party and you slipped out or got lost?* Neb sighed, shaking his head. "I give up."

"Oh, never give up, never, my dear boy," said Tict in an alarmed voice, but with a soft tone. "Look, I know all of this must be confusing at the moment and you're wondering what's going on. Who am I? Where did Halley's Comet go? Why am I not at home having a cup of hot chocolate watching reruns of *Star Trek*? Or running a hot bubble bath but then at the last moment you forget to add the bubbles because you decide to make a cheese sandwich and in the meantime your bathtub has overflowed and your downstairs neighbors who are watching *Star Trek* reruns start to notice drips of water falling through their ceiling while they drink their hot chocolate and eat cheese sandwiches. It's all so relevant, you know, when you think about it."

"Look, Halley's is back," Tict pointed upwards.

"That was a mouthful and yes a few answers would be nice and your analogy about the hot chocolate and cheese sandwich was interesting and *Star Trek* was oddly spot on. Have you been stalking me or something, because I'm feeling a little creepy just about now?" Neb stepped back.

"Stalking you? By no means!" Tict replied reassuringly. "Well, that's good to know," Neb said and looked down at his watch. It was 2:25 AM.

With no coffee left to keep him going and Halley's Comet not going anywhere, he thought perhaps he would try again the next night for another opportunity to observe Halley's. "It's been nice to meet you, Tict, but I am afraid it's time for me to pack it in." Neb yawned and proceeded to dismantle the telescope.

Tict sat on the grass watching him quietly. Neb's head was full of thoughts watching Tict as Tict watched him.

"You're not some kind of alien, are you?" Neb broke the strange silence between them.

"Alien?" Tict's voice shot up once again, alive with enthusiasm. "By Jove, no," he replied, "Not that aliens exist and, really, what does alien mean? To someone not from Earth, let's say, who would be considered the alien, the visitor or the native?" he said.

"I guess it might depend on the circumstance," Neb replied. "Does the alien look like, you know, human, or is it a big blue, green, ten-eyed creature? Then again, it depends on one's perspective. Just as long as it doesn't want to eat me or something like that," Neb mused.

"You wouldn't have to worry about that, Neb, everyone knows that big blue, green, ten-eyed creatures are vegetarians," Tict remarked solemnly.

Neb wasn't sure if he was being serious or not; it just felt that way. They both laughed.

"Now, on the other hand, I might be considered a foreigner as opposed to an alien, being British, "Tict said.

"Do you have your green card?" Neb asked. "Green card? What is that?"

"How long have you been in the country, then?"

"In the country? My dear boy, I've only been on the planet for less than two hours!"

"Tict, it's now 2:30 AM. I am really tired, confused and out of coffee. I am going home. I'll try and forget about all of this, take a warm bath, sans bubbles, no cocoa or cheese sandwich, and jump into bed. When I wake up after a nice restful sleep, excuse the pun, this will all be an odd dream of a strange alien encounter. By the way, you're not an alien from another world, are you?" Neb asked again, this time jokingly. They both laughed again.

"Wait!" Tict started. "Before we go, may I tell you a story?"

Before we go? We? Neb thought it strange of Tict to say this. Did this odd little, but likable, man figure on following him?

"It won't take long," Tict said.

Neb thought about it for a few seconds.

"OK. If you must." Neb sat down on a small chair. As Tict began his story, Neb started wondering where the chair came from. He also noticed Tict was sitting on a similar chair.

To hell with it, he thought, and settled in to listen. He didn't think this could get any weirder than it already was. Maybe a cup of hot chocolate and a cheese sandwich wasn't such a bad idea.

Tict straightened up in the chair and began.

2

"It's been such a long time since I last told my story that I sometimes don't believe it myself." Tict chuckled to himself. "The past, present and future lie above, which all intelligent beings strive to reach and understand." Tict stopped, looked to the starry sky, and then back at Neb. Neb could hardly believe what he had just heard.

"What did you just say?" Neb cut in, wide-eyed.

"I was saying, the past, present and future…" he opened his mouth.

"Yes, I heard what you said," Neb cut him off again.

"If you heard what I said, then why are you asking me to repeat it?" Tict gave Neb a dry look.

"My father used to tell me the same thing." Neb reached over to the telescope and retrieved the photo of his parents and handed it to Tict. Tict gently took the photo from his hand. He looked at it for a couple of minutes in silence and handed it back.

"Oh my, isn't that a coincidence. Though I don't believe in coincidences, or do I?" Tict slyly grinned and winked at Neb.

Question after question filled Neb's head. He wanted to ask them but thought it better to wait it out. He wondered what this strange pull was that Tict now had on him.

"Please continue," Neb politely motioned.

"Thank you," Tict replied, nodding. "The past, present and future lie above, which all intelligent beings strive to reach and understand. I was born in June of the year 1707. My mother was a house servant, a cook for the House of Stuart, Her Royal Highness Queen Anne of Great Britain. She died giving birth to me. My father remained unknown to me, though whispers floated that royal blood filled my veins. Whether that was true or not remains a mystery.

"After the death of my mother, I was raised by the house kitchen staff. Everyone was my mother, father, brother and sister. There was always plenty to eat. I did not want in that area, when so many others starved.

"I was trained to be a cook, a tanner, a gardener and stable hand, though mostly a cook. I was taught to read and write, which for a person of my status was unheard of at the time. Perhaps it had something to do with my unknown lineage? I never questioned it, though one or two did and, when they did, they somehow discreetly and secretly disappeared. Gossip of the day was best kept behind closed doors.

"On August 1st of 1714, Her Royal Highness Queen Anne passed away. Her successor, King George the First, was followed by King George the Second. In 1732, at the age of twenty-five and very content with my life, as one's life could be, on a particular midsummer July afternoon, I found myself soaking in the sun out in a pasture of knee-high grass a mile or so away from the kitchens and from everyone and everything, or so I had thought. I had brought with me a wine skin, some cheese and a small loaf of bread. Stretched out on the grass, staring up at the bright blue cloudless sky, a piece of straw hanging out of my mouth, all was well.

"My thoughts strayed from one thing to another and, thinking back, I really wasn't thinking much about anything except the blue sky above me. I thought I heard a wild dog running or was it a dog running wild? Suddenly, and without warning, a horse galloped over me.

"'What the hell!' I stood up, my anger burning, my fist pumped high.

"'Hey!' I yelled out at the top of my lungs. 'What's the big idea? You could have killed or injured me!' I raised my voice high enough for the rider to hear as he certainly did not see me and kept riding. The rider stopped the horse; slowly, he twisted the reins and turned towards me. Still shaking my fist and voicing my complaint, it wasn't long before I realized who the rider was. I fell to my knees. There was a long silence as I waited to be carted away to the gallows. The horse and its rider sidled up to me. I could feel the breath of the horse on my head. The rider eased himself off the saddle. Standing before me was King George the Second.

"'Rise,' the King spoke. I trembled. My knees felt like rubber. I did not know how long I would be able to stand as I rose, my face turned down, looking at my feet.

"'Your Majesty,' a mouse-like voice issued out of me. 'Forgive me, sire.'

"'Is there a young lady hiding about as well?' The King laughed.

"'No sire, just me,' I answered. 'I came out to enjoy the peace and quiet and gather my thoughts as I often do when the day allows me time from my duties.'

"'As I do, Tict, as I do,' the King smiled, thumping his chest, breathing in the fresh air.

"'How do you know my name?' I asked, quickly apologizing for speaking out of turn.

"'Some think that the King does not know what is going on in his realm, whether it be near or far, or that people, places or names escape his notice,' the King remarked. 'I, like any other man, can truly appreciate a day such as this. To get out and breathe in the fresh air, to admire a grassy plain, to feel the brush of a summer wind on one's face, to feel the power of one's steed beneath him, both hearts racing, seeking and awaiting a wanted or unwanted adventure. Do you seek such adventures, young Tict?'

"'When I can,' I answered, though I would rather have just been alone sans any adventure.

"'What's this?' The King bent down to pick up my wine skin. He proceeded to enjoy some of – make that all of – my wine. He gulped it down as I watched, downcast.

"'Thank you, Tict, that was very tasty indeed!'

"*I am sure it was*, I thought to myself.

"'Nice to have chatted. You must be more careful next time where you decide to picnic. We wouldn't want our best cook dead, would we?' the King said as he hoisted himself back onto his saddle and rode off.

"I picked up my empty wine skin and watched the King trot away. I wasn't really sure what had just happened.

"Fast forward to June 2, 1757. I was roused from my sleep to the sounds of banging on the kitchen doors. Upon opening the door, two royal guards handed me a note and told me to pack any belongings I had and that I would be going on a long voyage. I didn't even have time to read the note until I was well on my way to who knew where.

"The note read:

Archibald Tict, you are hereby now assigned as personal cook to General Pitt. P.S.: Perhaps an adventure awaits.

"It was stamped with the King's seal.

"I was taken aboard the HMS Pembroke. Destination – the North American Colonies. For 42 days, we crossed the Atlantic Ocean until we finally lay anchor. I set foot on dry ground in Halifax, Nova Scotia. I soon became aware that we were in the middle of a war, later named the Seven Years' War, also known as the French and Indian War.

"What had I done to deserve this? It was not an adventure I would have sought. I settled in rather quickly heading up the kitchen for General Pitt and his staff. I missed home but there was nothing I could do about it. I had learned a long time ago to adapt to situations when needed. I supposed it was in my nature to take the bull by the horns in such circumstances. In some ways, that is why I found myself where I was.

"Why did I have to tell the King, 'Oh yes, please, I would love an adventure.'

"A year later, in June of 1758, the Battle of Louisbourg was in full swing. It turned out to be a decisive victory for the British. French prisoners were taken back and forth from our position. I felt a deep sadness for them; some were either born here in the so-called New World, or were shipped here from France. They were good chaps who, like me in some ways, didn't want to be where they found themselves, that is, in the middle of a war. I would sneak them extra food when I could. If I had been caught, I too would have been between bars or, worse yet, shot. They called me 'le cuisinier d'ange', which translated to 'the angel cook'.

"However, that December 25th, 1758, I would be found out and the real adventure was to begin.

"The events of this night would forever change my perspective, not just on my own life, but on life itself!

"It was Christmas evening. After feeding the General and his guests, I set aside enough food for the prisoners so that they too could enjoy a little cheer. Plenty of fresh buns, butter, roasted potatoes, chicken, vegetables and much more. On my last trip, I was able to sneak out some ale and wine to wet their lips, which generated multiple hugs from everyone. They began to sing cheerful songs about their new homeland, toasting one another, some with tears, thinking about their wives and children left behind. There was a moment of silence in which I was able to slip away. I could still hear them singing as I walked into the night.

"A light snow began to fall and the cold seemed so far away. I looked up to the heavens with joy in my heart and a smile on my face. The clouds parted for mere seconds and I caught sight of it. It was as if the Star of Bethlehem appeared to me! I never considered myself an overly religious man, but I fell to my knees only because I tripped and, as I did so, a floating, glowing creature swooped over my head.

"A Christmas angel? I felt a tinge of fright, though remained calm as it hung above me. I could feel the air of it brush my hair. I watched it as it flew into a bank of snow. My first inclination was that we were under attack for some reason. I stayed down on my knees, waiting for the battle to begin, but nothing happened. Then I saw him walking out of the snow bank.

"I rubbed my eyes twice, not believing what I was seeing. He was walking towards me. I stood frozen as he staggered and fell at my feet. He looked up at me and held out his hand. I grabbed hold of it, pulled him up and shuffled off to the warmth of the kitchen house.

"Once inside, I noticed that his clothes were naval in appearance. I had never seen such a uniform. A short black coat, black pants, a white shirt with a bow tie and, on his feet, bright red shoes!

"I proceeded to sit him down on the rocking chair beside the fireplace, throwing a warm wool blanket over him. His teeth chattered, sweat poured from his forehead. There was some leftover broth on the stove, which I poured into a cup.

"He was staring into the fire, mumbling, and his eyes were keen on the dancing flames.

“’Who pushed me backwards? Who pushed me backwards?’ He repeated. I thrust the cup of broth into his hands.

“’Here,’ I said, ‘drink. It will warm you up.’

“Looking up, he smiled and took a few sips of the broth, and in a lonely voice he asked, ‘Where am I?’

“Where are you? That’s a strange question, I thought, but I guess if you were lost out in the winter cold with just a flimsy jacket and pants like he wore and tramping through the woods for who knows how long, you might not know who and where you were. But I wondered where he came from as I answered,

“’Well, at present, you are in my kitchen house.’

“’No, no, I mean place, date, place and date,’ he repeated.

“’Perhaps I should get you something stronger to drink,’ I said and rose to fetch a shot of warm brandy for him. Before I could, though, he grabbed me by my coattail.

“’Please, good sir, I am not crazy, please,’ his eyes pleaded.

“’Very well,’ I replied, ‘you’re on the shores of the Atlantic Ocean. Halifax, Nova Scotia, Christmas Day, 1758, to be precise.’

“’Of course! 1758! He shook his head. ‘It’s all starting to come back to me. Everything happened so quickly. One moment I am there and now I am here.’

“He then introduced himself.
“’My name is Lafil.’

“’Tict,’ I replied and shook his hand.

“’Perhaps this may be a good time for that stronger drink you mentioned, and you might want to pour yourself one as well,’ Lafil coughed.

"Who was this man? Something in me felt compelled to ask. I reached to find the bottle of brandy, pouring each of us a fine helping. For the next hour, Lafil told me his story, such as I am telling you, Nebula Yorker.

Tict paused, watching Neb's reaction thus far. "Please go on," Neb asked politely. His attention was riveted on Tict and Tict knew it.

"Step one completed," Tict smiled to himself. "Lafil continued with his story."

"I was born in 200 BCE in the ancient city of Babylon. I was a stone carver by trade. My life was a modest one. I did my work, had my friends, and minded my own business, prayed to the gods though they never seemed to listen. Then, late one evening in my 41st year of life, I was sitting under my favorite palm tree, looking up to the skies, thinking about all there was to think about. My mind never ceased to ponder and reach out for answers. Babylon had so many deities that were worshipped – in fact, well over 600 – I wondered if any were watching over me or anyone. I laughed to myself; perhaps one god would be enough if any existed. I did believe that there must be something or someone running the whole show, but again, what did I know and really still don't know. Well, actually, I do know who's running the show,' Lafil laughed for the first time.

"'Then it happened. As I looked upwards, it suddenly was upon me. At first, I thought it was a falling star shooting out through the night sky, as the many I have seen over the course of my life. It was above me, standing still in the air, a white floating creature…'

"Before Lafil could finish his sentence, we both heard the loud noise!

“It was a gunshot! Then voices shouting out. I heard one voice stand out among all the others. ‘RUN! Monsieur Tict, Run!’

“I recognized the voice of Pierre, one of my French prisoners and a friend at this point. I realized all hell was about to break loose. I had been found out.

“I dashed, bolting for the door, and in the frenzy, I forgot about Lafil. Panic started to creep in. I then felt a release of the fear that had overwhelmed me. I turned. Lafil was holding my hand.

“Don’t worry,” he said, in a calm, soft tone, ‘Everything happens for a reason.’ He unraveled the belt from around his waist. Handing it to me he said, ‘Press the buckle here,’ he pointed, ‘but not just yet’.

“I looked down at the belt in my hand and back at Lafil, dumbfounded to say the least. He could see the questions running through my mind. *Why is he giving me his belt? Does he want me to hang myself with it? It’s not a very big belt; I don’t think I could hang myself with it. It’s a nice belt; no one ever gave me a belt but it is Christmas. Perhaps it is a present of sorts. Is he giving it to me as a present?*

“I could now hear the guards shouting my name, louder than Pierre. ‘You bastard traitor, Tict!’ Large heavy thuds started to hit and kick at the sturdy kitchen door. ‘Open up, Tict!’ they yelled. Lafil and I retreated to the far end of the room. There was nowhere to go.

“They finally busted open the door, six guards and Pierre stared at us, guns pointing. Two of the guards had Pierre in their grasp and it was evident that he had been severely beaten. Poor Pierre, blood and tears poured down his bruised face.

“‘Is that him?’ One of the guards shook Pierre by the neck.

"'Qui,' he said in French. 'Forgive me, Monsieur Tict.' They threw Pierre to the ground giving him one last kick.

"'Who's that with you,' they barked, noticing Lafil. A warm blue light started to encompass Lafil. I stepped back, my eyes as wide as they could be.

"It's OK,' he said, 'I have lived a life beyond any man's wildest thoughts or dreams. You will also.' The blue light fazed in and out around Lafil, it was an amazing sight. 'You must do one thing for me, Tict,' Lafil said. 'Will you find out who pushed me backwards?'

"I didn't know what to say. 'Pushed you backwards?' "Who pushed you backwards? Hardly last words, I thought. Maybe I should be thinking of my own last words. I looked back at the guards.

"The blue light began to radiate outward. Lafil began to fade in and out of existence. I could see Pierre and hear him praying on the kitchen floor. The guards thought it was a trick of some sort. I thought I started to wet myself but I wasn't sure. I looked down at my pant leg. I had.

"Lafil asked again, 'Will you find out who pushed me backwards?'

"I didn't know what he meant, but said 'YES.'

"Lafil nodded with a smile. 'Thank you.'

"The guards by this time had had enough. They started to inch forward, guns ready. One fired! The bullet flew between Lafil and me, hitting the wall over the stove.

"Lafil's last words to me were, 'Now would be a good time to press the buckle.' With that, he vanished into thin air.

"I pressed the belt buckle. Pierre cried out in a loud voice, 'Le cuisinier d'ange!' A white pulsating light swooped through and over the guards straight out the door."

3

Neb was grasping clumps of grass with both hands as Tict finished his story. There was a long silence between them. Neb didn't know what to think. He looked down at the dirt and grass wedged between his fingers. He glanced back at Tict who was watching him, intently smiling the whole while. Neb opened his mouth to say something, stopped and started again, but nothing came out. This went on for at least five minutes. Finally, he spoke.

"OK, what does any of this have to do with Halley's Comet?"

"Everything!" Tict excitedly answered. "Look, you're a fellow who was raised to have an open mind, right? Even your parents were progressive before progressive became a type of sixties and seventies music. They had an open mind to the unlimited knowledge that expands all known worlds, galaxies, and universes past, present and future that may or may not exist," Tict enthusiastically expounded.

"For someone who for the time being may or may not have fallen from the sky or a loony bin, you seem to know a lot about my parents. And, if my calculations are correct, you're also telling me that you're 279 years old, which also may be possible if I am to keep an open mind. I know this might sound crazy, but are you Dr. Who?" Neb asked, feeling very unsure about all of this.

"Dr. Who? Why would you think I'm a doctor? I told you I was a cook.

"Are you then a time traveller?"

"A time traveller. I suppose you could say that. Never thought of myself as such, but if it makes you feel more secure then, yes, I am a time traveller." Tict folded his arms and smiled. "You see, Neb, time travel is not what people think it is."

Tict continued to explain. "What many don't know, mostly here on Earth, is that one can only travel back in time according to his or her own age. For example, I was born in 1707 and the present year is 1986. So, while I am on Earth, if I want to, I can travel back in time 279 years. In another 75 years, I could travel back 354 years. The real kicker is that one cannot travel forward in time because the future does not yet exist. Now some have questioned whether the future exists and those who have tried to go there have never come back. So, either they didn't get there or they found a party that was too good to leave."

"That must be one hell of a party," Neb interrupted Tict. "I suppose it could be thought along the lines of the teaching of many religions that when you die, your soul goes to heaven or to a fiery hell, depending on the nature of your life. To my knowledge, no one has ever come back from heaven, or from hell, for that matter. There was that one fellow, Lazarus, but he never mentioned heaven or hell or a party. He never said, 'Hey Jesus, why did you pull me out of that party?' So whether heaven or hell exists could be parallel to travelling forward in time. Either it does or it doesn't exist."

"Now that's using your brain power, my dear boy." Tict gave Neb a thumbs up.

"So you're saying," Neb continued, "that I could time travel back to the 1960s if I wanted to?"

"If you wanted," Tict replied.

"OK. Show me then. Make me a believer," Neb remarked with outward skepticism.

"That's not possible at the moment, Neb," Tict replied.

"I thought so." Neb shook his head in dismay. "I was starting to think there was a spark of truth to your story."

"It's not that it's impossible, Neb. There is a 24-hour waiting period and one needs to be off the planet for the process to take effect."

"Of course. How could I have forgotten? Yes, the 24-hour dilemma, and don't forget to be off the planet," Neb sarcastically snorted.

"Well then, are you ready to go?" Tict asked.

"Go where? I thought you said we couldn't go. You know, the 24-hour thingy," Neb replied as he turned to pick up his knapsack and telescope.

"Just a moment, Neb, I'm receiving an incoming transmission."

I bet you are, Neb thought to himself.

He watched Tict open his coat and lightly touch his belt buckle. "Tict here. Go ahead."

"Mr. Tict, are you ready for transport?" a crackly static voice asked.

"Is that you, Eno?" Tict answered.

"Yes sir," Eno replied. "TeeceeFore is asking for a progress report on your present situation."

"Please inform TeeceeFore that all is well and that we will be heading back aboard very soon," Tict replied. "Please stand by, Eno."

"Standing by," Eno stated.

By this time, Neb was starting to wonder if he was at home in bed, tucked under his cozy blankets, and all of this was just another bizarre dream, of which he'd had many. He had dreamt of faces and places he couldn't recall but that felt familiar.

It was as close to a déjà vu feeling as one could have, though it always felt like something more. He had now finished storing the telescope away into its case and he picked up his knapsack and flung it over his shoulder. As he did so, he looked back at Tict, and was sure he heard his father's voice. "MOVE FORWARD."

Neb thought, *what if he's telling the truth? But where did he come from? How does he seem to know so much about Mom and Dad? Is he a leftover party guest from Neil Young's place spaced out on magic mushrooms? And what does any of this have to do with me?*

He heard his Dad's voice again, as if he were standing next to him. "Remember, never discount the variables that seem unreasonable to the human mind. Work out the calculations. Sift through the possibilities. Become one with what the eye cannot see or feel. Let the moment take you. Move forward. In other words, it may sound unconventional but taking a leap of faith may be sounder than you think. Move forward, Nebula. Move forward."

"So, are you ready to go?" Tict asked, breaking Neb's train of thought.

"Excuse me? Ready to go where?" Neb came back to the present.

Tict smiled and pointed upwards with his other hand on Neb's shoulder. "Why, to Halley's Casino, of course, my dear boy!"

Tict touched his belt buckle. "Eno, we are now ready for transport."

"Transporting now," Eno replied.

"Halley's Casino! What?" Neb braced himself.

"No towel required," Tict laughed.

A yellowish-green hue surrounded them, covering them from head to toe until they transformed into two white jellyfish-like creatures that hovered in midair for a few seconds and then flew straight upwards into the early morning bright clear sky.

***

The inside of the hangar bay was busy as usual. Every docking port was full, with a wide range of incoming and outgoing ships and shuttles. Tict and Neb materialized at the far end of the bay. They both now stood within a glass-encased transfiguror booth. Tict was smiling as usual, watching and waving at the organized chaos that was streaming outside the booth.

A young slender blonde-haired woman dressed in a red jumpsuit tapped on the glass, giving Tict the thumbs up. “Clear,” she said. The glass doors swooshed open. Tict stepped out first.

Neb felt paralyzed, or was it traumatized? Whatever it was, he didn’t feel good.

“Come on,” Tict motioned to him.

Neb eyed his surroundings very coolly. It looked like a regular airport hangar, though it seemed to go on forever. He couldn’t see where it started or where it ended. It was as wide as it was long. The ceiling was high with a light shining down almost as bright as the sun. Hundreds of people strode about in every direction. He watched as hover cabs zoomed in and out, up and down the hangar bay. He pinched himself. Yep, he was awake. OK, keep it together, he told himself. He felt weak at the knees and wasn’t sure if he had peed himself either, but he was afraid to look down and embarrassed to find out. He did look down and patted his crotch and behind. All dry.

“What are you doing?” Tict’s eye caught Neb’s. He started to laugh. “You’re fine, my boy,” he said.

The glass enclosures slowly hissed open. Tict walked out and off the platform. He was a few feet away when he turned about.

"Come on, Neb, it's alright."

Neb stood frozen. He wasn't sure if he could move or if he wanted to.

"Medic!" Tict hollered. He walked back up to the booth. "Everything will be fine, Neb," he assured him. "You're experiencing molecular reconfiguration stabilization transfer, though I have never seen or heard of it happening to a human before. I guess there is a first time for everything."

"What do you mean it never happened to a human before?" Neb's whole body started to tremble inside and out.

The medic soon arrived with a hypo dart which he quickly pressed into Neb's left arm. "There," the medic turned to Tict. "He should be fine in a few seconds."

Neb's eyesight started to shift out of focus, blurred and went blank. He then blinked twice and all was clear again. He moved forward without even knowing he had and before he knew it, he was out from behind the transfiguror booth and standing beside Tict and the medic.

"Thank you," Tict said to the medic. The medic bowed his head in response and disappeared as quickly as he had appeared.

"There now, feeling better?" Tict asked, resting his hand on Neb's shoulder.

"Better, yes. Thank you," Neb replied. "Now where the hell am I?"

"You're welcome," Tict answered. "Where the hell are you? Is that all you can ask? I think it would have been better if you had pissed your pants," Tict huffed a little at Neb's questioning. "Look around, my dear boy. Where do you think you are? Kansas?"

A hover cab halted in front of them. The window slowly rolled down and a plump woman with a purple beehive hairstyle popped her head out.

"Hello, Mr. Tict. So nice to see you again!" the women excitedly yelped. "See you in the ballroom tomorrow evening?" she asked.

"I will be there," Tict replied, as the window rolled back up. The hover cab whizzed off.

"Now that's a question," Tict waved at the disappearing hover cab.

"What was that all about?" Neb asked. "And who was that?"

"Well, a couple of reasonable questions, young Nebula. That was Tnangy Rulipd, one of our most frequent guests. She might as well join the crew for all the time she spends here," Tict answered.

"Guests?" Neb was confused. He scratched the top of his head.

"Yes, guests, dear boy. You see, Neb, what you see in front of you is just a small portion of the Casino."

"Casino?"

"My, I must say you're getting good at asking the right questions. You see, Neb, you're not just on Halley's Comet, but inside it. It's otherwise known as Halley's Casino". Tict stood smiling with his arms stretched wide. "Welcome to Halley's Casino."

"Halley's Casino? Really, Tict?" Neb didn't know what to think.

"I guess I should have told you that Halley's Comet is not really a comet at all, but rather an intergalactic casino, the one and only in all of known time and space. It's disguised as a comet to avoid lesser technological worlds from catching on until they are advanced enough to join the club, so to speak."

"Really! An intergalactic casino! You're kidding, of course," Neb remarked in a snarky tone.

"I am not kidding. I never ever kid. Never," Tict replied quite assuredly.

Neb's mind was wide open to the possibility that anything was possible, though more questions would certainly need to be answered. It may well be some kind of elaborate trick, Neb thought, or perhaps he had fallen asleep beside his telescope waiting for Halley's Comet to appear.

He watched as the guests stood in line on conveyer belts that led them all to opening and closing swooshing doors where they were disappearing to who knows where. There seemed to be as many men and women dressed in red or white jumpsuits who were assisting the guests. They were helping with their luggage, hailing cabs, giving instructions and directions. Two-, three- and four-seat hover cabs were arriving every five seconds, filling up as soon as they stopped, and then flying off, ready for the next group. Everyone was very congenial as they waited their turn.

Overhead, a woman's voice could be heard from invisible speakers, welcoming everyone. "Welcome to Halley's Casino.

Whether this is your first time or perhaps your last, we wish you fun, happy times." Her voice was very upbeat. It was too upbeat for Neb's liking, not that he didn't like upbeat. He was usually a very upbeat type of guy, but he was very tired and needed some rest.

The overhead voice continued, "The Casino androids are happy to assist with whatever you need while aboard. For you first-timers, you will note them by their red or white jumpsuits. Please refer to your Casino brochure on tipping procedures.

Remember, everyone's a winner! Thank you and have a pleasant visit."

Neb took it all in. The organized frenzy was a marvel to watch. He'd never seen anything like it. Then he paused for a moment. Did she just say the androids would be happy to assist? He turned his attention to those individuals dressed in the jumpsuits. Androids! Neb thought they looked very human. He watched them work. There was nothing out of the ordinary that would make you think they were androids. He thought perhaps he had heard wrong.

Tict was standing a few feet away, watching Neb absorb the proceedings. He was thinking, *Boy, if he thinks this is something, wait until he sees the rest of the ship.*

Neb turned to Tict. "I know this might sound stupid, but did the overhead woman's voice say that those dressed in the red and white jumpsuits are androids?"

"Yes, androids," Tict replied. "They look fairly human to me."

"Yes, I believe that is the look they were going for when they were constructed," Tict replied.

Neb started to feel a little weary. His head thumped and he started to feel like he couldn't move again. Tict also noticed.

"Tict, I can't move again!" Neb was now getting seriously nervous about the situation of his surroundings and his body was telling him all was not well. "Why can't I move?" he thought he said, but it actually came out as, "Gripal cha cha whoop?" Unknown to him, he spoke in a clear ancient Pratt dialect which translated, "I know what you are but what am I?"

Tict stared into his eyes, not quite sure what he was looking for. He thought that something more was at play here. He had never met or heard of a fellow human being that had such a difficult time transporting. He decided he would keep it to himself for the time being.

"Everything is all right, Neb, your body's molecules are resetting," Tict assured him. "Give it an hour or so. In the meantime, I am going to give you another hypo shot. It should stabilize you."

Tict pulled out a small blue metallic vial from his right coat pocket. "Good thing I prepped one," he said to himself. He pressed the vial behind Neb's left earlobe and, as he did so, a low hissing sounded. After administering the hypo shot, Tict started to count down, "Five, four, three, two, one and we're done." Neb fell forward into his arms.

"There, that wasn't so bad, was it?" Tict helped Neb up. "Says who?" Neb replied. He looked around and muttered to himself, "Damn, it's not a dream and I am still here. I still have a splitting headache and I have to go pee!"

"Oh, so now you have to go pee," Tict ushered him along. "So much to take in, so little time," he sighed. "Believe me I know what you're going through, though back in 1758, I had no clue whatsoever where I had come to be. Now you have printed fiction, comic books, radio, television; it's easier for someone like you, Neb, to believe this is real but it took me some time, let me tell you. You should be sopping all this up rather than trying to think it's all a dream!"

"It's not that I don't believe all of this, Tict, but it's happening so fast and my brain can only digest so much. But it is sopping it up, as you say, very quickly for some odd reason, almost as though it were natural in some way. Man, I feel taller or something." He examined his hands and looked down to his feet.

"You are. Everyone here on Halley's is exactly five foot nine. It's part of the matrix. I will explain everything to you shortly, my dear boy, but for now let's get you something for your headache and to a washroom fast!" As Tict finished, his personal hover cab pulled up beside them.

"Welcome back." Eno, one of Tict's few non-android employees, was sitting at the wheel. He proceeded to press one of the buttons on the dashboard console that opened the back door to the hover cab.

"After you, Neb," Tict waved him in. They seated themselves and the automatic harness belts safely secured them in.

"My, that's kind of tight isn't it?" Neb tugged at the straps, "feels like a straightjacket."

"Have you worn a straitjacket before?" Eno asked, making small talk.

"No, not really," Neb laughed.

"Then how do you know that it feels like a straitjacket?" he asked again.

"It's alright, Neb." Tict turned to Eno. "It's just an expression of thought. Even though one has never experienced the experience, they may have seen the so-called experience expressed by someone who has experienced the experience, thus noting that, if they were wearing a straightjacket, it would feel as it now feels."

"I see," Eno remarked, "Much like if I hate fish but if a fish were to hate me it would make things even, even though I may not know the fish personally."

"What?" Neb shook his head.

Tict tapped Eno on the head. "Just drive, Eno. Drive."

The hover cab sped off, zooming up and down and all around the hangar bay, giving Neb a much better view of the goings on below. "How big is this place?" Neb looked out through the tinted windows of the hover cab. He leaned his head against the window and the coolness of the glass soothed his headache as he took in the fullness of his surroundings.

After five minutes, the hover cab came to a halt. "Here we are, sir," Eno peeked up into his rearview mirror at Tict. The door hatch opened slowly, making a watery stream-like sound that reminded Neb that his bladder still needed to be emptied. The safety harness retracted, releasing Tict first and he spryly hopped out. Neb tried to get up but the harness held him in place.

"Where is the damn button?" Neb twisted about in the cab trying to find a release button. "Tict!" he shouted, "What now!"

"Just give it a second, Neb, the seat is calibrating your cell structure. There are so few of us onboard, it needs to input your DNA code, then record it and store it. You won't have to go through any of this again after this procedure. You'll be clear to do as you wish, go as you want, anywhere aboard the Casino.

"OK, then," Neb nodded, waiting. "Hey, what do you mean, so few of us?"

"Humans," Tict replied.

The safety harness soon retracted, releasing him.

He got out and stood beside Tict. "Good to go." With that, the hover cab sped away, back into the deep reaches of the hangar.

"First of all, speaking of 'go', I really need to go, before I go inside my pants! And secondly, "What did you mean by 'us few humans'?"

"Yes, yes, the washroom, this way," Tict walked a few feet from where the hover cab dropped them off and said, "Open." A door swooshed open out of nowhere; at least it looked to Neb as if it came out of nowhere.

"Sometimes when you've got to go, nothing really matters, does it?" Tict remarked. Neb was definitely thinking that.

They walked into a very large white room. The first thing Neb noticed was the paintings on the wall. Leonardo da Vinci, Vincent van Gogh, Pablo Picasso, Pierre Auguste Renoir, and some he wasn't quite sure about. Having studied these artists with his father, Neb was all too familiar with their strokes and techniques, but no one had ever seen these pieces of art before, to his knowledge.

"Am I seeing what I think?" Neb turned about to face Tict. "Are these really what I think they are?"

"Those? Oh they're just some paint by numbers I did years ago," Tict laughed. "You'll find the washroom through the checkered black and purple door," he pointed out, "or have you forgotten?"

"Yes I did. Well, not really. I just lost my train of thought. These painting are marvelous! Checkered black and purple door. Right!" Neb made a beeline. Once at the door, he looked about for a handle but found none. "What's this, another calibration?"

"Just say 'open'!" Tict replied.

"Open." The door opened and Neb flew straight in.

4

Tict was sitting behind his large oak desk, his body resting in a high-back black leather Victorian-era chair. The wall behind him had a painted mural of space, the Earth prominent in the background. Thousands of points of lights (stars) gleamed in the background, surrounding the planet. It was truly a remarkable sight.

Two long, deep, red-covered chesterfields, with yellow buttons dotting the arms, separated by an oval Maplewood coffee table, centred the room. There was also a rocking chair with an orangish angora afghan thrown over the back. It was all very cozy looking.

As soon as Tict had sat down, calls and messages started to stream in. Minor sensor problems were being detected throughout the Casino. Some guests were complaining that it was either too cold or too hot in their rooms or that some guests were sent in error to their specific rooms. Everyone was always accommodated according to their special needs and wants and body temperature was always at the top of the list. Foods, liquids, lighting and sleeping arrangements were always a priority when booking. Each guest had to have their specific needs met; gas expulsion from some was not a pleasant experience, to say the least. The last thing anyone needed was an elephant or two in the room.

As soon as he stabilized a problem, another one soon crept up, Tick pondered. It was very unusual, indeed.

The sensor outside Tict's office door activated. He glanced at his desk console monitor to see who it was.

TeeceeFore, the Prime Minister of Telvon Three, was waiting at the entrance. He buzzed her in.

"Welcome, Madame Prime Minister," Tict stood, greeting her from behind his desk, bowing. Prime Minister TeeceeFore stood five foot nine, like everyone. She always maintained a graceful appearance and one would have guessed her to be in her mid-forties, though truth be told, for someone four hundred and three years old, she was very easy on the eyes. She wore a long grey dress with silver sparkles scattered about. Her dress touched the floor and Tict was never sure if she had feet because she would always glide across any floor as if floating on air. Perhaps she had wheels for feet, for all he knew. He'd never bothered to ask in all the two hundred and twenty-eight years that he'd known her but perhaps one day he would.

"How was your trip below?" she asked, sitting down on one of the chesterfields. Tict sat down facing her on the other chesterfield.

"The trip below was interesting, thank you. It was nice to fill my lungs with real air again. I may venture back down for a cup of good English tea with some old friends before the Casino is out of the range limit.

"Where is...? TeeceeFore asked.

Before she could finish, Neb was coming out of the washroom, head down, zipping up his jeans. "Man, you don't know how that feels! I think I just emptied Niagara Falls." At once, he looked up and saw Tict and TeeceeFore and his face blushed. "Excuse me; I didn't know there was anyone here but you and me."

"That's quite alright, my dear boy," Tict got up and walked over to Neb.

"Nebula Yorker, let me please introduce you to TeeceeFore, Prime Minister of Telvon Three and Head of the Casino Guild." Tict whispered in his ear, "Bow." Neb bowed.

"HOLY SHIT!" Neb exclaimed. His attention was automatically distracted. "Look at that wall mural. That's beyond fantastic! I have never seen anything like it in my whole life, not even at the Met!" It filled the entire wall behind Tict's desk. Neb walked over to the picture to get a closer look. "Wow!" he said and then proceeded to trip over his feet. He went face first into the mural. But wait! It wasn't a mural.

His face smashed up against a thick glass window. After a second or two, his face, now pressed up like a pug, started to drift down the glass making that sort of noise that one makes when your face hits a glass window and starts to slide down. He jumped back twice, three times and tripped again. He turned around to Tict and TeeceeFore, bewildered. He took a deep breath.

"Is that what I think it is?" he asked, his body starting to quiver with an uneasy excitement, not that it had stopped since he came aboard an hour earlier.

"Have you not told him, Tict?" TeeceeFore asked

"I have but I don't really think it has sunk in yet, though I believe he may be starting to think that something is afoot." They both stared in Neb's direction. Neb picked himself up from the floor. He looked blankly out into the space that really was space and not a mural.

"I need to sit down." Neb walked over and plunked himself down on the rocking chair, pulling the afghan over himself. "I know it might be early or late or whatever, but do you have anything to drink?" he asked Tict.

"I agree, a drink would be very fitting," answered Tict. TeeceeFore strolled over to Neb and gently took his hand.

"Now, Neb, do you know where you are?" she asked softly, with a motherly touch.

Tict was soon handing everyone a small glass. "Private reserve," he winked. Neb gulped it down.

"More, please," Neb asked.

"Here, have mine," TeeceeFore handed him her glass. "Thank you." He drained it down like the first. He could feel a smooth warm rush over his entire body as he relaxed into the rocker. He unknowingly rocked himself back and forth, back and forth. A nice little buzz took over.

"Is that what I think it is?" Neb asked, though he already knew the answer.

"Yes, Neb, that is the Earth." Tict slowly sipped his brandy. "You're in outer space aboard Halley's Comet or, should I say, Halley's Casino.

"Yeah, I sort of remember you saying something like that, but I didn't really believe it until now and I guess I am not dreaming any of this." Neb cupped his empty glass. "So, let me get this straight. Halley's Comet is really a spaceship?" he asked Tict.

"Yes, sort of. It's a ship, but not in the conventional way you might think of a space ship. It's a fully functioning travelling intergalactic casino, to be precise," replied Tict, finishing his brandy. "We adopted the *Halley's* name about one hundred years ago. It gave it that punch and pizzazz we have always been looking for. "BOOM! HALLEY'S CASINO!" Tict spread out his hands. "Very zippy, wouldn't you say?"

"Very!" TeeceeFore smiled. "I heartily agree."

"So, if I have got this right again," Neb began, "what we on Earth have thought for centuries was a comet is really an intergalactic casino and, if I remember correctly from this non-dream I'm having, you mentioned earlier that there are, I think you said, a few humans aboard? Yet everyone I have seen looks pretty human to me."

"There are actually three humans aboard," TeeceeFore joined in. "We have Mr. Tict, here, Marcus Apitippius, and yourself, Nebula."

"Four, if you count John Lennon," remarked Tict.

"Oh yes, I forgot. But he's not really human, is he?" TeeceeFore mused.

"John Lennon? Not human? And I suppose the rest of the Beatles aren't human either?" Neb smirked.

"Don't be silly, Neb, of course they are human." Tict and TeeceeFore looked at each other and laughed.

"So, let me get this correct, three humans, possibly four, if you count John Lennon. Then who or what are all those human-looking people out in the hangar?" Neb paused. Tict could see his mind working it out. "They're androids, aren't they?" rolled off Neb's tongue.

"Good one. Close, Neb, but, no, they are not all androids."

Not all androids? You mean some are actually freaking androids? Cool, thought Neb.

"First of all, those you saw wearing the red or white jumpsuits are the worker bees, the androids. Everyone else you saw, and will see, are from across known space."

"Hmm," Neb pondered. "That's a bummer." "How so, young Neb?" TeeceeFore asked.

"I guess from all the science fiction I've read, written and watched, our idea of intelligent life outside of Earth is usually of little green men, reptilian creatures, bulbous headed aliens and the like," Neb grinned, "but it doesn't look as though any of that was right."

TeeceeFore laughed along. "Oh, Neb, you're so funny. But, yes, little green men, reptilian creatures and bulbous headed aliens do exist, and much more."

"So, are you telling me that you're not human either?" Neb asked TeeceeFore.

"Of course not!" TeeceeFore exclaimed, sounding almost insulted.

"You don't exactly look alien to me."

"I am a Telvonnite from Telvon Three. You see, Mr. Yorker, some intelligent beings are humanoid in form; most are not. Some are green or purple or red and so on; some have two legs and stand upright, some three legs, four legs, and no legs. Some have one eye, two eyes, three, and four and so on. Some are gigantic in size, others so small they could fit in the palm of your hand." TeeceeFore held her hand out, palm up.

"You see, Nebula, the Vegastriopelia arranges and redistributes our molecules to the height restrictions of the Casino. The Triopelians programmed the humanoid configuration as the best fit. There would be no room aboard if everyone came as they were, so to speak. You will find that everyone is exactly five foot nine inches tall and proportioned to their original size in that if they're a little overweight or thin, the Vegastriopelia will compensate each one to fit its humanoid form."

"The Vegastriopelia? Triopelians?" Neb scratched his head. "Man, this is all too much! Halley's Comet is not a comet but a casino. Androids that look human. Aliens posing as humans to fit inside the Casino! And John Lennon may or may not be human?" Neb dropped his head into his lap.

TeeceeFore motioned to Tict and they walked away from Neb over to his desk. "Tict, do you think this may be too much for him?" she whispered, both of then eyeing Neb.

"I don't think so. I agree it is a lot to digest. He's actually a very smart fellow, more than he thinks he is. Otherwise, why would the Vegastriopelia have chosen him?"

Neb's eyes opened and closed, his body now stretched on the chesterfield, looking up, his mind in a half fog trying to work it out.

"What is that sound coming out of him?" TeeceeFore asked.

"That's called snoring," Tict grinned.

"Humans never cease to amaze me. They are so full of new experiences. Snoring, I guess there is a first for everything. Who knew?" TeeceeFore and Tict silently crept out of the office leaving Neb to sleep.

5

Seven hours later Neb awoke, his head resting on his pillows, the blankets pulled up covering his whole body. He was as snug as a bug as a bug could be snug, if you were a bug of course. Neb was not a bug. At least that he knew. He had been dreaming of being in a faraway place, having a picnic with a good looking girl. She had long blonde hair braided down to the middle of her back, bluer than blue eyes, a slender trim body dressed in a black and white miniskirt, and a smile to die for.

"Would you like a cup of coffee?" she asked fawningly. "Yes, please," Neb replied, "One sugar and plenty of milk, stirred." The smell of coffee was so real, so real Neb could almost taste it. He opened his eyes, still under the covers. "Now that was a dream," he said to himself. *Hey, that does smell like real coffee*, he thought. He rolled the covers down ever so slightly so only his eyes and his boney double-jointed fingers were visible. His eyes darted back and forth and he realized that he was not at home in his own bed. He pulled the covers ever so slowly back over his head. He peaked out again and dove back under. He took a deep breath, and then he heard her.

"Here you go. Coffee with one sugar and plenty of milk, stirred. I will leave it beside your bed here on the tray," he heard a female voice say.

Neb stuck his head out again to glimpse the back of someone in a red jumpsuit with long blonde braided hair exiting the room.

Did that really just happen? He sat up and looked around at his surroundings. The room was a modest size. The bed he lay in was queen size and very soft and comfortable. A wardrobe sat at one end of the room and beside it a small computer console desk with a wingback leather chair. As in Tict's office, a black and purple checkered door led to the washroom. There was also a rocking chair with an orangish afghan thrown over it.

It all started to come back to him. Not that it had left or that he had left or that right opposed to left was a good thing. In this case, he wasn't sure just yet. He eyed the steaming cup of coffee and then leaned over and reached for it. He sipped it slowly. Not bad. He took another. He felt well rested and assured himself that all would be fine.

Maybe it was the coffee but whatever it was, he had now come to terms with his surroundings, where he found himself having a cup of coffee on a spaceship. He laughed to himself taking another sip. He heard his father's voice again.... "Move forward."

"I think I have moved forward, Dad." He raised his coffee cup up in the air and, giving a wink, toasted his Dad.

That was the one thing about Neb. He could be very analytical about solving mysteries of all kinds that presented themselves out of the blue, so to speak. His present situation would be considered well out of the blue or, in his case, outer space. *Outer space*, he mused to himself, finishing his first cup of coffee.

Unknown to Neb, the deepest region of his brain was assembling the threads of the last twenty-four hours, making the connections, tying them together until they were ready to divulge themselves. So, he was on some type of ship or, rather, an intergalactic casino posing as a comet. Halley's Casino!

"What does this, if anything, have to do with me?" he wondered out loud. "There must be some variable I haven't seen or have yet to uncover. He looked down into his empty cup and wished he had another and, just like that, in through the door she came, coffee pot in hand.

"Good morning, Mr. Yorker. More coffee?" she asked. Neb held out his cup while she poured. She set the pot down and added the sugar and milk to the outheld cup.

"Might you know what time it is? Neb asked.

"11:45 AM, Earth time," she replied politely.

"11:45 AM! I never sleep past 8:00 AM. Are you sure?"

"Yes, quite sure. It is now 11:46 AM," she replied again.

Neb looked up at the girl from his dream and smiled, "11:46 AM and counting," he said.

"Obviously," she remarked.

He sat up in bed, coffee in hand, and noticed that he was wearing white silk pajamas. He wasn't about to ask how he got into them. His thoughts overwhelmed him as he stared at this blonde bombshell. To say he was taken by her was an understatement.

"You have me at a disadvantage," he said to her. "How so? she replied.

"Well, you seem to know my name but I do not know yours."

"My designation is KEL-345."

Designation? KEL-345? He hadn't put two and two together yet that she was an android. The jumpsuit should have clued him in, but he was smitten.

"I see. And may I ask your age, if I can be so bold?"

"My age?" she remarked, "That is an odd request. If you must know, I was activated nine thousand, one hundred and twenty-five solar years ago."

"Well, you don't look a day over nine thousand one hundred and twenty-four years." This was so unlike Neb and he knew it, but he couldn't stop for some reason and he still hadn't clued in.

KEL-345 stood mildly perplexed for a second or two. "Accessing," she said. "You are attempting a humourous anecdote." Her internal circuits skipped a micro-fraction. "I will have to look into this at a later date," she processed.

"You may call me Nebula, or Neb for short, if you wish." "Very well, Nebula or Neb for short." KEL-345 tilted her head in a robotic fashion.

"No. You may call me either Nebula or Neb. It's my first name," he replied.

"Yes, I see. Neb. Very well. Neb, Mr. Tict has asked me to inform you that you will find clean attire provided for you." KEl-345 pointed to the wardrobe.

"Thank you, he replied.

"You're welcome. I believe that is the correct response," she said as she turned to leave.

"Before you leave, may I ask you one more thing? May I call you just Kel?" Neb smiled at her.

"Just KEL?" She smiled back, imitating Neb's smile. After processing the request, she answered, "That would be fine. You may." She then turned and exited the room, the door swooshing closed behind her.

Neb crossed his arms over his head as he lay back grinning to himself. KEL-345 had made him forget where he was for the present time. He then looked back down at his white silk pajamas and it all came back. *I am not even going to ask how I got into these.*

He eyed the wardrobe. *Clean attire, eh?* He jumped out of bed – well, almost slipped out – and walked over to the wardrobe.

"Open," he said. The wardrobe opened slowly, with an almost eerie creak. Once the doors completely opened, he saw hanging inside three white turtlenecks, three red double- breasted suit coats and three pair of red pants. To the left were three shelves. The first had three pairs of socks and the second had a black red-trimmed belt with an oval brass belt buckle. On the lower shelf was a pair of black sneakers with a handwritten note that read 'Peter Pan Getaways'.

He rummaged through the wardrobe looking for the jeans, T-shirt, running shoes and windbreaker that he was last wearing. They were nowhere to be found.

He turned and walked towards the black and purple checkered door. *I hope this is a washroom like in Tict's office.* "Open," he said aloud. The door opened. Neb stuck his head in. *Yep, as I thought.* The washroom was no different from any other. Sink, bathtub, shower, towels, toiletries all laid out, soap, toothpaste, and shampoo. Neb decided a nice long hot bath was needed to rest up his new longer bones. He turned on the taps. It didn't take long for the tub to fill up. As the water was pouring out, he detected the scent of lavender. He held his hand under the tap and cupped a handful of water. He smelled it as it streamed through his fingers. Lavender scented water.

Neb lowered himself into the now full tub. He sat back, letting the soothing hot water seep into his pores. Yesterday, he was getting ready to observe Halley's Comet; now he was taking a bath on it, or on what he had thought was Halley's Comet. One never knows what one day to the next can bring. Even if you have life all planned, or think you do, there are so many variables that never even enter your mind. You can think you are setting out for the Grand Canyon and end up in Disneyland in Paris, France. Right now, though, he was more relaxed than he had been in a long time. Amazing what a hot bath can do for the mind and body.

"Time allotted," a voice echoed in the washroom. Within seconds, the water in the tub had disappeared down the drain, leaving Neb sitting there cold and stark naked.

"What the hell?" Neb looked down at the drain.

"Neb. Oh, Neb." He heard Tict's voice outside the washroom.

"I am in the tub. Or, I was in the tub." Neb came out of the washroom, now clad in a towel.

"What's up with the tub, Tict? I was very much enjoying the relaxing and soothing experience of the lavender scented water, then this voice said, 'Time allotted'."

"Limited time per usage, I'm afraid. We have over six hundred guests aboard. We must recycle, recycle, recycle," Tict replied, bouncy as ever. "Six hundred guests plus one android per guest, though the androids don't need to shower. They are self-maintaining."

"I see. Well, it was nice to meet Kel earlier. She sure knows how to make a great cup of coffee."

"Kel?" asked Tict.

"Yeah, you know the nice-looking girl with the long blonde braided hair, blue eyes, great smile," Neb's eyes lit up when he mentioned her to Tict.

"Interesting," Tict mused. "You mean KEL-345 and you do know that she is an android."

The android part just went over Neb's head again. "Yeah, that's her. KEL-345. But I asked if I could just call her Kel."

"And she said yes?" Tict asked, surprised.

"She did. I like being on a first-name basis with people. I'm a people person, you know." Neb darted back into the washroom. "I need to brush my teeth."

"You can call me Archibald if you want?" Tict said as Neb disappeared into the washroom. *Kel?* Tict thought. *That's a first.* "I have never thought of an android having a first name or of anyone asking if they could address one as such or of them responding to the request," Tict now thought out loud.

"What was that?" Neb stuck his head out, toothbrush in hand.

"Oh, it's nothing, Neb, just an old man lost in his thoughts."

"OK, Archie," Neb winked, ducking back in.

Tict smiled. "We have a busy day ahead of us, Neb. I'll let you finish up, get dressed and all that." Tict reached into his right breast pocket and pulled out his long chained watch. "It is now 12:25 PM," he told Neb.

Neb poked his head out again. "Wow, I'm surprised I slept as long as I did."

"It was almost 4:30 AM when you fell asleep on the chesterfield in my office. I'll pop back here in about twenty minutes to pick you up."

"OK," Neb yelled out.

Tict turned and made for the exit, still thinking about KEL-345, or now Kel.

Five minutes later, Neb was back at the wardrobe pulling out his clean attire. He reached for the red coat and pants, turtleneck, black shoes and socks. He did not have much choice, unless he wanted to go out in the towel still wrapped around him. He took out his new attire and laid everything on his bed, which was now made up. *Who did that? Tict? Kel?* He sat down on the edge of his bed and pulled on the socks. He always put his socks on first. Next he pulled on the red pants and then threw the white turtleneck over his head. It was a light turtleneck, the fabric one that Neb was not accustomed to. It was soft and cool against his skin. He liked it. Bending down, he slipped on the shoes. They looked like regular black dress shoes but felt like running shoes, very spongy and light on the feet. Lastly, he threw on the double-breasted red coat that hung down to just above his knees.

He walked back over to the wardrobe that had a mirror inside both doors. "Not bad!" he said, admiring his new look, "very sharp, indeed!"

"Don't forget the belt." Tict had slid up beside Neb without him noticing.

"How did you do that? I didn't hear the door swoosh."

Tict grabbed the hanging black belt from the wardrobe. "Of course you didn't hear anything. You were too busy admiring yourself." Tict handed the belt to him. "This belt is your lifeline, Neb. It's very important."

Neb took the belt from Tict and slipped it through his pants' belt loops. As soon as he had it fastened, he felt a charge go through his body. "I am calibrating again?"

"You're getting good at this, Neb. That's the Vegastriopelia effect."

"The Vegastriopelia effect? What is that now?" "Think of it as being inoculated," Tict said.

"Inoculated for what, I hate to ask?" Neb look worried.

"Well, it's not really an effect as in an effect. It's more of a surge of your body's electronic signature being inputted into the Vegastriopelia's matrix, thus inoculating you against any unforeseen circumstances where you may or may not need assistance. For example, when we arrived, I used my belt like a carrier wave to bring you aboard. Now you are able to come and go as you please, but you need the belt, always. The belt acts as a homing beacon and has a built-in communication module. Don't leave the Casino without it!" Tict patted Neb's shoulder.

"Is that how Lafil died?" Neb enquired.

"No." Tict's eyes saddened at hearing Lafil's name. "Lafil died because he was pushed backwards. We'll discuss that later, if you don't mind. We need to get you caught up on all things Triopelia and Vegastriopelia before the dinner tonight."

"I am sorry, Tict, I didn't mean to bring up such a painful memory regarding Lafil." Neb could see how it affected Tict when he brought up Lafil's name.

"It's OK, Neb. Lafil gave his life for mine and I will be forever grateful."

"Dinner sounds great," Neb changed the subject. "What's on the menu? I hope it's not me."

"No, Neb, you're too thin," Tict chuckled.

"You're not serious, are you, Tict?" Neb wasn't quite sure if he was kidding or not.

"No, but you are the guest of honour."

"Really? I've never been a guest of honour before. Cool. Why?"

"The Guild is very anxious to meet you." "The Guild?" Neb asked.

"Yes. They're sort of a federation of worlds representing the whole known universe, otherwise known as the Council of U." Tict waved to Neb to follow him. "This way, please." They exited Neb's room.

"You're kidding. Like *Star Trek*?" Neb's eyes popped. "Yes, just like *Star Trek*, which is a widely debated topic among the Guild members. We picked up a transmission of *Star Trek* from

Earth about fifteen years ago. It was all the rave here at the Casino and still is. The debate among the Guild is how closely they got it right. I mean it's so eerily close, it's mystifying to everyone. Who would have thought earthlings like us could come up with such ideas and throw off the Guild. Don't tell anyone, but I find great pleasure in it. To be honest, Neb, Earth at the moment is not highly regarded among the Guild either. Progress reports throughout the millennia have not favoured Earth. They're not sure if you're going to eventually blow yourselves up or become civilized enough to one day join the rest of the universe and Guild. The odds favour the former, I am afraid."

"*Star Trek* was an OK show. My parents were really into it. You should have heard them when they cancelled the show – they went ballistic!" Neb said.

"An OK show," Tict shushed Neb, "and cancelled? If you're asked about the show tonight, please don't mention the cancellation bit. There are few accomplishments the Guild likes about Earth. *Star Trek* is one. *Star Wars* is another conversation altogether. Though reaching the moon, that was given a thumbs up for Earth.

Neb thought about it for a moment, then chimed, "Seems as though this Guild is a little racist, though I can understand that, at the moment, Earth may be a little underachieving where technology is concerned."

"Technology is the least of Earth's problems," Tict said. "How so?" Neb asked.

"Where does one start, my boy! Let's look at it this way. In *Star Trek*, we have the Klingons, the Romulans, the Andorians and, not to forget, the Vulcans, for starters. Each of these worlds doesn't seem to be at war within their own worlds, though they are with each other. The earthlings, on the other hand, fight against their own people and have since the beginning. One fights another because of a different colour of skin, language, race, country, faith, etc. It's the only known world that does so. The Earth is doomed, some say, because it's not unified as a people. I mean we're all the same damn species! Human, for heaven's sake! Which leads one to ask, would you let such indifference into a club that does not tolerate this type of behavior? Or would you avoid them until they learned to adapt to the norm, if ever?" Tict vented for the first time in Neb's presence.

"Interesting, Tict. The Vulcans were war-like until they adopted logic."

"Yes, that's true, Neb, but you're forgetting one thing."

"What's that?"

"Vulcan is fictional; the Earth is real. It's not that they're hated by the larger universe. Actually, everyone is pulling for them to get it right. Earth is a marvellous planet. Its lush greenery, seas and oceans are envied by many worlds. When you mismanage it, someone is going to have to pay dearly. Earth and its people, I am afraid, may lose the right to exist. I would hate not to be able to visit home every 75 years," Tict said sadly.

"What about all those UFO sightings over the years, centuries, in fact? If what you say is to be believed and Earth is to be avoided, what accounts for these encounters?" Neb countered.

"The policy is you can visit but no contact whatsoever is to be made. That does not just go for Earth, but for any planet not up to speed with the rest of the galaxy. Though sometimes a ship or two is detected, there always seems to be an explanation by the authorities. You know, a weather balloon and the like. Not one world or its species is perfect, Neb."

"So, in the end, it's like the non-interference pact in *Star Trek*. Sometimes Kirk screws up."

"Yes. The Guild has set up an ongoing inquiry to find out how Earth got *Star Trek* so right. It's too much of a coincidence. So, if you're asked about *Star Trek*, please play it coy, will you?" Tict asked.

"OK, will do," Neb nodded, "though I have to ask, Tict, if not everyone is sold on Earth, why the human-looking appearance that everyone seems to have? I am also afraid to ask what everyone really looks like."

"That is an interesting question, Neb. When I first arrived, I thought that everyone was indeed human. You see, the creators of this vessel, the Triopelians, were also humanoid, much like us, but with longer life spans. So, when the specs were drawn up, they automatically incorporated their own form into the Vegastriopelia's matrix. Every being is set at five foot nine like all Triopelians. It makes perfect sense."

"Wait, you're confusing me a little. There's the Vegastriopelia, the Triopelia and the Triopelians?"

"Don't worry, Neb, we will get to them all soon enough." "So, if I may ask, what's with you? I mean what is your function here? Are you the greeting party?"

"Oh, did I not mention I am the concierge of Halley's Casino?" Tict bowed. "Welcome, Nebula Yorker."

"Concierge! How is that? You're human. I thought that humans were *persona non grata*."

"It's kind of complicated and we will get to that later as well. Suffice it to say Lafil was the first human concierge and he did a magnificent job for well over 5,000 years. He was the longest serving concierge, human, anyhow, to my knowledge."

"Five thousand years? You've got to be kidding me!" Neb loudly remarked. "How is that possible?"

"All in good time, Neb, all in good time," Tict assured his young new friend.

"TeeceeFore mentioned someone named Marcus Apitippius, along with both of us, as the only humans aboard. And, did I hear correctly, John Lennon?"

"You have a good memory, Neb. I know you have many questions and I ask you please, once again, to be patient. All will be answered very soon," Tict assured him. "Let me tell you something, Neb, that the Guild won't say in public," he whispered. "It's that we humans have something that they lack and do you know what that is? WE HAVE BALLS! Literally and figuratively!" They both laughed.

"That is the main reason why, for well over 5,000 years, a human, starting with Lafil, ran the Casino!" Tict gleefully and proudly said. "But it's gone mostly downhill from there with Earth. The Guild saw progress but, again, as humans, we take one step forward and two back.

"What about you, Tict?" Neb asked. "Lafil chose you to replace him, didn't he?"

"Not really. I was very fortunate to have found Lafil or to have met him when I did. Lafil had an assistant who was to be next in line to replace him when he retired or stepped aside. Though one benefit of being the concierge of the Casino is a kind of immortality clause; as long as you're concierge, or being groomed to take over at some point, all your cellular structure has been reconfigured. You become one with the Vegastriopelia. In Lafil's case, an unforeseen circumstance led to his untimely demise, which would have led to my death if it hadn't."

"Unforeseen circumstance?" Neb enquired.

"Yes. All departures must be requested, registered, imputed and coordinated before one can leave the Casino, to ensure that the immortality bubble is set in place when visiting Earth in present time and especially when time travelling. Lafil had not registered any request to leave the Casino back in 1758 and someone was aware of this. To make a long story short, this someone pushed Lafil backwards through the transport transfiguror. With no planned schedule to leave, once Lafil made contact with Earth, his molecular structure began to revert and deteriorate. I guess you could say I was in the right place at the right time, if that is any consolation to my present situation and occupation," Tict explained.

"But if you can travel back in time, can't you go back and save Lafil, Tict?"

"I wish I could, Neb. Unfortunately, I'm afraid that is strictly forbidden. Time could fold or collapse or the Earth's past, present and whatever future would be altered. Who knows what that could lead to! It would be the same on any other world if anyone tried or inadvertently changed their past. Don't get me wrong, Neb, time travel in itself can be fantastic. One needs to be very inconspicuous when doing so. Blend in and mind your own business. For example, I never knew my mother, as she died giving birth to me. Back in 1910, the last time we were in the solar system, I decided to find her."

"How is that, Tict? I thought that you could only go back in time according to your age."

"True. So when is one's existence determined? Is it at birth or perhaps at conception? I presented this question to the Vegastriopelia. It calculated that it could be both. It varies from one species to another. So, long story short, I met my mother while still in the womb, it was truly an amazing experience. I was watching her from afar at the market. She was very beautiful, cheerful and pleasant with all she met and spoke with. While sitting at the entrance to the market square, she breezed by me. I said 'Good Morning' to her. My voice triggered a reaction from the child inside her (me). The baby jumped. She looked at me grinning, laughed and went on her way. The best thirty minutes of my life." Tict wiped his eyes. Neb shed a tear as well on hearing his story.

"But enough about me. You know more about me than most do and I hardly know you."

Neb wondered if that was true. "What is this Vegastriopelia you keep speaking about? You'd think it was the Wizard of Oz, the way you speak of it."

“Well, get ready to kick up your heels, Mr. Yorker. You’re about to find out. Follow me, please,” Tict motioned with his finger.

6

They walked out of Neb's room and down the white- walled hallway. All the hallways of the Casino were long and white-walled. How anyone found their way around was nothing less than a miracle. There were no doors that Neb could see but every few steps a door would swoosh open out of nowhere. As quickly as they opened, they closed. Neb was able to take a quick peek and he could make out people milling about and some kind of games being played. *Of course*, he thought, *we're in a casino.*

Each room had a different game of chance. There were slots, bingo, baccarat, keno, roulette, blackjack, craps and, of course, poker of every kind. Neb's curiosity did not go unnoticed by Tict. One room had crib-poker, a mix of cribbage and Texas holdem poker. Tict asked Neb if he'd like to take a look inside.

"Sure," Neb jumped at the offer.

Tict said, "OK, but we're on a tight schedule."

They entered the room and walked over to the closest table. They observed the four opponents seated at the table, three men and one woman, along with the dealer in the centre. Player one's name was Vertal, player two, Mertal, player three, Jertal and player four, Zertal. They were a family, Jertal, the mother, and her three sons. The sons all looked ready for the old age home but Jertal had such young-looking features, she looked like she had never given birth

The game and betting had begun with a sizable pot visible to both Neb and Tict. The dealer had already dealt the first round of two cards each, face down. He was about to proceed with the flop, three cards up. He tapped the table, and then proceeded to turn over the cards. The first card up was the King of Hearts. Next, the dealer pressed down with two fingers revealing the following cards: the King of Clubs and, finally, the last card, the Ten of Hearts. The player to the dealer's right was first to call. It was

Vertal, a white-haired stocky fellow wearing dark round sunglasses perched low on his nose. He looked down at the flop with a slight grin that everyone at the table noticed. The cards he held in his hand were the Five of Spades and the Five of Hearts, a set. Stretching his hand out on the table he patted twice and said “Pass”.

His opponent next to him, Mertal, could have been his twin. Neb noticed that they were identical except for Mertal’s huge white handlebar moustache and knew there was a good chance they were. Mertal peeked at his cards that were face down on the table. He had the two other Kings, Spades and Diamonds. Strangely enough, he also passed on betting.

To Mertal’s right was their mother Jertal. Neb thought she looked like she was about to explode, with her flowing red fiery hair and her shifty eyes. He also thought she might be an alien. Jertal lifted up her cards from the table and peeked at a pair of Twos, Clubs and Spades. She played with her chips, lifting them up, then letting them fall back in place over and over again. When it seemed that she was going to bet, she also passed.

Tict was now thinking how strange a game this was turning out to be. *Aliens*, he mused to himself, though he knew better.

Finally, it was Zertal’s turn, the last player, who could easily have been a triplet, stocky and white-haired, though with a long black thick unibrow above his eyes. *What was it with these three guys?* Neb wondered as he looked at them. Zertal

held the Queen and Ace of Hearts. He had a possible Royal Flush. He didn’t flinch.

“One hundred thousand!” he said, pushing his chips into the pot.

“Really?” Vertal said, looking down at his cards again and back at Zertal. He had two pairs, another King or Five would make it a full house and a great crib hand. He studied his brother up and down for a few minutes, then announced, "I see your one hundred thousand and raise ALL-IN! Two million more!"

Mertal did not hesitate. "Call. Here's the initial one hundred thousand and my two million." Jertal, the fiery red- headed mother, laughed out loud. "What the hell, boys, no fun just watching. I call!"

Zertal scratched his head. What had he started? He played with his chips, started to pick his nose but decided against it and farted instead. "Well, someone's going to win and it might as well be me. I call!"

In total, there was well over twelve million dollars up for grabs. Neb couldn't believe it. Was it real money or alien money?

The dealer now asked everyone to display their cards up. The Fives, the Kings, the Twos and the Queen/Ace suited.

King of Hearts, King of Clubs and Ten of Hearts were now ready to go. The dealer held the deck of cards in his left hand. He tapped the table with his right. Taking the top card, he placed it to the bottom of the deck, burying the card, as it were. The next card he overturned -- placing it beside the King of Hearts, the King of Clubs and the Ten of Hearts in a nice straight row – was the Five of Hearts.

"Yes sir!" Vertal jumped up from his seat, pumping his fists into the air. The table was not amused.

Interesting, Mertal thought, looking back at his brother Vertal.

Zertal still had a possible flush waiting to be had to dash his brother's hope. Jertal needed a Three and was hoping it wasn't a Heart. The dealer once again buried the top card to turn over the last card of the game. He turned up the Three of Diamonds.

King of Clubs, King of Hearts, Ten of Hearts, Five of Hearts and Three of Diamonds, all face-up, completed the line. Jertal leaped up from her chair and danced around the table twice.

"YES!" she proclaimed.

"OK, lady and gentlemen," the dealer began, "I am now going to take this fresh deck of cards." He held it up for everyone to see and cut for the Crib. All eyes were on him. Neb had never seen such a tight game of cards, especially as this was his first Crib Poker game. The dealer cut the deck once and turned to Tict.

"Would you do us the privilege, Mr. Tict?" he asked.

Tict looked to the table. "Is that fine with everyone?"

Everyone smiled. "We would be honoured," Jertal spoke up.

Tict's hand reached for the top card. The entire table held their breath. He turned over the Five of Clubs. Vertal fell over on his chair and popped back up in seconds.

"What's happening?" Neb turned to Tict. "Who won?"

"Give it a moment," Tict replied. "In Texas Holdem, it would seem that the player with the Flush has won but, not so fast, not with Crib Poker. The dealer now adds up all the crib points. The player who has the most crib points is declared the winner unless the winning poker hand, along with his/her crib hand, is the better of all the hands at the table.

After adding up the cribbage points the winner was Vertal with KK1053 & 5 for 40 points. Mertal had KK1053 & 5 with a pair of Kings for 30 points; Jertal had KK1053 & 5 with a pair of 2's for 28 points; and, lastly, Zertal had KK1053 & 5 with Queen/Ace suited for 20 points.

Tict congratulated Vertal.

"Drinks on me tonight!" Vertal proclaimed.

"You bet your ass they are, and not just drinks!" Jertal and Mertal laughed. Zertal said nothing. He sat there and stewed as his brother reached for his winnings.

What an odd game, Neb thought. *Why not just play crib and poker separately?*

7

Tict and Neb exited the oval Crib Poker room and headed back down a long white hallway. The entire Casino was oval, every room from the games rooms to the bathrooms. The ballrooms were magnificent, especially the Green Room. They walked silently, a door opening every now and then. Then Neb noticed that no doors were opening and no guests were seen popping in and out. Tict again noticed Neb noticing.

"Don't worry, there, dear boy, we've passed beyond the games room into the restricted area of the Casino. You know, employees only," Tict assured Neb.

"Hey, I didn't say anything. How did you do that?" Neb asked.

"It's written all over your face." Tict stopped and held out his arm for Neb to stop walking.

"What's up?"

"Wait for it," Tict replied. The floor beneath them began to vibrate. A hissing sound came up from beneath them as a square of the floor they stood on began to slowly move downward. As they sank down, the floor above closed over them. A dark space now encompassed both Tict and Neb. Neb could feel the slight movement of the hydraulics as they descended.

"Tict?" Neb asked calmly, but a little nervously. "What's going on?" He wasn't sure if they were still descending or moving sideways. It felt like both. Were they picking up speed? Was that a left turn? Neb felt his stomach bouncing up and down and, well, yes, all around. He felt the plates beneath his feet start to slow down, then another quick turn. He could hear music or what sounded like music. Were the hydraulics humming a song? Whatever they were on now came to a halt. A crack of light appeared. Looking up at the floor, or what was now the ceiling, he saw an opening peeled away and they now leisurely ascended. Neb squinted as they rose from the dark, the light hitting his eyes, and he covered his face. As he did so, he looked over at Tict and noticed he was wearing a pair of sunglasses.

"I see you came prepared." Neb tapped Tict's sunglasses.

"Oh yes, I am always." Tict grinned.

They surfaced into an empty white oval room. Tict removed his sunglasses.

"Could use a little colour, don't you think?" Neb said as he looked around another white room. "Is everyone here colour blind by chance or was white paint on special when they painted?"

"I can't speak for everyone but I am colour blind. Or I was before I came aboard."

"Activate," Tict said aloud. The room now went pitch black.

"Is that the colour you were going for, Tict?" said Neb.

"Wait for it," Tict replied. "Patience is not one of your strong suits, is it?" A dim soft light appeared and, as it became brighter, the empty space was no longer empty. They were now in a completely different room, or so it seemed to Neb.

"How did you do that?" Neb scratched his head.

"Welcome to mission control," Tict said.

There were androids in red and white jumpsuits manning consoles, running with electron clip pads. Some were flipping switches and pressing buttons on the many consoles that were everywhere. In all, there were 42 male and female androids working feverishly, like honey bees or like ants marching up a hill. Neb had watched a documentary two nights before on honey bees and ants and this activity reminded him of it. It was all so very strange. Neb's mind could take him on a wild ride at times.

Tict now waved to Neb to follow him. Some of the androids nodded to Tict and Neb as they walked passed. Tict nodded in return. No one spoke a word.

"Everything here is programmed, transcribed, vented, invented and reinvented, sorted, resorted and digested," explained Tict. "The flow of data never ceases. From here at mission control, all functions of the Casino are monitored; every need is cared for; everything planned out in advance. Take the toilet paper, for example. We believe some of the guests might be hoarding and taking some home with them when they leave, though one cannot blame them because it's the softest throughout time and space. Coming from a place that didn't have toilet paper, that says a lot. I suppose that is why so many of our guests keep coming back."

As Tict was explaining, he thought he noticed Eno out of the corner of his eye exiting the far corner of the room. *That's odd*, he thought. He mentally registered it and continued on with Neb. He didn't notice that Neb also saw Eno. Neb didn't think much of it. He just recognized Eno from the hover cab ride.

"Is there any reason for the red and white jumpsuit for the androids? I've noticed that they're intermingled. Why not red for the males and white for the females or vice versa?"

"What's that, Neb?" Tict's mind was still on Eno.

"Hey, is that Kel?!" Neb's attention turned as he spotted her working at one of the consoles alongside two others, a male in white and a female in red. Neb forgot about Tict and was soon walking over to her.

"Hello, Kel. It's me, Neb!"

"Yes, I know who you are." She barely looked up from her console. The two other androids working beside her were

PIC-500, the male, and PIC-501, the female. They looked at each other quizzically, then shrugged their shoulders and continued working. Neb felt spurned.

"So, what's a girl like you doing in a place like this?" Neb continued.

"I don't understand the question," KEL-345 replied. "I am not a girl. I am, as you know, an android. Did you bang your head since our last meeting, impairing your memory banks? I have seen it occur with other humanoid species. Some never seem to be the same after such a trauma; others, though, seem to find themselves with a higher IQ than that they started with. Is this the case with you Neb?"

Neb wasn't sure what to say next. PIC-500 and PIC-501 let out a low static shrill that Neb swore was a laugh. He stared them both down for a few seconds, looking into their silicone eyes. *Androids, eh?* He still ignored that KEL-345 was one, though.

"Anyhow, what I meant to say was, Kel, what are you working on?"

"We are preparing the Vegastriopelia simulator for you and Mr. Tict."

"Vegastriopelia simulator? Is that anything like the Triopelia I have been hearing about?"

"They are one and the same." KEL-345 continued keying in data.

Tict shuffled up behind Kel and Neb. "Are we ready, KEL-345?"

"We will be in four minutes, three seconds, two seconds, one…." Tict cut her off.

"Androids, eh?" Tict said. "You got to love them!"

"Tict just gawked at Neb. For whatever reason, he could still see that Neb was either ignoring the fact about KEL-345 or that he was in need of medical assistance. He thought it better to wait it out and let Neb eventually figure it out. He found it very fascinating, to say the least. He thought he might even write a paper on the subject when he had the time.

"Have you ever had a dream so real, Tict, that it became true? I had a dream about Kel before I met her this morning. To dream about someone you've never met and then meet them is more than a coincidence, don't you think?"

That does explain a lot, Tict thought. "Have you ever had such a dream before this? About meeting someone and then actually meeting them?"

"Funny you should ask." Neb paused. "When I was younger, two nights before the Yorkers came for me, or should I say to rescue me, I dreamt of them. I never told them until my sixteenth birthday. The three of us were watching *Star Trek*, of all things. It was the episode 'Mirror, Mirror', my favorite, when Captain Kirk, Mr. Spock and Dr. McCoy, Scotty and Uhura are caught in a transporter malfunction that swaps their counterparts with each other from a parallel universe. That evil Spock really rocked it! Anyhow, for some odd reason, it triggered the dream of Mom and Dad coming to get me. I waited until the show was over to tell them. They didn't think too much of it, saying that every orphan had a wanting, a wish, a need, a dream about having real parents. It went with the territory. I accepted the reasoning. It made perfect sense that a parentless child would want real, loving parents. It wasn't a big deal, though I did overhear Mom and Dad talking about it later that evening before bed. So much was going through my head that, for a few days after that, I thought I was from a parallel universe. Funny the things we think of when we're younger, eh, Tict?" Neb smiled.

"Yes, indeed, young Nebula. Parallel universes can be very tricky at that. That is, if one were to find oneself in such a spot, one needs to be very careful so as not to interfere or be found out. It's much like time travelling. The consequences could be fatal, not just for the one, but for all," Tict replied with a very serious tone.

"Are you telling me, Tict, that parallel universes exist?" Neb asked, wide-eyed.

"I didn't say that, did I? What I did say was that if one found oneself in one, much like time travel, you wouldn't want to do anything that would change anything, that's all."

Now why don't I believe you? Neb thought to himself. KEL-345 looked up at Tict from her console.

"The Vegastriopelia simulator calculations are now complete and ready."

"Not a moment too soon," Tict muttered under his breath. He quickly grabbed Neb by the arm and led him away. "Open," he said. A door swooshed open and, looking both ways, he hurried Neb in.

Now this was a definite change. The room was multi-coloured, with shades of blue, green, red, yellow, orange, purple, and colours that Neb wasn't sure existed.

"What the…." Neb stopped.

"You did ask for some colour, did you not?" Tict proudly grinned. "You haven't seen anything yet, my dear boy!" he pronounced with his arms straight out. "Welcome to the Vegastriopelia!"

In the middle of the room were two rocking chairs, quite similar to the ones in Tict's office and in Neb's room, minus the orange afghans. "Let's rock, shall we?" Tict escorted Neb to the chairs. As soon as they sat down, the room went dark. *Not again.* Neb shook his head. *What's up with that?*

“Start rocking,” Tict called out in the dark. “What?” Neb asked.

“Just start to rock your chair,” Tict repeated.

Neb complied and, as he started to rock back and forth, the room began to lighten up, ever so slowly. He could see shadowy images moving in the background, two or maybe three, he wasn’t sure. He thought maybe his eyes were playing tricks on him. A twirling sound began to ring in his ears. It got louder and louder, and then stopped. It repeated itself twice. Suddenly the air cracked as if a plane were taking off.

“Attention. Attention. Transport completed,” a voice was heard. Those shadowy images now began to clear as Neb realized he was watching a viewing screen with TeeceeFore stepping down from a transporter platform with two male androids in red helping her down. Then the screen froze.

“Computer, play back initial time of arrival for TeeceeFore index 4550.5,” Tict ordered, while rocking back and forth. The two male androids now appeared back on screen standing away from the transporter platform. They were working at the prime console. This particular transporter platform was adjacent to the hangar that Neb arrived on. It had a square base with four columns holding up what looked like a hovering tent top.

“A square? That’s a first,” Neb commented.

The two male androids were speaking to each other. They nodded, agreeing on some procedure, by the look of it. “Ready,” one could be heard to say. The other pressed a few keys and held down a leveler and lifted it back up again. Inside the platform, a yellowish blue mass began to appear. It fazed in and out until the androids could get a solid fix on the transport. Nodding again, they pressed another series of buttons, looking up from the console. They fixed their attention on the platform. The yellowish blue haze appeared again. It started out small and then grew larger with a loud sonic pop. Neb’s eyes grew wide. Something the size of a grown elephant materialized on the platform.

It had five-inch quills sprouting from its leathery grey body, two huge, black shark-like eyes blinking non-stop. It had no nose, a wide mouth but no visible tusks that Neb could decipher. It wasn't an elephant.

"Phase one complete, initiating phase two," the first male android said to the second. The second repeated the sequence or so it sounded to Neb. The creature started to jiggle and bounce as the yellowish blue mass of light swirled counterclockwise around it. The whatever-it-was disappeared then reappeared instantaneously. It began to lose its form as it shrank before Neb's eyes.

"Attention. Attention. Transport completed," again was heard. There standing in full sight on the platform, in front of Neb, on the viewing screen was TeeceeFore. She was being helped down off the transporter platform by the two male androids.

"Computer, end," Tict ordered. Neb stopped rocking, his mouth agape. It took a few minutes for him to register what he had just seen.

"Who would have thought?" he commented. He turned to Tict who was watching his every movement, his every expression, indeed, his every tic. "To quote Mr. Spock, fascinating!" Neb marveled.

"Indeed!" Tict replied, his left brow cocked.

"Does TeeceeFore know that she looks like that?" Neb asked in disbelief.

"So, that is how we get everyone to fit aboard, though you haven't seen or heard anything yet, dear boy. This is just the beginning."

“Computer,” Tict called out, “commence with the history file on the Vegastriopelia.”

“Commencing,” the computer’s voice replied.

“May I ask, Tict, what is with the rocking chairs? I also noticed one in your office and one in my room with the orangish afghans.”

“The back and forth motion eases the brain waves while the Vegastriopelia configures the synapses, so as one takes in the information, the transmitted data stream flows through your whole body, not just your brain. You become one with the Vegastriopelia.”

“The afghans?”

“The afghans are there in case you get a chill and want to warm up,” Tict laughed. “You see, the Vegastriopelia and the Triopelia are one and the same, but not to everyone. You’ll get the hang of it once you have taken in the stream. I know it may seem somewhat confusing but, again, it will all make sense to you shortly. You only need to go through this procedure once. Don’t worry too much about it, Neb. If you were ever to experience the meaning of being brainwashed, hang on, keep on rocking; you’re in for a wash and spin cycle treat.

“Can I go to the bathroom first?” Neb nervously asked.

“Do you really have to?” Tict replied, a little annoyed.

“On second thought, I think I can hold it. May I ask one more thing, Tict? Is there any chance of getting some popcorn and soda?” Tict said nothing but smirked.

8

The room again went dark. All that could be heard was the sound of two rocking chairs swaying back and forth. A small white dot appeared. It grew and grew until a large explosion projected out from the view screen. Neb almost tipped over in his rocking chair. A deep voice echoed out, "Beyond the Plexus Rim, there exist the planets of Pratt, Lerxst and Dirk, whose people were all one." Shown on the viewing screen were the three named planets orbiting a yellow sun, much like Earth's sun. Neb took note of how these worlds also resembled Earth, the blue water and land masses almost equal. The Prattonians, the Lerxstonians and the Dirkonians were the first known spacefaring races. As universes grew and expanded, other species would take to space flight, some for scientific purposes or commerce, and others for war. The Lerxstonians were masters of all technology and science and witticism. The Dirkonians' strength lay in teaching, poetry, music, architecture, medicine, literature and witticism. Prattonians were agriculturists, environmentalists, oceanographers, ship builders, encompassing land, air, sea and space, yet void of witticism.

The screen now depicted the activities of these people hard at work and at play. Again, Neb noted their humanoid appearance, not much different from himself. Every manner of life on Pratt, Lerxst and Dirk was for the good of all. Never a disagreement, never a second thought, never war. Much of this was due to the fact that they relied only on themselves. Contact outside of the Plexus Rim was limited; those from the outer regions of space considered them hermits. They were far from being hermits. From time to time, delegations were accepted from visiting worlds and at times a small delegation would also venture out to show that they were an open people. Hermits indeed!

In time, there arose a devastating plague on Telvon Three that almost wiped out the entire population. Everything was tried, but to no avail. A planet-wide quarantine was imposed on all surrounding space, a subspace beacon notified, alerting the galaxy. Upon hearing of their plight, the Dirkonians, without fear of danger to themselves, set out on a mission to help the people of Telvon Three.

Rocking away, Neb peeked over at Tict. *TeeceeFore's home world.*

Within days of arriving on Telvon Three, the Dirkonians determined the cause of the plague and quickly synthesized a cure. A quill manicure, of all things, was to blame. This was quickly outlawed. It did not sit well with the beauticians' union but it was unavoidable. The Dirkonians implemented the use of sonic manicures, a procedure that would be soothing and painless for the Telvonians and far less expensive.

The news of what had been done for the inhabitants of Telvon Three spread quickly through the neighbouring star systems. The Council of U was then formed, patterned somewhat after the unity of the planets of Pratt, Lerxst and Dirk, and headed up by Telvon. All the worlds were urged to join. Delegates were sent out, treaties signed, ideas shared. Peace ensued where peace had never existed, although a few rogue worlds continued to resist, sometimes causing small skirmishes over petty disagreements; not against the Council of U but directed towards Pratt, Lerxst and Dirk.

The primary mandate of the Council of U was to assist any world in dire need of assistance, whatever the cause might have been. Though Pratt, Lerxst and Dirk signed on to the Council, they largely remained apart from the actual functioning of the Council, a decree agreed upon by all and included in its constitution.

As thousands of years passed, less and less was heard from beyond the Plexus Rim. A Prattonian ship's signature was detected now and then, but was left alone. Most thought that the Council of U was doing a fine job and who needed them anyway? Sure, they helped with the whole unity configuration but some quietly began to question the importance of their membership within the Council.

"Why aren't they ever here?" some would vent. "Are they too good for us? Do we smell or something?" Of course, it always came down to the clear thinking minds of the Telvonians to set matters straight. They were Defenders of the constitution. If it were not for the Dirkonians, they would not exist, nor would the Council of U. As with all things, time passes along with its old generation and a new generation is born, knowing nothing of its past but only its present.

In the Year of Confliction, as it has come to be called, and unknown to the Telvonians, a delegation was secretly formed. Led by Membob Kopp, a council member from the planet of Hilips, they left in two ships headed for the Plexus Rim. When Membob Kopp with his ships reached the Plexus Rim, they dispatched out a subspace message to Pratt, Lerxst and Dirk of their immediate arrival. No answer was received. Upon entering their star system, no planets were found. Not one moon or sun.

Membob Kopp and crew scrupulously dissected every known star chart at their disposal. According to the location and the proper coordinates imputed, they should have been orbiting Lerxst but found themselves staring into nothing but dark, deep space. More frustrated than ever, Membob Kopp turned his ships around and headed back to Hilips. But to his delight, by mere chance, halfway home while scanning an asteroid field, long-range sensors detected a small Prattonian vessel. Membob Kopp pounced on the vessel and its occupants, a young Lerxstonian male and a Prattonian female.

There were no pleasantries extended to them. Immediately upon their capture, the interrogations began. The question Membob Kopp wanted answered was, "Where had the planets of Pratt, Lerxst and Dirk gone to?"

The news of this violation soon spread to the Council of U. Some were outraged; others not. The disagreement began to split the Council. The Telvonians, of course, stood up for the rights of their saviours as did many other worlds. The Hiliponians managed to sway a third of the Council seats to their side. What were Pratt, Lerxst and Dirk hiding? Or why were they seemingly hiding? Of what business was it to the Hiliponians what they did? Upon the formation and signed constitution of the Council of U over two thousand years earlier, these worlds were well within their rights to be left alone as agreed by all. But that was no longer a reasonable answer to the Hiliponians and their followers.

The Telvonians sent out couriers to the Plexus Rim to inform the three planets of the perilous situation, yet they too received no answers. After numerous tries, a communication beacon was left behind in the region in case their message was finally received and acknowledged. It was eleven months later before it would be.

Meanwhile, the young Prattonian and her Lerxstonian companion were continuously tortured. The Council pressed for the release of the couple, but all pleas fell upon deaf ears. Finally, the Hiliponians resigned from the Council along with the planets of Dregonion, Graspton Six, Chocxivxix, Ekaveo and Themosjustic. All diplomatic ties to the Council of U were now severed. It was now feared an all-out war would ensue. Little information trickled in on the condition of the Hiliponian's captives. There were rumours that they had been executed, though nothing could be confirmed.

Reports filtered in along the Dregonion border of a buildup of warships. Graspton Six and Ekaveo troops were assembling on Chocxivxix and now word that Themosjustic was having second thoughts reached the Council. Indeed, one of the captives was killed, the young male Lerxtonian. Themosjustic's reverse course of action was met with force but not before the Themosjusticians were able to smuggle out the badly beaten Prattonian female. She would be taken to Telvon Three and cared for.

Furious with Themosjustic and the rescue of the female, Membob Kopp gathered his forces, along with his remaining allies, and headed full-on for Telvon Three. The armada was now bent on destruction, revenge and glory.

The Council of U convened on Telvon Three, knowing what lay ahead. All Council forces were activated and placed in orbit around the planet on the orders of Krule Kom of Jaloop, the new presiding chair of the Council of U who had only been sworn in for the cycle three days earlier. Jaloopians were known for their sincere demeanor and diplomatic skills. Krule Kom's mettle had been put to the test. How could anyone secure any kind of diplomacy with the undiplomatic Hiliponians?

Krule Kom paced back and forth, looking down to the council chamber floor, the arms of his thin, seven-foot frame positioned behind his back. The Jaloopians had a basic humanoid form, though most were seven to eight feet tall and had long, gaunt faces. They were extremely good listeners and problem solvers. The other fourteen council members sat around the crystal oval chamber table working their consoles, keeping in touch with each home world, and peeking up every now and then, eyeing Krule who was still pacing. Everything stopped when the chamber doors opened and the Prime Minister of Telvon 3, Thyee TwothyFore, walked in with the ex-captive Prattonian female at his side.

Many of the Council worlds were stunned and amazed at Thyee TwothyFore's humanoid form. A part hologram, part synthetic clone matrix gave him the freedom that most humanoids took for granted. This process was the beginning of the transfiguror, as it would come to be known, as accommodating Telvonian delegations at times could be a massive undertaking to their hosts. The process was revolutionary. It would change how inhabitants from all known worlds would meet. All it would take was a flip of a switch, so to speak, to adapt to any scenario that one could not previously envision or fit. Vacation planets would boom!

Thyee TwothyFore's newly enhanced humanoid six-foot frame, egghead bald, sailed briskly along the Council chamber floor, his red and blue robe lightly fluttering. Walking beside him was the rescued captive of Membob Kopp. Her name was Blulay. Everyone rose and bowed. Krule Kom approached Blulay, extending his long arms and fingers and gently tapping her forehead. She smiled as they communicated telepathically.

Blulay thanked the Council of U and the Themosjustic for her rescue from Hilips. The death of her companion, whose name was Ruban of Pratt, weighed heavy on her, as did the impending outcome of the present situation out in space. Never in her whole life or that of her civilization had they faced such conflict. Blulay asked if she could use a console to contact Lerxst, her home world.

"Of course, my dear, you may use mine." Krule Kom escorted her to his seat at the chamber table. Blulay sat and looked about the Council table, noticing that all eyes were on her. A wave of calm overwhelmed her. She knew that they had nothing but good intentions. Blulay smiled at everyone seated and said in a soft, warm tone. "All is not lost."

A surprised Krule Kom turned to the other Council members. *All is not lost?*

Blulay keyed in her transmission codes. She and the Council now sat back and waited for a response. Unknown to the Council, the year of confliction was about to end.

Blulay closed her eyes and thought about Ruban, her companion, her lover, her bond. They had set out on a two-year exploration of the Mentic Terran Star System. Life was in its earliest stages on most of the planets in the system. One in particular stood out. They began their adventure, landing on a planet similar to their own – blue with lively rivers, lakes, oceans and seas, snow-topped monstrous mountain ranges, long golden prairies, tall flowing grass tossed about like waves on a sea.

They had made base in the mid-temporal zone. It was warm enough that they didn't need to wear heavy clothes during the day and the nights were cool for sleeping. Their vessel sat atop a high hill overlooking a large lake shaded by red trees, 200 feet tall. The yellow sunsets were magnificent. It was where they made love for the first time.

One beep, two beeps, three sounded off from the console. It shook Blulay back to the present. Contact with Lerxst was made.

Meanwhile out in space, Membob Kopp now had Telvon Three well within his target range. Five hundred warships sat steadily behind his flagship waiting for the call to engage. The Council's fleet consisted of two hundred ships that formed a shield about Telvon Three. As Membob Kopp's forces edged closer and closer, his fat body grumbled for food. He had not eaten or slept for well over twenty-four hours. Sitting on his bridge looking out into the view screen, Telvon Three loomed closer and closer, as did the Council forces surrounding the planet.

"Orders, Sir?" His First Officer turned from his console to face Membob.

"Open up a channel to all our ships!" Membob Kopp snarled back.

"Channel open," the First responded.

"This is Membob Kopp. We stand on the frontier of history, new history, our history. No longer shall we be subjugated to the whims of the Council of U or those past idealistic pacifiers from Pratt, Lerxst and Dirk. Let those cowards hide and let them now hide in fear! Ask those on Themosjustic how traitors are dealt with."

Membob Kopp rose from his command chair. He stared down at his bridge crew.

"NO MERCY!" he cried out. "Commence the battle!"

An eerie hush resonated over the Council chamber. Everything and everyone stopped as if the air had just been sucked out of the room. Some of the Council members seemed to be praying to themselves; the intense expressions of others indicated they were all too aware of the seriousness of the situation. There was indeed a nervous tension.

A small bead of sweat rolled down Krule Kom's ivory face. Blulay reached over and tapped his hand twice with her finger. He sat back, smiled and relaxed. Blulay returned the smile and, as she did, subspace static echoed over the comm. Everyone's eyes at the table looked to Blulay.

A voice on the other end asked, "Are you well?"

"I am well," Blulay answered.

"Is Ruban with you?"

"Ruban is fine, though not with us at present," Blulay responded.

Shock and surprise filled the room. Had the Council received the wrong information regarding the Lerxstonian?

"If he is not with you, may we enquire where he is?" the crackled static-filled voice asked.

"He is aboard the flagship of the Hiliponians which sits five hundred kilometres from Telvon Three, along with approximately five hundred battle-ready war cruisers intent on destroying the entire planet and all of its inhabitants and then moving on to the Plexus Rim. Telvon Three defenses will be no match for the Hiliponians fleet," Blulay relayed.

"Understood," the voice at the other end replied.

Within seconds, a yellowish blue swirl of light began to fill the Council chambers. The entire Council stood watching what fate might await them. They all gazed at the forming figures slowly coming into focus. As the yellowish blue haze dissipated, it revealed three men. It was not Membob Kopp materializing as they had feared.

Blulay rushed to the men, falling into the arms of all three. They hugged each other and tears of joy fell on all their faces.

"What is going on?" Krule Kom asked.

"Forgive me." Blulay turned and faced Krule Kom and the others in the room. "This is my father, Traep." He stepped forward from the centre and bowed, as did Blulay's brothers, Yddeg and Xela.

"Welcome to Telvon Three, said Thyee TwothyFore as he and the entire Council bowed.

"Thank you," replied Traep. "It has been a long time."

"You have been here before?" Thyee TwothyFore asked.

"Yes," smiled Traep, "a very long time ago but now is not the time to reminisce. The Vegastriopelia has located Ruban aboard Membob Kopp's ship, as you reported."

A hush fell over the room hearing the name the Vegastriopelia.

("Finally!" Neb muttered under his breath, "the Vegastriopelia.")

"His condition is somewhat depleted but fine. He thinks of you even now," Traep assured Blulay and then turned to the Council members.

"On behalf of our people, the Pratt, Lerxst and Dirk, we send greetings."

The entire Council stood in awe. They could not believe their eyes and ears.

"We thank you for your patience over all these years since our last encounter. We commend you and your ancestors for your continued compliance agreed upon in the Constitution regarding our arrangement with the formation of the Council of U. Though we may not have been present in person over all these years, be assured you have never been far away from our sight and thoughts. We have been watching." Traep bowed to all. "The Hiliponians have always been a rather testy race. We are saddened by their less than ideal approach. We know that they somehow feel slighted by our absence."

Xela stepped forward. "The Hiliponians feel slighted, but they have no reason for this. We are, and always have been, watching you through all these millenniums and we feel very proud of all your accomplishments."

Yddeg added, "Let us now begin to repair this rift."

The Council chamber rocked with the sound of explosions. Tiny bits of debris floated down from its high ceilings. The Council members ran for cover. Traep, Yddeg, Xela and Blulay stayed put.

All hell started to break loose. Krule Kom's comm alerted. He pressed the comm channel open.

"The Hiliponians have begun firing at our fleet. We intercepted two suicide scout ships over the Capital. Scanners detect more on the way. What are your orders…."

Another explosion was heard as the comm cut out. The Council chamber shook once more. This time, cracks began to appear in the walls. Traep walked over to Krule Kom's console and waved his hand over it.

"This is Traep. Is everything in place?"

A voice replied, "Yes."

He then walked over to his family. They all held hands. The yellowish blue light swirled about them and engulfed them.

"You don't intend to leave us, do you?" Thyee TwothyFore cried out.

"No, Prime Minister. We mean to end this battle before any more lives are taken," Traep coolly replied. "Have faith."

With that, the yellowish blue hue shot upward through the chamber ceiling and disappeared.

9

Membob Kopp walked around the bridge of his ship, his chest pumped out proudly for all to see, not that they couldn't; it was hard not to notice. Reports began to trickle in. Telvon Three's defensive shields were down to thirty-five per cent. Their four moon bases had been captured and prisoners were being rounded up. Telvon Three's capital, Barkemin, where the Council of U presided, had had minimal damage. Suicide squadrons there continued to penetrate their shields. Membob Kopp was very pleased with himself. Everything was going as planned.

"Incoming transmission, sir." His First Officer looked up at Membob Kopp from his console. "It's Krule Kom!" His eyes widened with a sleazy smile.

"On screen," Membob Kopp ordered, grinning from side to side.

"Screen on," the First Officer replied.

The screen on the bridge flickered on. Krule Kom was standing in the Council chamber. There were small wisps of smoke as debris floated in the background. He watched the Council chamber rock again as his forces continued to pound the city, centring on the Council chamber. The fourteen other council members slowly came into view and gathered around him.

"Have you decided to surrender before I inflict any more damage on you?" Membob Kopp asked, his hands on his hips, his black fanged teeth snarling out from the corner of his mouth. He watched as the Council members parted and stepped aside. As they did so, Traep came into full view before him.

"Who are you?" Membob Kopp glared and snarled.

"Membob Kopp of Hilips, the people of Pratt, Lerxst and Dirk bring you their greetings!" Traep said, his head held high. "I am Traep of Pratt." He bowed.

Membob Kopp's eyes lit up. He turned to his First and whispered to bring the prisoner.

"How delightful," Membob Kopp replied. "So you have finally come out of hiding, have you? I thought you would."

The bridge door swooshed open and there stood a chained Ruban. His face was scarred, his lip split with a dab of blood drooling down, his left eye puffed and closed. His legs were shackled. The chains rattled as the First brought him before Membob Kopp. He threw him to the floor of the bridge. Membob Kopp looked down at Ruban, then back up at the screen. He gave Ruban a vicious kick to his mid-section. He looked back up at Traep, standing unfazed.

"Lagmag Kopp would be so disappointed in you," Traep spoke.

Membob's eyes glowed demon red. "What do you know of Lagmag Kopp?" Membob Kopp retorted, kicking once again at Ruban.

"Lagmag Kopp of Hilips was the first to sign on to the Council of U. In fact, it was he who wrote up the clause regarding our participation within the Council those many years past, and he was a friend." Traep stared directly into the screen at Membob Kopp.

A long, cold shiver wavered down Membob's neck. It sank along down his back and through his legs to the tips of his toes. He paused for a few seconds. For some odd reason, it seemed like days. The crew all looked to Membob, dazed and confused at Traep`s words.

They were all very aware of who Lagmag Kopp was. Every Hiliponian knew. They had been taught Lagmag Kopp's accomplishments, his involvement with the constitution, his four cycles as chair of the Council of U and his heroic death saving his family from certain death after crash landing on Jaloop.

"How is it that you call my ancestor a friend? He has been dead for well over two thousand years," Membob Kopp screamed at the top of his voice. "How dare you invoke the name of Lagmag Kopp! I will personally kill you as I will now this scum." He bent down and picked up Ruban by the neck, lifting him up high enough for Traep to see. As he started to squeeze his neck, a swirl of yellowish blue light enveloped Ruban. The next moment he was standing beside Traep, free from his chains, no scars, no blood, looking as though nothing had happened to him.

Membob Kopp, now in a rage, grabbed the nearest person who, unfortunately, was his First Officer. Membob Kopp lunged at him, tearing off his right arm and throwing it at the view screen. His First thumped to the floor of the bridge, writhing in pain.

"Obliterate them!" Membob yelled, falling back onto his command chair with a primal scream heard throughout the fleet. No one on the bridge made a sound or a move. They were all too frightened.

"Did you not hear me? FIRE!" Membob screamed.

Still no one moved.

"I ordered you to fire!" Membob stumbled from his chair over to one of the firing consoles. He pushed aside one of his bridge crew who just fell to the floor. He didn't notice that the whole crew was frozen, suspended in time.

"What is going on here?" Membob felt panic seeping in. He then noticed that his First Officer's arm was reattached, though he was still lying on the floor of the bridge, immobilized like the rest. He pressed the firing button. Nothing happened. He pressed again and again, finally pounding on the console, smashing it to bits.

The Council of U convened on Hilips two days later. All warring parties were present. Hilips, along with representatives from Dregonion, Graspton Six, Chocxivxix and Ekaveo attended. Themosjustic stood alongside, although previously acquitted. Ruban and Blulay gave testimony as to their incarceration and they forgave their captors. Their captors breathed a sigh of relief, as did all.

Themosjustic forgave Hilips and Membob Kopp for the destruction of half their home world and the death of many of its people. Membob Kopp was sentenced to cryo state, though it was rescinded soon after with an offer that astonished all present. Membob Kopp was invited to visit Pratt, Lerxst and Dirk for as long as he wanted.

"We somehow feel at fault for all that transpired during this year of confliction. Our keeping our distance from your worlds should never be thought of as our feeling superior to another world or race. It is just our way, as your ways are yours. We can now see that we gave this impression and apologize for any real or imagined slight." Traep approached Membob Kopp, his hand held out to him.

"It was never our intention. As we have forgiven, we ask also that we be forgiven." Membob Kopp and Traep shook hands.

A thunderous applause erupted, but Traep was not finished.

"Please, please," Traep raised his arms to all assembled. "We have one more surprise for everyone, a gift to all worlds and their people. Screen please," Traep asked.

The viewing screen in the Hilips Justice Hall activated. "We give to you the Vegastriopelia!" Traep announced.

A silence overwhelmed the Hall. No one in attendance knew what to think as they viewed with bated breath and outright exhilaration.

Many have heard the stories of the Vegastriopelia being a myth, stories heard from our youth, legend told from long ago.

The Vegastriopelia is the most immense power source ever to be created, its energy so far-reaching that it could see into the past, though not the future. An omnipresent power, part organic, part machine, created by Pratt, Lerxst and Dirk, who came to be known as the Triopelians.

More applause erupted, louder than the first. There on the screen glowed the Vegastriopelia, turning, emitting a hue of yellowish green rays, a circle within a triangle within a box within a circle, it hung.

It took some time, though a plan was conceived on how to use this power source for the enjoyment of all. An intergalactic resort was proposed, one that did not have a precise destination but one that would visit worlds, universes and galaxies far and in between so that no single one would have control over it. Of course, rules and regulations would be implemented as to the size of the vessel, capacity, accommodations and so forth. A committee was set up and it took four years to determine all the necessary equations. Finally, a blueprint was sent to Pratt, Lerxst and Dirk to begin the construction. Thirty-six months later, the vessel was complete and ready for launch. Instead of a resort, it would now be the first and only intergalactic travelling casino. The Council of U would oversee its operations.

The first piece of business was to put in place a concierge and an assistant to run the day-to-day functions of the establishment. A celebration was held on Lerxst and transmitted across all worlds. As many delegates as were able attended the Casino launch ceremony. The capital city of Hsur was chosen for the event. Hsur was situated in a deep valley between the two mountains of Tor, a spectacular site for the launch. Membob Kopp was introduced as its first concierge and Unix Baff of Themosjustic as his assistant concierge.

The long awaited time had now come. As many as could stood in the city square and nervously looked heavenwards. The planet's sun began to set, as light and dark merged. The ground beneath the square rattled and rumbled. Small beams of light shot up between the two mountains. The beams of light grew and widened. Specially made sunglasses had been handed out earlier in the day for this precise moment. Others throughout the universe watching on viewing screens could dim their screens for the same visual effect.

It rose without sound up into the twilight sky, as if another sun had just been born. A hush fell over all those watching, in the city square and in faraway home worlds. The hush seemed to reverberate through time and space.

The vessel (the Casino), now in high orbit, began to swing around, a sleek tail of white emanating from its body like a shooting star. In fact, the Lerxstonians tweaked the design to resemble the shape of a comet to disguise it from non-space-faring worlds that were not evolved enough for contact. When found in the vicinity of these worlds, it would appear as a heavenly moving body or comet to unsuspecting viewers. In time, when these worlds were able to travel in space, they would be welcome to join the Council of U and enjoy all of its benefits.

It did not take very long to book accommodation for its inaugural voyage. Many wanted the opportunity to be first, though not everyone could be.

Dressed in his shiny new black tuxedo and red shoes, Membob Kopp really did look like a new man. Indeed, he was, as the first transfiguror process configuration candidate. During the last three years, he had taken up the invitation from Pratt, living and learning among his new friends. They helped him control his temper and to improve and enhance many other good traits. After hearing that the council was seeking a concierge, he offered his experience as a ship's captain and his knowledge of space travel, knowing that the job would be a lifelong service. With his new, improved and bubbly, yes bubbly, personality, how could they refuse?

Consulting with Traep, the Council agreed to offer Membob Kopp the position. Krule Kom could not believe his transformation, nor could the Council members. Neither could Membob Kopp himself or the whole of Hilips, for that matter!

With the Casino ready to venture out among the stars, the people of Pratt, Lerxst and Dirk now had one last matter to address. Traep acted as spokesperson for his worlds, as he had done for so many years. Stepping up to the podium, he waved politely to the gathered crowd. He turned to Krule Kom on his right and asked him to make sure that this message was being sent out on all subspace frequencies to the assembled worlds of the Council of U. Traep then began.

"Fellow beings, on this joyous occasion, let us be joined in continuous unity as we of Pratt, Lerxst and Dirk have been and always will be. We extend our deepest inner appreciation through our gift of the Vegastriopelia. From this day forward, our worlds of Pratt, Lerxst and Dirk will no longer exist. Under the adopted name of Triopelia, we will henceforth be known as the Triopelians. We Triopelians have never been as proud as we were at the formation of the Council of U. Your accomplishments are a record to the universe and speak for themselves. We no longer need to speak for you. As a parent lets go of a child's hand to allow him to walk alone, so we also do today. Our paths will one day cross again, somewhere out beyond the Plexus Rim. We will never be far away; our eyes will always be watching with fondness as you continue to grow and, yes, even evolve more than you think."

Traep finished with the following words: "The past, present and future lie above, which we all strive to reach and understand."

Everyone listening had no idea it would be the last time that the Triopelians would be seen or heard of for a very long time. Traep faded from the screen to be replaced by the casino making one last orbit around Lerxst, then soaring off into deep space.

The celebration continued for many days. Those who attended thanked their hosts, the newly minted Triopelians, and took leave for their home worlds. Soon after, Pratt, Lerxst and Dirk silently ebbed away. How they were able to cloak themselves, no one really knew. Yet everyone knew that they were never far away.

The screen faded to black …

10

Neb sat with his head bobbing to the rocking of his chair. Tict watched him, not saying a word.

"Remarkable," Neb uttered under his breath. "Can I actually see the Vegastriopelia?" he asked as he stopped rocking.

"Of course, Neb," Tict replied happily. "Reveal," Tict said loudly.

A side panel opened. A yellowish blue hue engulfed the room like that of a mirror ball twisting and shooting out specks of light. Neb reached out his hand to touch the stream of dancing light. It tickled him and made him giddy with delight. He had never felt this way before. It was as if the Vegastriopelia were singing to him. He was completely lost in its wake.

Tict marvelled as he observed. It seemed that the Vegastriopelia was interacting with Neb on a level he had never witnessed with anyone else, not himself when he was first introduced, nor even TeeceeFore.

The Vegastriopelia hung aloft in midair. It almost looked like a hologram, a circle within a triangle within a box within a circle. Waves of a yellowish blue hue enveloped Neb. Tict stepped back.

What is happening here? Tict thought to himself. *This is extremely unprecedented! Perhaps the truth is not as farfetched as TeeceeFore had said.*

The Vegastriopelia made one last sound akin to a killer whale happily swimming with its pod. The wall closed. There stood Neb and Tict and the two rocking chairs.

"Far out!" was all Neb could muster.

"Far out, indeed!" Tict said to himself.

They walked out of the room. Tict noticed that Neb had a certain reddish brown tint about him, as though his skin had changed colour.

"Let's hurry, Neb, shall we? We're running a little behind. Our guests will be patiently waiting for us in the Green Room." Tict tugged at Neb's shoulder, ushering him out.

"OK, OK," Neb said, still reeling from his experience with the Vegastriopelia.

Neb saw Kel standing beside her console and waved at her. She walked over to them.

"Was everything satisfactory?" she asked Tict.

"Yes, very," Tict answered. "Thank you. And now, if you don't mind, KEL-345, we are running somewhat late for our engagement with the Council in the Green Room.

"By all means," KEL-345 nodded. She walked back over to her console to continue her work.

"Will Kel be popping by the Green Room later?" Neb asked Tict.

"KEL-345 has diagnostics to run, Neb. I don't think she will have time." Tict rushed Neb. "Let's go."

"Oh, OK. Maybe later then, eh?" Neb mumbled. He took one last look at Kel as they exited the control room. KEL-345 also took a peek. They left. Tict's quick eye also noticed. He noticed everything.

PIC-500 and PIC-501 watched Kel as she watched Neb leave. PIC-501 approached Kel-345.

"PIC-500 has detected an anomaly that requires your immediate attention."

PIC-500 gave Kel a hand-held view pad.

Kel's eyes grew wide. "This is impossible!"

The Green Room was the main ballroom and the centre of the Casino. Everyone who was someone or who wanted to be someone was always there or, as some would say, they were there so they could say they were someone to someone who might be someone. Tickets were always booked so far in advance that some guests, depending on the lifespan of their species, may have waited hundreds of years. In some cases, their beneficiary would be the so-called lucky ones to inherit the tickets to dine and enjoy a fabulous Casino show. On this night, as always, it was filled to capacity. If there had been rafters, they would either be hanging from them or heading down river.

It was a special evening for a few different reasons. First of all, the entire 14-member Council of U was in attendance. Secondly, the Green Room's musical show for the evening was going to be a mind-blowing spectacle, hosted by none other than the super supreme emcee Sy Dyloup. Not even Mr. Tict knew who the special guests were and that said a lot about Sy Dyloup, who was very tightlipped about such events. The last time he pulled such a feat, the entire Green Room had to be renovated, much to the dismay of Tict and the service androids who had to clean up. Last, but not least, the Council of U's guest of honour, Mr. Nebula Yorker. Neb was unaware of his newfound status.

The balcony, as always, was reserved for Council members and their guests. Their view looked out at the entire oval floor below where there was a sea of tables. Three golden lit chandeliers hung from its ceiling.

On the stage were a few clues to the night's entertainment. A small drum kit sat centre stage. To its left sat an electric guitar on a metallic, silver-plated stand, along with what looked like a Marshall amplifier. In front of the drums was a stand equipped with a blue microphone. A shiny red bass guitar standing upright beside a Fender amplifier and a synthesizer filled the left side of the stage. A light blue hazy mist flowed out and over the stage.

The room was busy with android waiters and waitresses running about, filling water glasses, taking orders, spilling a drink or two on annoyingly loud guests. The androids could be very human in nature at times. Mimicking the guests happened only occasionally, though in the last few months it had increased by 15 per cent. Tict was not amused.

Kel-345 determined that nothing was wrong. Even androids were not as perfect as one would like them to be.

"Always treat the help as you would treat others and you won't get water down your pants," Tict jested.

KEL-345 didn't get it. "The guests didn't always see it that way, especially if you had been waiting a hundred years or so to get in only to get water down your pants."

Tict would always find a way to soothe those wetted. "It's part of the experience! Have a drink on the house," he would say cheerfully.

Tict and Neb entered the Green Room panting, a little out of breath.

"We're not too late, 30 minutes or so." Tict grabbed a glass of water from the tray of a passing waiter who gave him a look of disdain. He emptied the glass and placed it on the tray of another waiter who gave him the same look.

I really need to look back into this, Tict made a mental note to himself, *android waiters with far too much attitude.*

Neb also tried to take a glass but the waiter, anticipating his move, swung left and out of his reach. The waiter then suddenly turned back and paused. He looked at Neb, tilting his head, then handed him the glass of water.

"My apologies," the waiter said.

"Thank you," Neb replied, downing the water.

This also did not escape Tict's notice, adding more mental notes to his previous mental notes, some of which he thought he had forgotten but really hadn't. *Perhaps I should start carrying a notepad*, he thought, making another mental note.

Tict directed Neb to a winding staircase that led up to the Green Room's balcony. "You go ahead up. They are waiting for you. I will be up shortly. I need to find Sy Dyloup and find out what he's up to. I don't need another renovation on my hands." Tict rushed off, leaving Neb alone.

Who? What? Neb watched Tict zigzag through the busy ballroom as he crept slowly up the spiral stairs and, looking upward, wondered what was waiting for him when he reached the top.

"Welcome! Welcome!" TeeceeFore exuberantly greeted Neb as he reached the last step. "Everyone!" exclaimed TeeceeFore, her arms wrapped around Neb as she lead him to the full table where the Council of U sat. They all stood, clapped once and then sat down again.

How strange, Neb thought. *One clap, not even two. No rhythm at all. Unlike, say, if you're in a room with a hundred people and you close your eyes and listen to the clapping, it sounds like French fries cooking in hot grease.* Something picked up in his stoner days, which now reminded him that he was hungry.

"Has Mr. Tict brought you up to speed on everything? Everything Triopelia?" Neb nodded yes. "That's very good to hear, very good indeed. Then, without further ado, I officially welcome you on behalf of the Council of U!" TeeceeFore waved her hand, introducing the table to Neb once again. They all stood up once more, though this time they did not clap. Instead they bowed. Neb in turn bowed to the table.

TeeceeFore summoned the attending waiters. "Drinks for everyone!" She happily clapped her hands twice.

"OK, that's more like it!" Neb said, aloud this time.

"Here, you may sit beside me," TeeceeFore motioned to the empty chair to her left, which also happened to be the head of the table.

The 14 Council members sitting at the table were:
TeeceeFore, Prime Minister of Telvon Three

Luapyentraccm, Viceroy of Dregonion

Prince Cirderf, Holder of the Keys from Graspton Six

Esyparells Ish, High Baron of Flaga Rex

Tregot the Dan of Lanoisthull

Messill Di, Magistrate of Themosjustic

Snilloc Lihp, Fifth Master from Oootopopah

Notlen Hoj, Duke of Landanphishfri

Queen Mercury, the White Sovereign of Chocxivxix

Van Ohic, Ard RI the Tenth from Emerald Prime

Jonibleeuw, Duchess Samrajni of Ekaveo

Ellakeepar, the Rose of Mary from Balaster II

Bac Roew, Dauphin of Ctieaps Nova

Mleh Novel, Premier of Sasnakra Prime

And John Lennon, chatting away with one of the waitresses.

Another chair sat empty at the end of the table.

"Why the empty chair at the end of the table?" Neb asked TeeceeFore.

"That chair represents Pratt, Lerxst and Dirk, the fifteenth member or, if you like, the Triopelians," TeeceeFore replied.

"Interesting," Neb mused.

"How so?" enquired TeeceeFore.

"Well, has the Council ever had a dispute where seven Council members agreed on one solution and the other seven for another?"

"To my knowledge, never, but what are you getting at?" TeeceeFore asked, intrigued.

"I don't know, it seems kind of funny, you know. Wouldn't you need a member from the Triopelians to settle the situation should one come up?"

The table fell silent at Neb's question. Neb now noticed all eyes were transfixed on him.

"It's alright, Neb. Everyone's personal comm links are always activated, so when we are together, no one misses out on what anyone has to say. We are very open that way. Guests included." TeeceeFore smiled. "To answer your question, we never have any such disputes. It's written in our Constitution. No disputes allowed ever. Clause 5, paragraph 650.

Everyone at the table laughed, except for John Lennon who hadn't a clue what was going on.

"I see. I guess you could say you've covered all bases, haven't you?"

"Bases?" Queen Mercury asked.

"It's a baseball metaphor," Neb explained. "Baseball?" They all looked at each other, perplexed.

"Go Yankees!" John Lennon shouted from the far end of the room.

"Yes, baseball. It's a game played on Earth. It's been around for at least a hundred years, if not more," Neb explained. "A bat, a smooth wooden club, is used along with a small white ball. It's played by two teams of nine players each, who take turns hitting the ball with the bat and fielding or catching the ball, or trying to catch it, when it's hit."

"You mean Ssakwatchoubit," Van Ohic interrupted.

"Ssakwatchoubit?" It was Neb's turn to be perplexed.

"Yes, Ssakwatchoubit," Bac Roew chimed in. "It's outlawed now. Too many players were accidently getting themselves killed during play. It kind of messed up a totally fabulous game."

Everyone laughed.

"Of course it did," Neb laughed, not sure if they were making fun of him or not.

"Go Yankees!" John Lennon shouted out again, giving Neb a thumbs up.

Wow, John Lennon just gave me kudos! Neb returned the gesture.

The lights of the ballroom dimmed. A huge spotlight shone on centre stage and out walked Tict to thunderous applause.

Well, at least the folks on the floor know how to clap. Neb watched keenly.

"Hey, everyone, close your eyes," Neb said to the table. No one heard him except John Lennon.

"Cool! Sounds like French fries," John Lennon winked at Neb and Neb laughed, but wondered how John Lennon knew what he was thinking.

"French fries?" TeeceeFore eyed John Lennon and Neb. "Humans," she said fondly.

Tict sauntered up to the microphone. He took the mike off its stand and got an electric shock. The shock frizzed his white hair up, giving him that Albert Einstein appearance, minus the moustache. He dropped the mike and looked to the stagehand, who was now picking it up.

"Hello. Hello. Is this thing on?" He tapped the mike. Feedback zipped through. He waited a few seconds before trying again. "Here you go, Mr. Tict," said the stagehand. "Sorry about that. We weren't exactly ready for you. Sy Dyloup had me working on extrapolating his program matrix for our special guest's arrival."

"Extrapolating?" Tict asked. "Forget it," he added and grabbed the mic from the stagehand.

"Good evening. Good evening," Tict repeated jubilantly. "The Green Room is pleased that you could make it for tonight's festivity. Sy Dyloup has informed me that no renovations will be needed after tonight's performance, for which I am grateful." He looked to the side stage to see Sy giving him a thumbs up. He didn't really know whether to believe him or not. Sy was always up to something new.

"The Council of U sends their greetings," Tict pointed to the balcony. A spotlight beamed up to the balcony where the Council now stood. Everyone on the floor stood and applauded as the Council applauded back.

"Well, at least they know how to clap," Neb remarked to himself again.

"On behalf of the Casino and the Council, we ask that you remain seated during the course of this evening's entertainment to ensure your total enjoyment."

Sy Dyloup giggled to himself listening to Tict. *Stay seated? I don't think so.*

"First drink is on me tonight!" Tict offered, which garnered more applause even though no one really paid for anything. Tict then exited stage left, tripping over the microphone stand cord, causing some laughter as the stage curtain closed around him.

"Marvelous, just extremely marvelous, our Mr. Tict is!" Queen Mercury cheered. "Don't you think, Nebula?"

"Oh, he's something," Neb smirked, "and speaking of something, here he is now." Tict walked in and joined the table sitting down beside Neb.

"Did you miss me?" he asked, lifting up a glass of blue Ekaveoion wine, toasting the table. The Council members all raised their glasses.

"Tell us, Mr. Tict, what has Sy Dyloup in store for us tonight?" TeeceeFore enquired.

"I wish I knew. He tells me that Neb should particularly enjoy the show."

"Really!" TeeceeFore sipped at her wine gingerly, her eyes on Neb.

Soon the android waiters and waitresses were hurriedly bringing the table guests their specific dishes and drinks. Everyone began to enjoy their meals, tasting a morsel from each one's home world. Some meals moved on the plates; others just sat there wishing they were somewhere else. The strong aromas filled Neb's nostrils and, not wanting to be rude, he made a point of tasting each dish that was passed his way, even smiling when he disliked whatever he was eating. He was very diplomatic. His manner did not go unnoticed and it impressed the Council.

"What do you call this dish?" asked Tregot the Dan of Lanoisthull.

"Fish and chips," John Lennon replied.

"Very crunchy. I like it." Queen Mercury added.

"You're quite the diplomat," Tict leaned over whispering to Neb.

"Diplomat? No, that's your job," Neb replied, finishing up his last bite of Dregonion chicken rat. Neb was about to ask what he was eating but thought better of it. *As long as it isn't rat*, he thought.

Now resting back and rubbing his stomach, Neb had never felt so full in his entire life. He let out a loud burp, which roused the whole table in laughter.

"Waiter!" TeeceeFore called out, "a small glass of Vilit for Mr. Yorker, please."

"Straight away, Prime Minister," the waiter replied. He returned a few minutes later with a small two-inch high cubed glass filled with a greenish white black liquid. TeeceeFore asked the waiter to hand it to Neb.

"It's OK, Neb. It's a Telvonian aperitif," Tict explained. Neb waved the glass under his nose. He could smell a tinge of mint and orange.

"Bottoms up!" he said, holding up the glass and gulping it down.

"Wait!" TeeceeFore tried to stop him, but it was too late.

"What's wrong?" Neb asked, letting it slide down his throat.

"It's not the type of drink you just gulp down like that. It must be savoured, sipped slowly, so that it can adapt to your cellular structure as it soothes your mind and body."

"More cellular structure hooey," Neb thought out loud. "It's not hooey, as you say," TeeceeFore remarked.

Neb once again blurted his thoughts out. "I got to get hold of that."

"You see, Vilit has been used for millenniums for long-range space voyages. It helps with the nerves before one is put into cryo-sleep," TeeceeFore said, observing Neb. "Are you sure you're fine?"

"Couldn't feel better," Neb replied.

No sooner had Neb spoken than a heavy rush blasted his head like a brain freeze after eating cold ice-cream. He closed his eyes and fell into a kind of dream state. By all outward appearances, he looked fine to everyone around him. It only lasted about ten seconds. He thought he saw himself walking up long, wide, white steps that led into an atrium with four marble columns. Then, as quickly as the dream began, it ended. He opened his eyes.

"Are you sure you're OK?" TeeceeFore asked once again.

"That Vilit has a bit of a kick to it, doesn't it," Neb smiled.

11

After everyone had finished eating, the real dialogue with Neb began to open up. Jonibleeuw, Duchess Samrajni of Ekaveo, spoke first.

“Nebula Yorker, on behalf of the Council of U, may I be so bold as to ask a question or two on a matter that has dumbfounded us?” she asked, very seriously.

Neb picked up on her tone as all around the table listened. “Sure, go ahead,” Neb hesitantly replied.

Jonibleeuw continued. “For some time, 75 years to be exact, since we last orbited Earth, we have monitored your species very closely. In fact, we have monitored Earth and all worlds as they have progressed from their beginning, in hopes that one day they will be able to join us. Earth, we are afraid, is a long way from doing so. No offence,” she nodded.

“None taken,” said Neb. “Please carry on. I find this fascinating.” He rested his chin on his clasped hands.

Mleh Novel, Premier of Sasnakra Prime, took over from Jonibleeuw. “Our world, like many others over the thousands and thousands of millenniums, has evolved to where we stand now, but not without conflict, whether through commerce, technology or, yes, sometimes even deadly war, though never with each other of the same species.”

“Excluding the Year of Confliction,” Neb added.

“Of course; that goes without saying,” Mleh Novel nodded. “I see you’re up to speed. Each of our worlds has never even experienced a civil war. Our worlds have always been unified, one people, one world.”

"Only after the Year of Confliction," Neb again said.

Mleh Novel cocked his right brow. He was starting to feel a little perturbed with Neb. "As I have said, we have had many differences with other worlds which have led to war. It was not until the Council of U was conceived that we have been unified as a universe for the greater good of all intelligent species. Earth is the only world we have ever encountered where there is war among its own species for various reasons. We often wonder what will become of Earth. Will it progress to one day joining us or will it destroy itself? You show great sympathy at times for your fellow beings, yet you can be so harsh and unrelenting in your actions towards one another. Why this happens continues to baffle us. When Earthlings become a space faring people – and that is inevitable as all life one way or another reaches out beyond their limitations – how they will react to first contact with other worlds also worries us."

Neb stared at Mleh Novel. He wasn't sure what to say.

"Though it must be admitted, from what we have witnessed, that may not be for a very long time," Mleh Novel smirked – something Neb did not like at all.

"No disrespect intended," Mleh Novel asserted.

"None taken," Neb smiled through his teeth, remaining diplomatic.

Tict took notice, as he always did. *This Nebula Yorker is amazing,* he thought.

Mleh Novel then added, "It's kind of funny, but many worlds much younger than Earth have already reached the stars. Thus far, your world has only reached your one moon."

"Good thing you don't have two," someone whispered. No one was sure who it was.

Neb started to boil inside. *How dare this pompous alien to make such statements*, he thought. He wasn't sure if he should just try to remain calm or if he should knock him out of his chair. The latter was starting to feel like a good idea.

"But the most confusing of it all," Mleh Novel paused. *Here it comes*, Neb thought now clenching his fist beneath the table. "How did *Star Trek* get it so right?"

A silence overwhelmed the table. Neb's jaw dropped. He was starting to feel as though he was on trial for something he didn't do or didn't know anything about.

"I beg your pardon?" Neb finally asked.

"Yes, *Star Trek*. The United Federation of Planets, the Prime Directive, Warp Drive, the transporter. We could go on and on."

Tregot the Dan of Lanoisthull joined the conversation. "Is it merely a coincidence that *Star Trek* closely mirrors our own Council of U and much more?" he asked.

Neb couldn't believe what he was hearing, though Tict did warn him not to say anything on the topic. As he was about to try to reply, the lights of The Green Room dimmed. Above each table, small balls of light hovered, much like the light that Neb had encountered when he first met Tict, though a little smaller. Each of the balls began to change colour as they rose, humming as they floated upward. They floated until each ball exploded into a stream of dancing fire descending down to the seated guests. The dancing fire transformed into something that resembled a light falling snow, then disappeared before touching anyone's head.

The ballroom floor erupted into applause and laughter. A drum roll sounded, spotlights moved over the crowd and the stage. The red stage curtain slowly inched open, revealing someone standing centre-stage, his back to the crowd. The Green Room hushed. The figure, dressed in black, started to move. Like wings, his cape opened outward. White-gloved hands appeared at the cape's edge. The figure began to rise above the stage. When in midair, he turned to face everyone.

"Greetings, fellow beings!" A smiling Sy Dyloup flew out over the ballroom, his hover shoes spurting out little puffs of vapour. His black cape, with its red flashing inseam, rolled like a wave as he circled about, waving to everyone. His slick purple zoot suit and yellow shoes and belt dazzled as they reflected off the spotlights.

"What a lovely group we have this evening! We have an amazing treat in store for you all tonight," Sy teased. He hovered over to the balcony and touched down to chat with the Council, much to the amusement of the guests on the floor. He sat on the balcony railings, the spotlight on him as always.

"Look everyone, it's TeeceeFore, the Prime Minister of Telvon Three." Sy kissed her hand ever so gently, then, looking up, gave the crowd below a wink. "So, what brings you here tonight, Prime Minister? And don't say it's me!" Sy laughed along with everyone. Before TeeceeFore could answer, Sy was off to his next chat.

"Why it's Luapyentraccm, Viceroy of Dregonion. And how are we tonight, Viceroy? You really need to shorten your first name or is that your last name? Luapyentraccm, is that your real hair? Before the Viceroy could utter a single word, Sy zipped away to more laughter.

"I like your hair," John Lennon said to Luapyentraccm.

"Well what do we have here?" Sy slinked up beside Neb. "Spotlight, please!" The spotlight flashed across Neb and Sy. "So, what's your name?" Sy cheekily asked Neb. The spotlight shone so brightly in Neb's face that he had to lift up his hand to block it out to see Sy's face googling over him. "Don't be shy," Sy teased some more. "Ladies and gentlemen and bisected species," Sy laughed, "let me introduce to you this fine young Earthling." A hush fell over the ballroom. "Mr. Nebula Yorker."

There was no applause, just one little mousey voice from the floor that echoed, "Who's that?"

“Exactly!” Sy replied. Again the floor erupted with laughter.

Tict gave Sy a stern look as he hovered back down to the stage.

“I apologize, Neb, Sy Dyloup can get carried away sometimes,” said Tict.

“No need to apologize. I don’t think there is much more that can faze me.”

“Be careful what you wish for or say,” said Tict. “I wouldn’t hold my breath if I were you, dear boy,” Tict reached for the full bottle of Telvonian red wine and poured himself and Neb a full glass. “To adventure!” Tict raised his glass.

“To adventure!” Neb replied. They clicked glasses.

Sy Dyloup had now landed back on stage after taking one more jaunt around the floor. “Is everyone ready?” Sy leaned into the crowd his hand cupped around his ear.

“I have been all night!” A voice yelled out.

“Oh yeah? Try two hundred years!” another cried.

A stagehand was now trying to get Sy’s attention. “Psst. Psst. Psst.”

Sy just happened to lean to the right and noticed the stagehand waving to him to come over.

“I think someone needs to go to the washroom. Excuse me for a moment.” He zipped off to see what the stagehand wanted.

“What is it?” Sy demanded. “Can’t you see I am in the middle of a show?”

"We have a bit of a problem transfiguring the coordinates. It's temporary at best, sir, but they keep fazing in and out. Never had a problem like this before," said the stagehand.

"Can't you boost the signal?" Sy asked.

"We're in the process, sir," the stagehand scratched his head. "We're getting a chemical interference strain looping through the buffers that doesn't want to let go. It's very odd."

Another stagehand came running to the first. "Sorry about that, Sy. I mean, Mr. Dyloup. We're good to go," he relayed.

"OK. Don't ever bother me again unless my life is in danger, especially during a show!" Sy bowed and turned his attention back to the waiting ballroom.

"Just a little technical difficulty, folks. We're good to go, I'm told. Without further ado," Sy began…

"The Green Room is proud, very proud, to welcome our very special guests tonight for your entertainment. All the way from Earth, please welcome THE ROLLING STONES!!!"

Neb dropped his glass of wine. It crashed to the floor, shattering into bits.

"THE ROLLING STONES!" he gasped, wine spurting out of his mouth.

There was Mick Jagger strutting his stuff about the stage, breaking into the "Harlem Shuffle". Cigarette slumped out of the corner of his mouth, Keith Richards slid up beside Mick Jagger, strumming his guitar. Bill Wyman thumping on his bass, Ronnie Woods bouncing around, playing away, and Charlie Watts, keeping the beat on the drums, holding it all together.

John Lennon stood and yelled "Hey Mick, it's me." No one heard him.

Queen Mercury was up on her feet with TeeceeFore dancing, swaying to the beats and rhythms.

Is all of this really happening? Neb thought as he watched everything going on around him. He reached for another glass of wine. Forty-eight hours earlier, he was getting ready to go out and observe Halley's Comet, only to find out it's really Halley's Casino dance bar and grill. Maybe he was at home in bed dreaming, for all he knew. With everything going on around him, he really wanted to speak with John Lennon. What was John Lennon doing here? The man died about six years ago. What was this? John Lennon not being human? TeeceeFore had said he was but wasn't. What did that mean?

After a few more songs Mick addressed the ballroom. "Good evening." He paused, looking somewhat unsure of himself for some reason. He strode over to Keith.

"Hey man, like what city are we in anyhow?"

Keith shrugged his shoulders. "I don't know, man, but it's a blast!"

"Yeah, great crowd!" Mick went back to his microphone. "Alright then, here's another new one off our new LP 'Dirty Works.' 'One Hit (To the Body)'. Mick looked back at Charlie, then over to Bill and Ronnie, and jumped into the song.

Two hours later, the show ended to thunderous applause. The band waved, thanking the crowd. Ronnie Woods, sweat pouring down, wiped his forehead with a very large pair of women's panties thrown up at him from the floor. He had at first thought it was a towel.

"Yikes! Bloody hell!" Ronnie let out and threw it back only for it to boomerang back in his face.

"Nice place, I don't think we've played here before, have we?" Bill Wyman said to Charlie Watts.

"Yeah, it doesn't seem that familiar," Charlie replied. "But a great crowd and vibe for sure!"

The Stones all gathered at centre stage and took a bow. Sy Dyloup hovered over the crowd. "Well, folks, what did you think?" Mick and Keith watched Sy hover above the floor.

"I can't see any strings, can you?" Keith watched dazed. Sy floated back up onto the stage beside Mick. Mick passed his hand around the back of Sy. He looked at Keith.

"Hey, man, no strings, Keith? What's up with that?"

"Well, man, I got to get me some of that, whatever it is," Keith lit up a fag.

"Excuse me, my good man," Mick tapped Sy on the shoulder. "When do we get paid for the gig?"

Sy Dyloup looked to the stagehand, making a cutting motion with his hand across his neck. The hand understood and nodded. The stage curtain began to close on the band and Sy. A few seconds later, the Rolling Stones, with Mick still questioning Sy about their pay, started to faze in and out until they were gone. The stage curtains reopened. Sy stood blushing.

"Well, wasn't that spectacular? What did you think, Mr. Yorker?" Sy pointed to the balcony, asking rhetorically. "We hope to see you tomorrow night for another exciting extravaganza!" Sy Dyloup bowed as the curtain started to close again. He looked down to the stage floor and saw the large pair of women's panties. He picked them up and stuffed them into his coat pocket.

The Green Room was abuzz, electrified by the Stones' performance. Never had they seen or heard such a musical blast. Neb was still in shock. He too had thoroughly enjoyed the concert along with the Council and the entire ballroom.

"I know it's only rock and roll, but I love it!" Tict raised a glass.

The ballroom floor emptied quickly, everyone satisfied with the evening and now dashing off to their favorite game rooms to continue the night. They couldn't stop talking about it as they left the Green Room.

12

With the Green Room now emptied, except for the Council of U and John Lennon up in the balcony, the questioning regarding *Star Trek* resumed. Neb looked down at his watch. It was 2:00 a.m. Earth time, he reckoned. Who knew what time it was aboard the Casino - or if they even kept track of time.

The Council went through every episode of *Star Trek* with Neb, asking a bounty of questions. Neb tried his best to answer. He surprised himself on how much he knew or perhaps they were just asking questions that he knew the answers to. He wasn't quite sure what they were after.

At one point, now getting tired, Neb said, "It's just a TV show, people." This caused some members to gasp, it seemed to Neb, in terror.

"Wow," Neb muttered under his breath, "Trekkies/Trekkers everywhere."

Neb did concede that there were far too many coincidences that did parallel the universe he now found himself in. It was decided that a panel would be conceived in the near future to get to the bottom of it.

"How could such a backward planet like Earth be so exact yet so far from achieving interstellar travel themselves?" Mleh Novel huffed.

"Now, look here!" Neb took a stand. "For such an advanced people, it looks to me and in my opinion, your attitude almost borders on racism towards my home Earth. You do know what racism is? From what I have seen, heard and learned from the Vegastriopelia, the main goal of the Council is to unify, not deify yourselves before so-called backward worlds to the point of disregarding what a world's potential may or may not be. Who of any of us has the right to tell another what to do or say? How to live or not to live? Evolution, creation, each world has and will find its own way through this vast universe and at some point all will converge as one. Dare I say, to boldly go where no one has gone before?"

The Council sat wide-eyed and silent as Neb asked one more question before finishing.

"If the Earth is such a backward planet, as you say, why then have you had human concierges running the Casino for well over four thousand years, starting with Lafil? And though you look very human to me, I find that you're being very disrespectful of the Triopelians who, by the way, were also humanoid in appearance like the people of Earth."

Neb crossed his arms and sat back eyeing the Council.

"Well said, Neb!" John Lennon stood and clapped as one should clap.

"You must excuse our young Mr. Yorker. He's not quite up to speed with the protocols of the position yet." Tict calmed the scene even though there was no scene to calm.

"No. Mr. Yorker is quite correct. We apologise," TeeceeFore spoke up on behalf of the Council. They all nodded in agreement.

Tict cocked an eyebrow. "Really?"

"Yes, really," she smiled.

There seems to be more to this Mr. Yorker than we know, TeeceeFore thought to herself.

"With regard to the choice of human concierges, it is not we who have chosen but the Vegastriopelia itself that does the choosing," TeeceeFore added. "We may not at first have understood why the Vegastriopelia chose as it did but we have never doubted its decision and never will. You see, for all intents and purposes, the Vegastriopelia is entirely a sentient life form. It does not rule us nor do we rule it. We follow its guidance, not blindly mind you, but with deepest respect, as we should. And, as we should have for your home world, Nebula. The first human to actually board the Casino was Lafil. At first, we were totally perplexed. It was something new and, might I say, alien. It took us days to figure it out. It would seem that humans have a higher aptitude for organization than any other race. Who knew? Simply put, you really know how to get things done. You can be very orderly when needed. Unfortunately, however, and sad to say, your orderliness does leave much to be desired when it comes to running your own planet. Your First and Second World Wars come to mind. To date, we have had only one problematic situation with a human. It happened just before Mr. Tict arrived, to be precise. Lafil's assistant, Marcus Apitippius," TeeceeFore sighed.

"You've mentioned that name once before," Neb said. "I gather, then, he did not take over for Lafil?"

"No, he did not and if it were not for our dear Mr. Tict," she laid her hand on his shoulder, "I shudder to think what may have happened."

Tict looked up at TeeceeFore sadly.

"It was Marcus Apitippius who pushed Lafil backward, wasn't it?" Neb asked Tict.

"Yes," Tict answered.

"What era was Marcus from?" Neb enquired.

"Rome, 12 BCE," TeeceeFore replied to Neb.

"Rome. I visited there once with my parents," Neb mused.

"We were in orbit at that time," Tict said, "and Lafil took a mini-vacation down to the planet to visit, to breathe in some real home oxygen, as he put it."

Snilloc Lihp, Fifth Master from Oootopopah, joined the conversation. “He could have gone back to his own era and time-travelled to Babylon. He decided on Rome instead. I can now see why he did. He posed as a Babylonian astrologer, not too far a stretch for Lafil in case he should have any dealings with the inhabitants and he did. He found himself brought before the August One, Augustus Octavian Caesar, the first Roman Emperor of the Principate era, whose ascension ended the republic rule of Rome, as Lafil would inform us later. It was there that he first met Marcus Apitippius.”

Before he could finish, a warning chime rang out three times. The entire Council stood. Neb looked on, perplexed. They rose from their chairs in an orderly manner and walked out one by one, down the balcony stairs and out of the Green Room. Not a word was said, not even a goodbye.

“What’s happening, Tict?” Neb asked, wondering what was going on.

“I am not a hundred per cent sure.” Tict said. He then called out to TeeceeFore, as she was the last to leave. “Madame Prime Minister!”

She turned and said, “The Vegastriopelia is calling us.” With that, she disappeared down the stairs.

“That’s very unusual, indeed!” Tict looked very startled. “The last time the Vegastriopelia called out to the entire Council, they just happened to all be gathered as they are tonight. It was the night Lafil died.

“When was that?” Neb asked.

“December 25, 1758, the night I arrived,” Tict gulped. He nervously tapped the top of the table with his finger tips.

One, two, three, four.

One, two, three, four.

One, two, three, four. His fingers hit the top of the table as if he were playing a piano. Neb reached out to stop him.

"What does it mean?" Neb held Tict's hand, staring him straight in the eye.

"That night I arrived was also the same evening Marcus pushed Lafil backwards through the transporter configuror. He tried to take over and hijack the Casino. The Council was completely taken aback with the situation or, I should say, the situation concerning Marcus's failed coup. The Vegastriopelia had alerted them to Lafil's death on Earth. It wasn't like Lafil not to have told anyone in advance of his plans to visit Earth. Marcus acted so concerned about his mentor's death that he had everyone fooled. He had falsified the transport log to make it seem that Lafil was going for a trip down to Earth, even cutting and splicing the video log to make it look as though Lafil had tripped backwards on his own. Though the Council wondered, why 1758? It didn't make sense. Why would Lafil want to visit that time period? He thought he had it all worked out. That is, until I appeared. Suffice it to say, he was not expecting me. I stood on the platform, wet pants and all. I did not look or smell my best. Marcus almost went ballistic on seeing me. If it had not been for TeeceeFore coming through the doors at that moment, I fear he would have killed me as well. It was a total frenzy. I didn't know where I was, who these people were or what was going on. Was I dreaming? Was I dead? I think I may have peed myself again but I was afraid to look back down. So I did the best thing I could think of and collapsed. The next thing I knew I woke up in bed with tubes sticking out of my arms. Marcus was standing at the foot of the bed. I knew one thing for sure and that was I did not like this Marcus character from the outset. During my stay in sickbay, I played the mute card, pretending I had lost my voice. I watched and listened for days to try and get a grip on my situation. Marcus ascertained that I was some kind of fool and thus harmless to his plans, so he left me alone. It was a very big mistake on his part. Soon enough, by observing TeeceeFore, I found her to be someone I could trust and still do very much. Finally, I came out of my shell, explaining to her how I had met Lafil, what he had told me about someone pushing him backwards, and that I had promised to help. I was completely lost on the whole being pushed back thing, yet determined to help in any way I could. I am one who keeps his promises and, even though I did not know who this Lafil was, I always keep my word."

"Lafil would have been proud, I'm sure," Neb consoled Tict.

Tict continued. "TeeceeFore then informed the Council about our discussion. There was some hesitation from a few Council members. After all, who was I? For all they knew, I murdered Lafil. Though, in the end, after more medical tests and re-evaluations, I was found to be just this human caught up in a mystery. They didn't know me from Adam, as the saying goes, but I earned TeeceeFore's trust. My story took some on the Council by surprise, though they had to admit, how would I know anything about Lafil had I not met him? It wasn't something a human from 1758 would know anything about. The Council decided they would carefully and covertly watch Marcus as, due to my story, they now felt that all truths were not adding up. They went over the video and transporter logs to determine the cause or malfunction, if any. They found none. They questioned Marcus again and not once did he stray from his original account. The Council had devised a plan that the members would say they were leaving the Casino to return to their home worlds. Soon after, thinking they had left, Marcus decided to take over Lafil's office. He had not yet been officially named the new concierge. Without permission, he began wearing the official attire – the black tuxedo and red shoes – and enjoying all the perks that went along with being the concierge. At this point, Marcus was informed by an unidentified source that I could in fact speak and had done so with TeeceeFore, though he knew nothing of what was said between us. His next step was obviously to get rid of me. Presuming that all of the Council had now left, he made his way to the infirmary where I was still undergoing my acclimatization, as it were. Neither Marcus nor his snitch knew that he was under surveillance, which was to our advantage. Marcus entered the infirmary and immediately had the two android medical staff leave, assigning them fake duties elsewhere.

He sat down beside me, his blonde hair falling over his left eyebrow, and with his twisted smile, he glared at me with his steel blue eyes. I will never forget that smile. You could see his mind working, the villain that he was and still is."

Neb stopped Tict. "What do you mean? Still is?"

"I will get to that," Tict said. Neb sat riveted.

Tict went on. "Marcus pulled up a chair and said, 'I understand that you are now able to speak. I know this must be confusing for you, all of this.' He said this in a gentle, soft tone, waving his hands around the room. He sat back, oh so relaxed, and said, 'I remember when I first arrived. I thought that I had been blessed by gods. Never in my wildest dreams could I have thought what wonders awaited. I looked to Jupiter to welcome me. I prayed to Juno, Neptune, Apollo and Mars to reveal themselves. Not even Pluto, the God of Death, dared to appear. Then it dawned on me. It was I who had ascended over all of them. I have waited a long time!' He grinned mischievously. He then took me by the hand and smoothly rubbed his hand over mine. 'Tell me,' he said, 'what did Lafil say to you?' I didn't know whether to continue playing dumb or not. I decided to stay mute for the time being. 'Come now, there's no need to be afraid. You are afraid, aren't you?' Marcus let go of my hand. I don't know why and I really at this point didn't understand what all the fuss was about being pushed backwards. All I could see was Lafil's eyes looking into mine if as I had known him all my life, asking with his last words to find out who had pushed him backwards. 'You!' I finally said to Marcus. 'You pushed Lafil backwards!' Marcus's eyes widened bigger than I had ever seen on a person. 'And there you have it!' Marcus slapped his thigh and stood up. 'Why?' I asked. 'If you must know,' Marcus answered, 'and because I am feeling charitable at this point, and this doesn't happen very much but, make no mistake, this will be your last moment of life.'"

"All villains spill the beans before they're caught," Tict cautioned Neb. "Keep that in mind."

"Marcus continued, 'With Lafil out of the way and the Council gone back to their home worlds, now is the perfect time to head back to Rome, my Rome, and change things up a bit, with this marvelous vessel at my command. A change to the whole of time and space is due, not just the Earth but all worlds to be, with myself at the helm. You see, I really am god! Nothing can stop me.' Marcus pulled out a small photon phase gun from his pocket and took aim. '*When knaves betray each other, one can scarce be blamed or the other pitied. Goodbye, knave,*' Marcus spewed out and fired.

"Nothing happened. The door of the infirmary swooshed open and there stood TeeceeFore. The Council members were bunched up closely behind her. Marcus tried again to fire the gun, this time at her, and again nothing happened. He dropped the gun to the floor. The Council had been viewing the entire conversation. The Vegastriopelia had also disabled Marcus's weapon. Two guards grabbed Marcus by the arms. He didn't resist. He said nothing as they led him out. Only his twisted grin remained. Before Marcus left the room, I shouted out to him. He turned to face me. 'Look, even the gods have become mortal.' I pointed at him. His smile disappeared as the door swooshed closed behind him. And that is the last time the Vegastriopelia summoned the entire Council while aboard."

"That's incredible!" Neb sat startled at what he had heard.

"I agree. Incredible!" John Lennon shook his head.

"You really need to fill me in on him," Neb nodded in John Lennon's direction. "So you said that Marcus was and still is. Does that mean he's alive?"

"He is. He's imprisoned within this vessel far below deck, the only one ever found willfully guilty of such an act since Membob Kopp." Tict looked down at his feet, his mind drifting.

"Tict, it's OK," Neb said. "I can see how hard that was on you to relive that episode. You saved the Earth, the Council and the Casino. Hell, the universe, for that matter. You're a hero in my books!"

"Thank you, Neb. That means a lot to me. Not sure if anyone has ever told me that before."

"Never?" replied Neb.

"No, never, and to be honest, I never thought about it that way. Marcus was so sure of himself, he never expected that little old Tict would foil his so-called, well laid-out plans, or so he thought. I guess you might say I was in the right place at the right time."

"A real working class hero," John Lennon began writing down notes. *The Ballad of Tict* he scribbled at the top of the page.

"OK Tict, really, what's up with him? Is that really John Lennon?" Neb asked.

"Well, it's kind of hard to say," Tict replied. "There are some beings in the universe that transcend worlds. It doesn't always happen, but John Lennon was one of them. When he was dying, his essence alerted the universe. The Casino was the closest portal to which his essence could flow, even though we were almost six years away from entering the system. The Vegastriopelia alerted us and made all of the arrangements for his impending arrival. In most cases, the essence travels through space, which can take some time, until it reaches its final portal destination, which is, funny enough, beyond the Plexus Rim. In this case, the Vegastriopelia acted as the portal. For some reason, it decided to intercept John Lennon's essence. Not that we mind. He's a very cool dude, so I am told."

"But is he flesh and blood?" Neb asked.

"He's actually a clone embedded with John Lennon's essence. He kind of knows and doesn't know who he is. It's like he has an assorted type of amnesia but, other than that, he's fine. So you might see him wandering about from time to time. He's a very sweet guy."

"I would love to jam with him." Neb watched as John Lennon continued scribbling.

"Jam?" Tict enquired.

"You know, play music together."

"Oh yes, I see." Tict had no idea about jamming and still wasn't all that sure.

Tict stood up, tugged at his jacket and straightened it. Neb slapped Tict on the shoulder.

"Let's go, hero, and find out what's going on. "You coming, John Lennon?" asked Neb.

"If you don't mind, I think I'm going to stick around awhile and write some more."

13

Tict and Neb made their way down the staircase. As they went, they could hear John Lennon singing in the background. *The Stones and John Lennon! Anyone else I should know about?* Neb thought to himself.

The Green Room door closed behind them as they walked down the hallway.

"I have to ask, Tict, how did you get the Rolling Stones tonight? Are they part of all this?" Neb looked around.

"Oh no, they weren't really here tonight. I mean, they were, but they weren't."

"OK, that doesn't make sense. Then again, what does around here? Yet they were here. I saw what I saw and heard what I heard, right?" Neb asked.

"Yes, you did," Tict replied. "It was another one of Sy's brilliant schemes. It's a cellular faze manipulator Sy Dyloup invented, or so he said. I am not a hundred per cent sure how it works. From what he told me, it centres on the intended subject or subjects' REM pattern. Once the connection is made, it extracts the brain's aura shell, then filters the neurons through the cellular faze manipulator, then re-filters it again, zoning in on what he called the in-between memories, and finally processing it through a bio clone anti-holographic stream loop resulting in having your subjects, or in this case the Rolling Stones, live for your entertainment. For all intended purposes, they were here tonight. Tomorrow when they wake in their nice cozy beds, or wherever they wake up, they will think they played a concert the night before when actually they were at home sleeping. Anyhow, that's how Sy explained it. I don't think he knows himself how it works. He gets his stagehands to do all his dirty work. Though it was a great show!"

Meanwhile, back in London, Mick Jagger is calling Keith Richards asking about the gig they played last night and when they're going to get paid. "What are you talking about, Mick, what show last night?" Keith replied.

Tict and Neb entered his office. "Coffee?" asked Tict.

"Sure." Neb plunked himself down on the chesterfield. "You know, Tict, its 3:00 o'clock in the morning Earth time and I don't feel tired at all."

"That's something you get used to up here." Tict handed him a cup of hot coffee. "One can go on for days without sleeping. I mean, you can sleep if you want but you don't really need to." Tict sat down opposite Neb, sipping his coffee.

"Tict, can I ask you a serious question?" Neb asked.

"Knock your socks off." Tict leaned back.

"I'm not going back home, am I? I mean, if I have figured this all out, the Vegastriopelia has chosen me to be your assistant, correct?"

"Yes, Neb, the Vegastriopelia has chosen you, but it's up to you if you want to stay. It's not like you're being held against your will."

"You mean I can go?"

"If you want. Your memory would be wiped and the last forty hours would be nothing but a dream, or a nightmare, depending on how you see it. Do you want to go, Neb?"

"I don't know, Tict, to tell you the truth."

"What would your parents say to do, Neb?"

"That's easy, they would say 'Nebula, move forward!'"

"Well, there's your answer, dear boy." Tict leapt to his feet as his comm system beeped. Neb watched Tict saunter over to this desk to answer the call. Tict pressed the comm systems button.

"Tict here," he said.

"Your presence is required." Neb recognized Kel's voice. "Please proceed to the Vegastriopelia control room.

"Will do. Tict out."

Neb finished his coffee. "OK, I am ready."

"Sorry, Neb, you'll have to sit this one out for now. I'll be back soon enough to fill you in."

Neb sat back down, disappointed. "What am I supposed to do then?"

"Do whatever you want, Neb. Why don't you go and find a game room and enjoy yourself a bit. Or go to bed if you want. Or wait here. No one is holding you. It's not like you're a prisoner here. Why don't you go find John Lennon and jam?"

"That's an idea! Sounds like fun." Neb gave a thumbs-up to Tict. They both left Tict's office. Tict went off one way and Neb the other.

14

Eno hurried through the corridors of the Casino. He was late again for his shift, the third time this week. The name Nebula Yorker raced through his mind over and over as he dashed between guests, running from gaming room to gaming room. He had been working at the Casino for well over three hundred years, give or take a day or two. As one of the few non-android workers on board, he thought at times the androids were treated better than he was. Of course, it was all in his mind, put there by someone else. Two hundred and twenty- eight years ago, he had thought for sure he would have been chosen to be next in line to be named the new assistant. He honestly felt he had made a connection with the Vegastriopelia but, no, another Earthling got in his way.

His personal wrist comm beeped. "You're late, again!" the voice on the other end echoed. It was HIP-001, the hangar bay android crew chief. That's all he needed.

"Hover cabs can't fly themselves. They could if we adapted them but, for the time being, we need drivers."

"I will be there as soon as I can," Eno unhappily replied.

"You know that I will have to write up another late report and, this time, submit it to Mr. Tict," HIP-001 dryly replied.

"Do as you must." Eno shut off his wrist comm. Eno had no intention of showing up for his shift. Never again. He waited for the hallway to clear to make his way out from the games room, past the Green Room and into the restricted area. He hadn't noticed Neb until he bumped into him. He knocked Neb off his feet. Eno, his head down, kept on going. He looked back once and saw Neb flat out on the floor.

"Neb Yorker!" Eno huffed to himself, out of Neb's view.

"That was kind of rude." Neb sat watching Eno disappear down the hall. He picked himself up from the floor and noticed a small green metallic case the size of a playing card staring back up at him. *Eno must have dropped it when we bumped into each other*, Neb surmised.

"Hey, Eno!" Neb yelled, but Eno was now gone. *I guess I should run after him and return it to him even though he ran over me and didn't even say 'sorry' or 'can I help you up'. Why must I always be the good guy? Because that is the way you were raised*, he thought to himself. Neb set out to find Eno and return his case.

15

"That's impossible!" TeeceeFore exclaimed.

"One would think so. Yet the data would state otherwise. The impossible has become possible," KEL-345 explained matter-of-factly.

"Are you one hundred per cent positive, KEL-345?" she asked again.

"I have run the equations three million point five times, ending with the same result. There is no error," KEL-345 added.

The Council sat in complete silence, each member mystified by the news. Tict entered the Casino's Council chamber and was brought up to speed on the situation. Like the rest, he didn't know what to think.

He asked, "Are you sure?"

KEL-345 tilted her head to the right. "Yes."

"Has this in any way affected any of the Casino's functions?"

"Nothing at the moment has been detected, sir," KEL-345 assured Tict and everyone. "We are currently running every possible diagnostic and simulation, though we have never gone through such circumstances. It may be difficult to determine what type of action should be taken, if any. Look here." KEL-345 called up the view screen to show everyone the problem.

"See here," KEL-345 pointed. "Computer, magnify section RL0025.3." It was such a small, minute, micro- puncture, even KEL-345 could not believe it. But there it was.

Everyone was glued to the screen and not everyone believed it or thought it was even remotely possible, yet there it was.

"Everything wears down over the course of time and it would seem that the Vegastriopelia is not any different, or so it would seem," TeeceeFore said.

"Yes, but we are talking about the Vegastriopelia. The Vegastriopelia does not wear down, does it? Who would have thought?" Tict looked to TeeceeFore and KEL-345.

"Any idea what may have caused the puncture?" TeeceeFore asked.

"Several, but until we conduct a more thorough investigation, I dare not say," answered KEL-345.

"This is highly unusual. Something doesn't add up. Why would Vegastriopelia decide to blow a tire?" Tict wondered aloud. "I don't buy it."

"Blow a tire, sir?" KEL-345 asked, confused.

"It's not important at the moment, KEL-345. I am just trying to reason this all out."

"Something, Tict?" TeeceeFore saw that look on his face. She had seen it before when something was afoot, though not on a scale like this.

"I'm not sure," Tict replied.

A mild vibration shook the entire Casino. Some didn't feel it but everyone in the Council chamber did. They looked at each other, wondering what it was all about. Reports started to come in from all over the Casino.

"What was that?" TeeceeFore, startled, reached out for Tict's hand.

***

Whoa, that sort of felt like an earthquake. Neb stretched his arms out against the wall. Living in California all his life, Neb knew a little about earthquakes. He'd been through two or three in his life. He waited for a few minutes before he felt it was OK to move on.

"How does anyone find their way around here?" he said aloud. "Everything looks the same."

"Destination, please," a voice echoed down from the ceiling.

Neb looked up. "What? Who said that?"

"You have activated the Casino's Interface program guide," a bland computerized voice replied.

Casino Interface? Why not? Neb thought, glancing up. "OK, Interface, where am I?"

"One moment, initializing voice commands protocols," the computer droned.

"Voice pattern, Nebula Yorker accepted," the Interface replied. "Please continue and repeat question."

"Where am I?" Neb asked again.

"Junction sixty, restricted area, zone forty-two," the Interface answered.

"Restricted zone? Why is it restricted, Interface?" Neb asked.

"Junction sixty by forty-two restricted to authorized personnel only."

"Am I restricted, Interface?"

"Working…" A few seconds later, the Interface answered, "You are not restricted. You may proceed, Nebula Yorker."

Neb then asked, "Interface, can you please locate Eno?"

"I will need more information on the request for subject Eno," the Interface replied.

Neb thought for a few moments. *Did Eno have a last name? Was there more than one Eno aboard?*

Finally Neb asked, "Interface, the Eno who drives a hover cab?" Neb asked tentatively.

"Searching," replied the Interface.

As Neb waited, he stared down at the metallic case in his hands.

"There is one Eno Low registered with the docking bay unit HIP-001, function hover cab chauffeur," came the answer from the Interface.

"That must be him," Neb said. "Please locate."

"Eno Low is presently fifteen metres ahead and one hundred metres below your present location, Nebula Yorker."

Neb walked fifteen metres ahead and stopped. Then it dawned on him. *One hundred metres below?*

"One hundred metres below?" he once again asked out loud.

"Yes," replied the Interface.

As soon as the Interface said "yes", the floor beneath Neb started to descend. Unlike Neb's previous encounter with the floor opening, which zigged and zagged its way to the control room, this time it just descended straight down. It didn't take long for the hydraulics to descend and then stop.

"Eno Low is five metres directly ahead. Approach with caution," the Interface, still active, informed Neb.

Caution? He thought to himself.

Neb stepped off the floor lift and he watched it ascend back up. As he did, he heard muffled voices just ahead. The floor shook again, like the last tremor. Neb stopped and waited for it to end. *I wonder what's with the shaking*, he thought.

"Interface?" he called out. "Interface?"

There was no response. Neb could still hear the muffled voices and this time he heard the sound of glass shattering. Then he heard a voice loud and clear. A door swooshed open in front of Neb and out came Eno, down on all fours, creeping, a foot pushing him out all the way.

"Eno!" a startled Neb yelled.

Eno looked up and, seeing Neb, lunged at him, drawing both of them back into the room he had just been kicked out of. They rolled around, Eno swinging his fist, missing and hitting the cold floor. Green blood oozed from Eno's knuckles. He shook his hand in pain.

Neb stood up and got ready to throw a punch back when a strong forceful hand stopped him from behind.

"Enough!"

Neb turned around. "Who are you?" He did a double take. He couldn't believe who he was seeing. *That face! I have seen that face in one of my dreams.*

"I am Marcus Apitippius."

An icy cold shiver ran down Neb's neck. It continued down his back and right down to the tips of his toes.

"Marcus Apitippius!" He backed up a step.

"Who are you?" Marcus demanded.

"That's Tict's new assistant Nebula Yorker," Eno said, now standing beside Marcus and wiping the blood off his hand onto his pant leg.

Marcus pushed Eno out of his way. "What did I tell you about standing so close to me?"

"Tict's new assistant. Well, well." Marcus slowly circled Neb. He eyed him up and down and even smelled him.

"Not officially, yet. I haven't accepted the position. I'm still mulling it over," Neb nervously said.

Marcus picked up on Neb's trepidation. "I see. Not officially. Still mulling it over, eh?"

"Wine!" Marcus commanded, snapping his fingers. Eno ran like a little panting dog. A few seconds later, he brought Marcus a glass of red wine. Marcus stood there, dressed in a red and white toga, his blond hair now long and braided in a ponytail hanging down his back, sipping his wine, glaring at Neb.

Neb remembered what Tict had said. You could see the wheels turning in his head.

"So, what brings you here, Nebula Yorker?"

"Actually, I was following Eno." Neb was just about to reach into his pocket to retrieve the case Eno had dropped when Marcus furiously threw his wine glass at Eno, missing his head and hitting the wall. Red wine and glass shards hit the floor. He pinned Eno up against the wall with one arm. With his other hand around Eno's neck, he lifted him up off his feet.

"What did I tell you about being followed?" Marcus released Eno from his grip, leaving him to fall to the floor.

"It won't happen again," Eno whimpered, looking up at Marcus.

Marcus turned to face Neb. "It's so hard to get good help these days. So, Nebula Yorker you were saying, you were following Eno. Go on. Why were you following him?"

Neb was feeling more uncomfortable with every passing second in Marcus's presence. "I think I may have come at a bad time. I'll just make my way back up and forget any of this happened," Neb said, making a beeline for the door.

Marcus stuck out his foot, tripping Neb as he tried to get away. As he fell, the metallic case slipped out of his breast pocket and slid across the floor, resting at Marcus's feet.

"The case, Eno!" he cried out excitedly.

Marcus bent down and picked up the case. "Finally!" He clutched it in his hands, cradling it like a baby.

OK, that didn't work out so well. Neb got back to his feet. He looked down at the palm of his right hand. It was glowing yellowish-green and then it disappeared. Only he saw it.

Holding up the case, Marcus asked, "I gather this is what you were intending to return to our little inept friend?"

"I was and then I wasn't. But yes," Neb replied.

"Come here," Marcus ordered Eno.

With trepidation, Eno inched his way over to Marcus.

"Well, is it?"

"It is, as you asked," Eno said, looking down at the floor.

"You are a fortunate man, Eno. You should be thanking your new friend here for his kind gesture in returning my property; otherwise, I may have had to kill you and you wouldn't want that, would you?"

"He's not my friend." Eno spat at Neb.

"Of course he's not. And don't spit on my floor again or I will make you clean it up the same way it came out. Do you get my drift? Now go and get me some more wine and bring a glass for my new friend."

Friend? I don't think so. What is he up to? Neb thought.

"Please sit." Marcus motioned to a small table with two curule chairs.

They sat as Eno returned and gave each a glass of red wine. Neb swirled his glass, hesitating to take a drink before Marcus did. Marcus raised his glass and said "To success" and took a drink.

Neb took a small sip of the wine as he looked about Marcus's room. It didn't look too much like a prisoner's cell, he thought. It was very much Roman in style. Paintings filled the walls, depicting Roman gladiators in combat, orgies, chariot races, and even one of a family eating a meal out on a beautiful blue sky terrace. In the other part of the room was a bed or, rather, a bed of cushions surrounded by light, white curtains. And the familiar black and purple checkered washroom door.

"Do you like the paintings?" Marcus asked, following Neb's eyes.

"They're exquisite, very detailed," Neb noted.

"Thank you. I painted them myself." Marcus seemed genuinely touched by Neb's comment. "You have an eye for art, I see."

"You might say that." Neb looked down into his glass. "And much more," he added.

"A scholar! I do enjoy a good chat though there hasn't been much of that lately." He looked towards Eno now sitting on a small stool in the corner.

"So tell me about Earth, Nebula Yorker. Has it changed much? Still full of death, deceit and politics, I hope? If there is anything you can count on, it's death and taxes." Marcus finished up his glass of wine, laughing.

"Unfortunately, the people ruling our governments have not changed much since your time. I am afraid it may even be worse to some degree, considering the nukes they have at their disposal. But, yes, to answer your question, death, deceit and politics are as rampant as ever," Neb replied.

"Just as I thought. It gives me a happy, warm feeling to hear it." Marcus sneered. "It can only get better and it will, I assure you."

What was Marcus up to, Neb wondered again.

"I'll let you in a little ole secret of mine." Marcus pulled away.

"Do you mean the one when you think you're a god and you plan on time travelling back to Rome 12 BCE to change history with this vessel's technology?" Neb slyly replied.

"Very good, Mr. Yorker. I can only imagine that Tict has filled you in? You're almost correct, but not quite. I did at one time feel as though I needed this vessel to accomplish my goal of universal and world domination and, yes, perhaps the whole of time and space, but I grew somewhat selfish in that regard. Too much, too soon, some would say. After spending two hundred and twenty-eight years locked up in this room, I've had plenty of time to work on my new plans. Eno is to be thanked for his help.

Neb gathered that it was Eno who had been Marcus's snitch all those years ago.

"Having someone free to come and go has been very useful," Marcus said. "That is, if he isn't followed." Marcus leaned back in his chair, staring at Eno.

"As I was saying," Marcus continued, "I don't really need this vessel, as I first thought, to accomplish my goals." Marcus held up the green metallic case. "This is all I need. So, yes, if you must know, I do intend to travel back in time, kill the Emperor and take over, or I should say, make over, Rome and then maybe the world."

"That's very enterprising of you, Marcus. What makes you think you'll succeed this time?" Neb asked, taking another small sip of the wine.

"Did you feel those two tremors earlier? Within seventy- two hours, this gaseous, fake ball shall begin to melt away everything and everyone aboard. Except myself and Eno, of course. Isn't that right, Eno?" Marcus grinned. "They think they're all so much smarter than us. When I say 'us', I mean us humans and, in turn, myself. Boy, are they in for a treat! Actually, what will happen is this. Halley's Comet/Casino will implode. They don't know it yet but, by the time they do, it will be too late, I am afraid, to reverse the ensuing chaos. You see, the Vegastriopelia has already begun to break down. Those two tremors you felt are nothing compared to what will happen next. I have left some systems onboard functional just because I am a nice guy. Others, though, will gradually fail, especially when everyone starts to regress back to their original forms. And poof! No more room to move. TeeceeFore's race, the Telvonians, will dismantle half of the decks alone. I wish I could see it all, but one can't have everything. But I do try," Marcus sighed.

"You know, some might think you're a madman, Marcus. I don't think you are. But there is always time," Neb said. "It must have been hard on you, as well as Tict, I imagine, being pulled out of time and brought here. Wondering where you had come, if you were dead or alive or dreaming, only to embrace your new surroundings for your own personal gain and selfishness. Unlike Tict, who moved forward, embracing this new challenge not just for his own benefit but for the benefit of all."

"Oh, please," Marcus spat out, "your wholesome gooeyness is so like all the other weak and mindless that I have trampled on. One needs backbone, Nebula Yorker, if one wants to succeed in this or any world or time. You see, time means nothing if one does not take advantage of it and, in my case, timing is everything!

"I am sorry that your time here has been to your disadvantage. You could have learned so much about the universe out there. You know, Marcus – may I call you Marcus? – I can see now why the Council has a dislike for Earth or, rather, for some of its inhabitants. I think it is people like you who give the Earth a bad name out here. Earth's history has shown this through time. Evil and malicious men and women have cropped up, only to be defeated when they think they have everything worked out. You, though, are something different. I don't know if you're a product of your time or if time is a product of yours. Did you evolve or were you created by time? Is it even possible to fathom?" Neb finished.

"Such profound words! If you are trying to impress me, you needn't bother. It won't work. But thank you for the compliments."

Marcus turned his attention to Eno. "Have you set the coordinates?"

"All imputed and ready at your command," Eno replied.

"Go then. Take your shuttle as planned and wait on Earth's moon until I call for you. It shouldn't be more than two thousand years or so."

"What?" Eno asked.

"It's a figure of speech. Keep watching the Earth. You'll know when it's time. Really, why do I even bother with you?" Marcus shook his head exasperated. "Once you have cleared the Casino, signal me. That will be my cue to leave as well. Go now!" Marcus ordered Eno.

No sooner had Eno left the room than the Casino shook for a third time.

"They must be going crazy up in the control room," Marcus clapped his hands in laughter. "Home, here I come! Oh, how I wish I could take you with me, Nebula Yorker. You would love Rome."

"I have been to Rome, thank you." Neb eyed Marcus.

"Yes, but not my Rome! Since you're not old enough to travel that far back, you would end up dissolving within an hour, if not minutes. Such a shame. But, you know what?" Marcus paused, tapping his fingers on his lips, "I think I will take you with me just to witness that. I didn't get the chance to see Lafil dissolve, unfortunately. It's mostly painless, from what I have heard," Marcus said sarcastically, miming a sad face.

"I'm not going anywhere with you!" Neb shifted in his chair. "What's going on now?" He looked up at Marcus, who was smiling that evil smile.

"Oh, by the way, that wasn't wine you drank. It may have looked and tasted like wine, but it wasn't. What did Eno call it again? Oh yes, Tilsmasbacs, a little something from his home world. When ingested, it renders one unable to move. You're cognizant of your surroundings, but that's it. It should only last an hour or so, but you don't have the luxury of that much time. Now, if you had some Vilit, it might help cushion the fall when we time jump. But I'm afraid I poured the last bit into my wine glass. Oh well, it would be only wasted on you anyhow," Marcus nonchalantly whispered in Neb's ear.

Twenty minutes later, a low hum beeped twice on Marcus's wrist comm. Eno was now out of range of the Casino and about to land on the moon.

"Just one more thing," said Marcus. "I'll be right back. When you've got to go, you've got to go." Marcus went to the washroom.

Neb sat paralyzed. Was this going to be his last moment of life? If so, who would have thought? Certainly not himself. One day, you're looking forward to a little star gazing and the next, you're out among the stars, literally, and the next day, you're found dead in 12 BCE Rome. Who would believe it? Neb couldn't believe it, yet here he was living it. *I guess there are worse ways to go,* he thought, *though, for the life of me, I can't think of any at the moment. Dead is dead.*

Marcus soon reappeared, with a pale brown satchel hung over his shoulder. "Ready?" he said. "Just so you know, as soon as we pop out of here, I have programmed a message for Tict and the gang to let them know what I have been up to. You know how irresponsible it would be of me to have gone through all these plans and not let them know. I really wish I could see their faces! Any last words before we go, Mr. Yorker?"

"You won't get away with this, you villain." Neb could hardly believe he had just uttered those words. Batman came to mind, for some reason, perhaps because it was the last television program he had watched before leaving the house. The Joker had tied Batman and Robin up and Batman said to the Joker, 'You won't get away with this, you villain!'

"Villain? I kind of like the sound of that. Thanks." Marcus reached into the satchel and pulled out a small triangular silver belt buckle. Neb's belt buckle was oval. *New and improved,* he thought.

"You know, for all the time that I was free on this damn ship, casino, whatever you want to call it, I never did time travel back home to Rome when I had the chance." Marcus paused and thought to himself. "I have visited many other worlds, tasted new food, drink and women. Mind you, it opened my mind to possibilities that I could never have imagined, but it also gave me insight into what I could accomplish when I did go home, and that plan is now finally about to come to fruition. Not bad for a Roman from 12 BCE, eh, Mr. Yorker? Soon, I will be back in my villa near Ostia by the Tiber. And, you know what? I will get to meet Lafil again for the first time. Well, his first time."

Neb's eyes lit up.

"Yes, Mr. Yorker, Lafil. I guess I should have said that the first time. I can't change time without him, I'm afraid." Marcus salivated with pleasure at his own words. He proceeded to stretch out his right hand and lay it on top of Neb's head. With his left hand, he pressed the buckle. With that, they were gone. Two white orbs shooting out of the Casino into space, heading for Earth.

***

The view screen froze with an image of Marcus Apitippius blowing a kiss.

The entire room, Tict, KEL-345 and the Council of U sat bewildered, stunned at Marcus's farewell message, as he called it.

"Shut that off!" A frustrated Tict raised his voice.

"Unable," KEL- 345 responded.

"Throw a blanket or something over it!" replied Tict.

"We must evacuate the Casino at once." TeeceeFore stood and addressed the Council.

"How?" Mleh Novel asked. "You heard Marcus. He said he has shut down the main hangar bay and he's disengaged the transfiguror converter. He's basically sealed everyone and everything on board; nothing can get in or out. We're going to implode and there's nothing we can do."

"Please settle down, everyone. This is exactly how Marcus wants us to react," Tict said.

“I heard what Marcus said,” TeeceeFore slammed her fist on the table. “Damn the day he came aboard!”

Tict had never seen TeeceeFore so emotional.

“We’re going to have to say something to our guests. We can’t just lie to them.” Tict looked up at Marcus’s grinning, evil face beaming down on him. “Didn’t I tell someone to throw a blanket over that!” he pointed.

KEL-345 walked over and tore the view screen off the wall.

“Thank you.” Tict sat back down, his hands to his face. “How did he bypass all our protocols? He must have had help. KEL-345, do we still have access to the main computer?”

“It would seem Marcus has left our internal systems functional. All Casino rooms are operative, Interface intact, ship’s logs open,” KEL-345 answered, as she worked her console.

“Why would Marcus leave all these systems functional?” asked Tict. “Send out a Casino-wide message, KEL-345, informing our guests that we have been experiencing sonic tremors associated with ongoing engine maintenance. We wish to convey our sincere apologies regarding this matter and expect to have it fixed shortly. In the meantime, Happy Hour will be extended until further notice.” Tict then addressed the Council, “with your permission, of course.”

They all nodded yes.

“That should keep everyone occupied until we can find some answers and a solution,” Tict added. “KEL-345, I want you to go over the video logs from early this evening just before Neb and I entered the Vegastriopelia. I feel there is something there that may help. Look for anything out of the ordinary, no matter how minute. Marcus may be brilliant but he’s not as perfect as he likes to think he is. He had to have orchestrated his plan with some help, no doubt, but from whom?”

TeeceeFore saw a look on Tict's face that she had seen before.

"Is something afoot, Mr. Tict?"

"I don't know. It may be nothing but something tells me there is." Tict pondered, mulling through his mental notes.

"I think it would be prudent if the Council were to go out among the guests. We don't want them to get any more suspicious than they may already be. I hate to say this but we need to put up a good front, especially if we don't get this under control," TeeceeFore said.

"You and KEL-345 need to concentrate on solving and undoing what Marcus has done. We on the Council will do what we do best."

"Which is?" Tict asked, smiling up at her.

"You never mind," she affectionately smiled back, kissing him on the head. Tict blushed.

TeeceeFore directed her attention to the Council. They spoke briefly and, one by one, calmly left the chamber room.

"I almost forgot about Neb! Interface," Tict called out, "locate Nebula Yorker please."

"Working. Nebula Yorker is not aboard the Casino," replied the Interface.

16

The warm October evening breeze blew across the city. The moon sat full and bright in the cloudless night sky. The constellation of Libra danced in full view. Orion watched nearby as countless gleaming stars looked down. Augustus Gaius Octavius Caesar looked heavenward, marvelling at the celestial ceiling. By his side, his wife, Livia Drusilla, also looked up at the vastness. Their home on Palatine Hill overlooked the Tiber River. On the other side stood the Circus Maximus. *How many nights together*, they wondered, looking up at the gods' playground. Their day had been long, with an endless parade of senators petitioning their long-winded proposals, poets, doctors, and even slaves, vying for Augustus's and Livia's attention.

"We should take a holiday and visit the provinces. What do you say, Livia?" Augustus put his arms around his wife, holding her tightly.

"Oh, I am too tired to think of a holiday right now, my dear. Besides, there is so much work and so little time." She tugged at his arm.

Augustus sighed, patting her hand.

"Perhaps early next spring we can plan a little vacation," Livia said.

"Yes, next spring would be good." Augustus breathed in the fresh night air. They snuggled as they stood rocking back and forth on the porch.

Their eyes caught it at the same time, high up in the eastern sky.

"What is it?" Livia gasped.

"I am not sure, but it is fantastic!" Augustus watched.

What would become known as Halley's Comet came into view, its tail dragging behind. As they watched, it looked like the celestial object was breaking up. A shooting star flew out of it. Then, it seemed as if the star broke in two. Two shooting stars looked as if one were chasing the other. They both fell east of the Tiber River.

"What does this mean?" Augustus asked his wife. "Have Romulus and Remus been reborn?"

Livia felt a tinge of fear trickle down her spine. She kept it to herself. The last time such an event had marked itself was the prophecy that Claudius, Livia's fool of a grandson, would one day become Emperor. It was long ago when he was just a child. But this was something different. She could feel it in her old bones. Livia knew that occurrences such as these were no mere acts of coincidence. Everything had to be mapped, star charts gleaned, astrologers questioned. Seers sought out. One star shines; two fall. What can it mean?

"There is someone who could help us," Livia remarked. "Who?" Augustus asked.

"An astrologer I met by chance recently. It was strange. I felt as though we had met before somewhere, some time long ago. His name is Lafil, a Babylonian seer."

***

A beam of moonlight shone through the hole in the thatched barn roof; dust and straw shimmered in and out of the lone ray. Inside the barn, two cows were munching hay. One gave a quick look up, while the other didn't bother. A small turtle-coloured round barn cat cautiously slinked over to the two entwined bodies lying motionless in the centre of the dirty barn floor. They had fallen in through the roof moments before. It sniffed at the bodies, one facedown and the other facing up. It pawed at the back of the head of the one facedown. The sound of a moan startled the cat. It leapt up into an alcove and looked down as one of the bodies started to move.

Neb opened his eyes. The first thing he saw was the hole in the roof above him. His body ached all over. *What happened?*

Gradually, he raised his upper body. His head was pounding. Raising his hand to his face, he felt a warm trickle. He pulled his hand away and saw blood on his fingertips. He looked around. The cat softly meowed above him. The two cows ignored him. The last thing he could remember was eating a cheese sandwich, or so he thought. He rolled over on his left side and was met by a pitchfork that could easily have pierced him if he hadn`t stopped. Thankfully, the moonlight coming down through the roof reflected off the fork.

Slowly, he raised himself up with the aid of the pitchfork. He was unaware that Marcus lay at his feet, out of the light, and at the moment he didn't remember what had happened with Marcus aboard the Casino. Actually, he wasn't sure of anything.

He hobbled over to the cows, almost tripping over Marcus, whom he still didn't know was there.

"Excuse me," he said to the cows, as he splashed himself with some of the water from the trough. This did get the attention of the cows, which mooed at him as if they were saying, 'Hey, that's our water. Get your own trough! Humans! All they want to do is milk or eat you!'

The barn cat jumped down from his perch and started rubbing himself up beside Neb. When Neb looked down at the cat, he saw that his pant legs were ripped up to the crotch. That explained the cool, airy breeze he felt. It caught Neb off guard, causing him to fall down, almost crushing the poor feline who just wanted to be friends.

Neb lay back on the floor, his face towards Marcus, still out cold on the floor.

"Oh, shit!" he muttered.

Everything came back to him like it had been a dream or, in this case, a nightmare. He sprang back up, looking over at Marcus, figuring that any moment now he would start to dissolve back into the earth from which he came. Closing his eyes, he waited and waited for it to begin. Nothing happened. He opened one eye and then the other. He did it twice to make sure.

"Yep, still alive!" he said turning to the cows. The cows continued to ignore him.

He hovered over Marcus looking for any sign of life. He gave him a light kick on the backside. He made no movement.

"Hmmm." He kicked him again. Neb thought, *can he be dead?* He walked back over to the water trough finding a small cup. He filled it with water and took a drink. It was warm and tasted awful and he spit half of it out. The cows looked at him, unimpressed. He threw the rest of the water onto Marcus's face. There was a little movement from Marcus. Neb found a much larger pail and filled it and dumped it all on Marcus. This time Marcus awoke.

"What? What?" Marcus shook his head and arched his body up. "What's going on? Where am I?"

"Don't play that game with me, Apitippius," Neb growled at him. "Look, I am still alive! What do you think of that?" Neb danced like a boxer back and forth.

Marcus sat wild-eyed and stunned. "Who are you? And what are you talking about?" he asked.

"Who am I? What is that supposed to mean?" Neb replied back. "I'm still alive, Marcus. Bet you didn't count on that. I didn't either, for that matter."

"Look, fellow, I really don't know who you are and what you're talking about."

Was Marcus trying to fool Neb or was something wrong with him?

"OK," Neb said. "What is the last thing you remember?"

Marcus sat silently, scratching his head. "I don't know, I can't remember." He looked around the barn and saw the cows. "Was I milking them?" He pointed to the cows.

Neb bent down and looked into Marcus's eyes. He lifted up two fingers and passed them in front of his face.

"How many fingers do you see?" Neb asked.

"Four?" Marcus answered.

"Do you know who I am?" Neb asked again.

Marcus replied, "Are you a priest?"

"A priest?" Neb was taken aback. "Why would you say that?"

"Your red garments." Marcus touched Neb's jacket. "Hey, that's a different kind of cloth. Where was it spun?"

Neb thought for a moment, looking up at the hole in the barn roof and back at Marcus. *Could he really have amnesia from the fall? I did fall on top of him. Can it be?* He wondered, looking at Marcus skeptically.

With Neb's help, Marcus stood and brushed off the excess straw and dust from his toga.

"Wow, nice toga. Where did I get it?"

Marcus's satchel hung over his shoulder. *The satchel!* Neb reached for it.

"Hey, what are you doing?" Marcus moved a step back and clutched the satchel closer to his body. "You're not a thief, are you?"

"No, I'm not a thief." Neb again tried to grab at it.

"Thief! Thief! Thief!" Marcus screamed out loud.

Neb punched Marcus as hard as he could in the face. Marcus fell back and hit the dirt floor, unconscious again. Neb was reaching for the satchel when he heard voices yelling outside the barn.

"Who's in there? What's going on in there?"

Neb forgot about the satchel and dove immediately into the nearest haystack, just as the barn door burst open. He lay all covered under the haystack. He moved a bit of the straw just enough to see what was going on. Two burly men entered. One had a sword in his hand and the other held a lance.

"Who's in here?" The man with the sword asked. "Come on, we heard someone calling out for help!"

They spotted Marcus sprawled out on the floor. Neb watched as one of the men picked up the pail, drew water from the trough and splashed it over Marcus, reviving him once again.

"Why do people keep doing that to me?" He sat up in his drenched toga.

The burly man with the sword said to the other with the lance, "Isn't that Marcus Apitippius?"

"It can't be? Is it?" the other replied.

"Did you catch him?" Marcus stood up slowly, touching his aching head. "Who are you?" he asked.

“Rufus,” the one with the sword said. “And this is my brother Germanus. You are in our barn, now with a hole in the roof.” He looked up.

“The thief, didn’t you see him?”

“There’s no one here but you, good sir,” Rufus answered.

“He does not look well,” Germanus whispered to his brother. “Maybe he had a few too many glasses of wine last evening.”

“Bring the horses around and let’s take him back to his villa before anyone else sees him like this,” Rufus said back to his brother. “Perhaps he will reward us for our discretion. Make it quick.”

Germanus sped off to retrieve the horses.

“It will be OK.” Rufus helped Marcus over and sat him down on a milking stool.

“Are you sure I wasn’t milking the cows?” he asked Rufus, who rolled his eyes. “The thief! He was all dressed in red. You couldn’t miss him.” Marcus looked down at his satchel. “He tried to take it.”

“I am very sorry. When we came in, there was no one but you here. We’re going to take you home now, sir,” said Rufus.

Germanus soon returned. “Ready, brother!” he called out to Rufus.

“You didn’t happen to see anyone dressed in red outside, did you?” Rufus asked Germanus.

“Dressed in red?” Germanus replied, stumped. “I really think he may have had too much of the red.” Germanus smirked.

“Perhaps so,” Rufus agreed.

"My brother is going to help you to the horses and bring you home, sir." Germanus steadied Marcus up onto his feet. "Go ahead. I will be with you in a moment." Rufus nodded to his brother.

Rufus took one last look around the barn. The cat darted out from behind the cows. It startled Rufus, who picked up the pitchfork and threw it at the cat. It landed in the hay where Neb was hiding, missing him by a mere inch.

"Damn cat!" Rufus fumed. The last thing he needed was to have to tell his mother he killed her cat. He again eyed the hole in the roof. How did that happen? He turned to leave and noticed a piece of ripped red cloth near the water trough. He picked it up and felt its smooth texture. After one last look around, he left.

Neb listened from underneath the hay pile to the horses galloping away. After waiting for 30 minutes or so, he crawled out from his hiding place. The cows watched him poke his head out and then ignored him again. It was still dark, though light on the far horizon indicated that morning would soon arrive. Neb knew for sure he needed a change of clothing. Walking around in a ripped red suit and a white turtleneck with black shoes was a dead giveaway, now that Marcus had described his outfit and Rufus had found that torn piece from his coat pocket.

How long before Marcus regains his memory, he thought. *How long before Rufus and Germanus make their way back to give the barn a more thorough search?* With his own memory intact, Neb was surprised at how cool, calm and collected he was, what with all he had been through in the last two days. He knew he had to find Lafil for starters and Rome was a big place. But first, a change of clothing was needed if he was to blend in. Of course, if Marcus didn't regain his memory, it might make it a little easier. History one way or another may have already changed or, for all Neb knew, it was right on course. And if and when Marcus regained his memory, what would that lead to?

Paradox, paradox, paradox, Neb thought.

And if he found Lafil first, how would he go about explaining who he was? Where he was from? Would Lafil even believe it? Neb thought so hard it hurt his head or was he experiencing the after effects of falling through the roof with Marcus. It looked as though history was about to change, whether it liked it or not.

Relax, he told himself. *Breathe in. Count to ten. Breathe out. Breathe in. Count to ten. Breathe out.* He closed his eyes and rubbed his temples lightly to reduce the pain.

"Move forward." He heard his father's voice so clearly he opened his eyes expecting to see him standing in front of him. Instead he saw the small fat barn cat staring up at him. It meowed at him. Neb picked up the cat. It purred in his arms as he rubbed it behind its ears, giving both the cat and Neb some comfort.

He thought about staying in the barn until daylight broke so that he could get some sense of his bearings and plan his next step. Then it dawned on him for the first time in a moment of clear thinking. Why was he still alive? It was well over an hour, almost two by now, and he hadn't disintegrated as Marcus had said he would. He was going to pinch himself when the cat did it for him, digging its nails into his arm.

"Yeow! What did you do that for?" Neb jumped up. The cat leaped off Neb and raced out of the barn. "OK. Well, that verifies it. I'm still alive. Flesh and blood."

Neb then decided not to waste any more time trying to figure it out. The sun would soon be up. He was alive, even though he thought he should be dead. First on the agenda, find some suitable clothing and some food. He knew he must not be too far from Ostia where Marcus said his villa was and where he overheard Rufus say they were bringing him home. At least, he now had a direction to head for. Rome hadn't changed that much, he thought, even though thousands of years had passed (or were ahead of him). It was all a bit confusing, but he was pretty sure he could find his way around. All he needed was daylight to break and then he'd set out.

17

"What do you mean, he's not aboard the Casino?" a confused Tict barked out.

"Interface, are you sure?" KEL-345 asked again.

"Affirmative," the Interface replied.

"Where did he go?"

The Interface responded without being directly asked, "Nebula Yorker has left the Casino with Marcus Apitippius. Destination, Earth. Rome, 12 BCE, to be exact."

Tict laid his head down on top of the table.

"I'm sorry, Neb," Tict muttered to himself and cried.

KEL-345 observed Tict crying. She knew that Neb could not have survived the time jump. She felt a pinch of emotion for the first time in her life. It was sadness. It was very uncommon for an android to feel such emotion, though this rare occurrence had been noted from time to time. The last listed record was two years after the launch of the Casino. Some oil had spilled over in the docking bay when Android 5501 suddenly started to cry. The android was sent for a diagnostic evaluation but nothing was found. Another time, Android 4200 was found laughing uncontrollably. Again, the cause was never found.

Emotion in an android was indeed rare. KEL-345 decided to keep this to herself. She wasn't sure if the sadness she felt was for Tict or for Neb. Perhaps it was for both or maybe it was for herself. She turned back to her console, imputing codes, pressing buttons, entering keys, doing everything she could think of to help with the present situation.

“Nebula Yorker’s homing beacon located,” the Interface blurted out.

“What? What was that?” Tict looked up.

“Nebula Yorker’s home beacon located, the Interface repeated.

Tict stood up, wiping the tears from his eyes, and walked over to KEL-345’s console.

“That’s impossible, isn’t it?” he asked KEL-345, his voice filled with grief and confusion. “Could it be possible he somehow survived the time jump?”

KEL-345 swiveled in her chair to face Tict. “Interface,” KEL-345 asked cautiously, “what are Nebula Yorker’s vital signs if any?”

“Working,” said the Interface.

After a few minutes the Interface responded, “Nebula Yorker’s vital signs detected. Core body temperature: 37.0 C. Normal. Blood pressure: Stable. Pulse: 90 beats per minute and falling. Respiratory: Normal. Fifth Sign: Headache.”

“Interface, are you one hundred per cent sure?” Tict could hardly believe what he was hearing.

“Affirmative. One hundred per cent sure, “the Interface replied.

KEL-345 looked up at Tict from her console. “How is that possible, Mr. Tict?” she asked.

“Well, it seems the impossible has become the possible.” Tict let out a long sigh. He went over it again and again in his head. The time travel restriction limit should have fallen into place. Tict thought long and hard.

"What is it, Mr. Tict?" KEL-345 asked.

"Interface, are you able to open Nebula Yorker's homing beacon's communication comm?" he asked hesitatingly.

"Working," said the Interface.

"Why didn't I think of that?" KEL-345 nodded sideways robotically.

"Nebula Yorker's communications receiver temporarily experiencing time static interference. Working on connecting," the Interface responded.

"How long before we can get a clear channel?" asked Tict.

"Unknown at this time," replied the Interface.

"Interface," Tict continued, "is Marcus Apitippius with Nebula Yorker?"

"Working. Negative. Marcus Apitippius is approximately 15 kilometres away from Nebula Yorker's present location.

"Interesting." Tict rubbed his chin. "What are Marcus Apitippius' vital signs?"

"What are Marcus Apitippius' vital signs? Working," the Interface again repeated "Marcus Apitippius' vital signs are erratic. Body temperature: 38.5 C. Small fever indicated. Blood pressure: Fluctuation found. Pulse: Detecting 110 beats per minute. Respiratory: Fluctuation found. Fifth sign: Headache associated with fluctuating amnesia."

"It would seem that Marcus is experiencing some difficulties," KEL-345 noted.

"It would." Tict gave a hint of a smile, but was still worried.

"Beep. Beep." KEL-345's console sounded.

“Mr. Tict, the computer has finished scanning the video logs you had requested earlier. It has found something you may want to look at.” Tict and KEL-345 watched Eno on the console’s view screen creep out of the Vegastriopelia room, looking back and forth to see if anyone was watching, then disappear off screen.

“Well, well. Eno, I always thought it was you! Not too bright, are we?” Tict shook his head.

“Interface, locate Eno.”

“Eno is aboard a shuttle which is stationed presently on Earth’s moon. His vessel is encased in a time bubble.”

“Time bubble?” Tict muttered under his breath. “What for?”

“Gadzooks!” Tict shouted out.

“Gadzooks?” echoed KEL-345.

“It’s an expression of surprise,” Tict said.

“Accessing.” KEL-345 scanned her memory banks. “Gadzooks. First used on earth in the 1690’s. Possibly derived from ‘God’s hook’, referring to the nails of a cross. Which god are they referring to?” KEL-345 asked Tict, “and why would he or she be surprised?”

Tict gave KEL-345 a disappointing look. “Just keep to the work at hand, KEL-345. Let me worry about surprises, which you are full of these days, I must say!”

“Surprises, sir?” KEL-345 replied.

Tict ignored her last comment. Eno must be waiting on Marcus for some strange reason. Why else would he be encased in a time bubble?

"PIC-500 and PIC-501," Tict addressed the androids, "I want both of you to start monitoring the Earth for any sudden changes in temperature, seismic activity, radio waves, video broadcast, governmental upheavals, anything out of the ordinary.

***

Before Neb could decide if he should stay in the barn under the cloak of darkness, the day had begun to break. A rooster crowed in the distance, shaking Neb out of his thoughts. He didn't feel as though he'd fallen asleep. It was more of a trance-like state.

Neb was fortunate that Rufus and Germanus hadn't returned to find him in his daze. He thought for sure they would have returned by now but, whatever the case, it seemed someone or something was looking after him.

In the meantime, without Neb realizing it, the stubby little barn cat had returned and was now all curled up on his lap and feeling quite contented, warm and secure. It looked up at Neb and meowed. Neb meowed back and laughed.

With the morning light brightening, Neb could see much better, both inside and outside the barn. It wasn't as big as he had thought it might be, perhaps the size of a two-car garage. The cows were off to the side sleeping, or at least it looked as though they were. Above a small loft sat a few pigeons, cooing and dropping a few morning drops. Neb sneezed loudly and frightened the pigeons that now flew up and out through their new skylight hole in the roof. The commotion also caused the cat to once again dig her claws into his lap before springing off him onto the window ledge and disappearing outside. Neb gritted his teeth, feeling the effects of the cat's scratches.

"That really stung! I was just starting to like you," said Neb, watching the little furball dart out.

A single ray of sunlight beamed down through the hole in the barn roof. Neb moved over to sit in its warmth. It gave him a sense of new hope and determination to get on with whatever needed to be done. He wasn't Superman, but it helped him. He almost felt as though he was on a knightly quest. He bathed in the sun for a few minutes with his face turned up and his eyes closed.

"Move forward," he heard his father's voice once again.

Like the last time he opened his eyes, the cat was staring back. It meowed back as if answering him.

"You again! What's with you?" He picked up his new friend and walked over to the open window. The cat jumped out of his arms onto the ledge, this time without scratching him. Neb peeked out. To his right, he saw a dirt road leading out among some sycamore trees. To his left was a small villa.

"It's now or never," he said. "Sorry, buddy." He pushed the cat off the ledge and lifted himself up and over and out.

Neb slinked along the outside barn wall as if he were walking on a ledge. When he reached the corner of the barn he had a much better view of the villa. He didn't see or hear anyone, but saw clothes hanging on a line, blowing in the warm morning breeze. There were a couple of white and red fringed tunics and some sheets, or maybe togas. Neb ran over and snatched what he needed. As he was pulling the clothes off the line, he also saw a pile of sandals on the villa's side porch.

***

Rufus and Germanus came riding down the dirt road on their horses. They could see their mother's small villa up ahead. They passed by the barn and Rufus eyed the hole in the roof. He knew he and his brother would have to get to work and patch it up. He was not happy about that.

With Marcus Apitippius now safely home and his pledge to assist the brothers for their discretion and a promise of some work when Marcus was feeling more like himself again, and his extra incentive to find the red-clad thief, Rufus and Germanus felt that the gods were finally looking after them after their life of servitude and sweat. They were ex-gladiators who had been set free three years earlier. Despite all their combat victories in the arena, they had incurred a huge debt. They did enjoy the celebrity status they experienced as gladiators, though, as time passed, they were recognized less frequently. But, when it happened, they beamed with pride.

Now living with their aged mother, they took on work here and there, sometimes as bodyguards for a day or two, other times working in a farmer's field. Mother would make extra money washing clothes or baking.

"What do you think, Rufus?" Germanus asked. "Do you think this thief in red exists?

"At first, like you, I thought that Marcus may have had too much to drink and that he was dreaming the whole thing up," answered Rufus, "until I found this piece of red cloth in the barn." Rufus pulled it out from beneath the gladiator belt he still wore. He handed to his brother to take a look.

Germanus rubbed it beneath his thick fingers. "Funny feel," he said, handing it back to his brother. "Seems like an expensive type of cloth for a thief, don't you think?"

"Possibly." Rufus shoved it back into his belt.

***

KEL-345 worked ardently, trying to connect with Neb's communication module. It was only a matter of time before she'd be able to open the link. Time was ticking -- 7 hours and counting of Marcus's 72-hour deadline had passed. Tict had returned to his office. If it was important for the Council to be visible to everyone, it was even more important that he be. He had asked KEL-345 to keep him updated every 30 minutes so that he in turn could inform the Council.

In the last seven hours, the Casino had rocked eight times, almost once per hour. For the time being, though, all was calm. A strange odour had recently been detected throughout the Casino. It could be smelled from the gaming rooms to the docking bays and everywhere in between. It wasn't a bad smell, but sweet and orangey. It didn't seem to bother any of the guests and no effects were being reported. With the help of PIC-500 and PIC-501, KEL-345 kept an eye on it.

KEL-345's comm beeped. It was Tict checking in. "Any news?"

"Nothing yet, sir, though I have been able to clean up 52.9 per cent of the time static," KEL-345 answered.

"Keep working on it, Kel," Tict replied, for the first time not using her call numbers.

Interesting, KEL-345, or now Kel, processed to his reply.

"I am heading off to the Bingo Darts Games Room to meet up with TeeceeFore. I will fill her in on your progress. Tict out."

Kel returned to her work. Neb had been the only one to ever address her as just 'Kel'. Now Mr. Tict had done so. It gave her more of an incentive to reach Neb. For hours, with the assistance of PIC-500 and PIC-501, she worked at cleaning up and clearing more of the time static. They were down to 15 per cent when they thought they made contact.

"Kel, I am picking up a signal. It's weak, low frequency indicated, sub-equating, boosting the time ratio variant stabilizers," PIC-500 alerted his cohorts, now also picking up on Tict's preference in calling her just 'Kel'.

"Hello, hello," a voice crackled. Just then Tict and TeeceeFore entered the room.

"I think we may have something!" Kel turned to Tict and TeeceeFore.

"Nebula, Neb is that you?" Kel enthusiastically asked. "Nebula? Who is that? To whom am I speaking?"

"It can't be!" TeeceeFore turned almost white.

"What can't be?" It was now Tict's turn to see TeeceeFore frazzled.

"It's ... It's ..." TeeceeFore paused. "Lafil! Disengage the transmission now," she ordered. "Now!"

"Ending transmission." Kel cut off the connection as ordered.

PIC-500 and PIC-501 were totally confused why, after working all this time to successfully break through the time static, it would be abruptly shut down.

"May we enquire why we ended the transmission, Kel?" they asked in unison.

"Unsure," Kel replied.

"Kel?" TeeceeFore looked to Tict.

"Yes, Kel," he said, without explaining.

"Madame Prime Minister?" Kel looked up at TeeceeFore from her console.

"Don't you see?" TeeceeFore looked about the room. "You have somehow, inadvertently, made a connection with Lafil's homing beacon communication module from the past."

"How is that possible, TeeceeFore?" Tict stopped himself. "Unless Lafil …." He thought about it.

TeeceeFore could see that Tict was coming to the answer. "Unless he was visiting the planet. Specifically, Rome of 12 BCE. Kel, access Casino's historical records."

Before she was able to relay that Lafil was indeed on earth in that time period, TeeceeFore answered the question.

"He was," TeeceeFore replied, sitting down to take in the information. "Every time we swung by Earth, Lafil would pop down to visit Rome of that era, never his own. He loved Rome and made a few friends, including the Emperor Augustus's wife Livia."

"Shouldn't that time stream have been locked after Lafil's death?" Tict asked, sitting down beside her.

"Yes, the time stream should be locked. But nothing seems quite right, does it? Earth's history may have begun to change as we speak."

"How is Nebula alive? How were we able to connect with Lafil?" TeeceeFore asked. "Is this all part of Marcus's plan or is there something more at play here? Lafil is dead. You saw him die. We shouldn't be picking up his time stream. It closes at death. Yet, somehow, Lafil's time stream is open. We've heard it and, by doing so, we may also have changed whatever history was in the making. Kel, is there any report of Lafil picking up another signal and reporting it?"

Kel accessed the history data banks again. "None," she replied.

"Could Marcus have already changed history, or has Neb?" TeeceeFore wondered.

"If I may?" Kel interjected. "It would seem that history, regardless of our point of view, has already changed, whether or not it was Marcus's initial plan. The big question is, how did Nebula survive the time jump? He should be dead for all intents and purposes, yet he lives, according to his vital signs. Let us assume that Neb knows of Marcus's plan. If so, he also knows that Lafil is visiting the Earth's Rome of this time period. I have called up the data on Lafil's first contact with Marcus. It would seem that the dates are correct. Also, if our updated data on Marcus's vital signs are correct, he may not remember anything about his time on the Casino or his initial meeting with Lafil. If so, therefore, history may continue as it is, or was, in this case. Should he regain his conscious state, I would say all bets are off. Again, Neb is the one variable we have not accounted for. It poses a series of questions that only time will answer. Regardless, if I were Neb, I would be looking for Lafil to warn him about Marcus."

"There is only one flaw in your assessment, Kel," added TeeceeFore. "You're forgetting one thing. The Vegastriopelia chose Marcus and Nebula."

"Did it?" Tict joined the conversation.

TeeceeFore marvelled at Tict's words. "You can't be serious?"

"I am quite serious," Tict said matter-of-factly. "Let me explain."

"Please do!" TeeceeFore replied, sounding somewhat offended at Tict's words.

"Say that Marcus somehow manipulates the time stream when he meets Lafil," Tict began. "Does he kill Lafil or does he let history repeat itself? The latter wouldn't make sense to Marcus. Why play out the sequence over again? What would be the gain? No, Marcus needs to kill Lafil. He doesn't plan on returning to the Casino. Why would he? He doesn't care. He wants to wipe the Casino from all of history. He wants to use what he has learned while aboard the Casino – Earth's history from his time until now, 1986, and any technology he may have stolen – to change the course of Earth's history solely for his own benefit."

"If that is true, Tict, what about us? Will we have ever existed?" TeeceeFore asked.

"Perhaps in a parallel world, though, if Marcus succeeds, not in the present one," Tict answered.

Kel added, "Marcus's last message to the Council did allude to this, though his gleeful message was mainly concerning the destruction of the Casino. That may explain why Eno now sits encased in that time bubble on the moon. He's waiting for Marcus."

"If what you say is true, then everything we thought about the Vegastriopelia choosing our concierges all these years has been wrong," TeeceeFore replied, leaving her with more questions than answers.

"Not entirely, Madame Prime Minister. If Marcus succeeds or has already succeeded, our Vegastriopelia may have never existed, nor any of us. That is, if our time frame is to be wiped out of existence," Kel calmly replied.

"I am not sure how to take that, Kel," Tict interrupted. "That may well be, though it still doesn't explain why Neb is alive and, hopefully, well."

During all this time, PIC-500 and PIC-501 were busy working away, half listening to the ongoing conversation. Human interactions were at times perplexing to them. Most of the time they didn't even bother to eavesdrop but today was different. They had to applaud Tict and TeeceeFore for how they were handling the present situation. Of course, their lives were at stake as well as those of all the other beings on the Casino. They wondered if anyone would really miss them.

One possibility led to the next, with each equation having a different solution and yet they found themselves in the same quandary as their human and non-human counterparts concerning what could be the correct explanation. It was fascinating to them that they both were stumped but they were sure that they would ultimately find a solution. They knew that time paradoxes were not something to trifle with and wondered if one paradox ever overlapped another. Such are paradoxes, the ifs and buts of the universe.

"We now have a clear signal to Nebula Yorker's communication module. PIC-500 has rerouted the time variant relay echo stabilizers. Static feedback should be minimal, if any," PIC-501 relayed. PIC-500 looked at PIC-501. They nodded to each other.

"Ready in five, four, three, two, and one....." Tict and TeeceeFore held their breath; the androids would have, too, if they had needed to breathe air.

"Nebula? Do you copy? This is Kel."

18

The road was dusty and the weather warm for October. Neb wasn't sure what time it was. He had to have walked at least three hours. He was tired and his feet were getting sore. He thought a break would help.

He had encountered a few travellers along the way, some pulling carts holding what seemed was all of their belongings and, in some cases, their livelihood. A group of six heavily armed soldiers on horseback had sped by earlier. That had given Neb cause for concern, though they continued on their way.

His newly acquired tunic fell to just above his knees. It was an off-white, light wool garment with two faded red stripes running down the front. He'd wrapped his belt around his waist to give it more of that Roman look. He also had unhooked the buckle and looped it through some thread he'd torn off the toga. He threw the makeshift necklace around his neck. It fell to just below the neckline and he hid the buckle inside his tunic. On his back, he'd slung a rolled up toga which held the remnants of his red suit, white turtleneck and black shoes. His very own Roman knapsack, as he called it. Though he loved the sandals he'd found back at the villa, he hated the feeling of the little rocks that always seemed to find their way between his toes.

The Tiber River ran to the left of the road Neb was on. He edged down the embankment to the river and, just as Rufus and Germanus rode speedily by, he slipped and fell out of their view. He scratched his legs along the way but thought, what was one more scrape to his already bruised body? He got up, dusted himself off and limped over to the water where he found a log to sit on. He pulled off the sandals and sank his tired, sore feet into the cool waters of the Tiber. The refreshing undercurrent rushed between his toes as he wiggled them.

"Yes!" he cooed.

As he sat back, he thought about where he was and how in the world he was going to find Lafil. He didn't even know what he looked like. He didn't recall the Vegastriopelia history introduction movie he watched with Tict saying anything about him. He now found it odd that it was skipped over. After all, Lafil was the first human concierge. Wasn't that piece of its history worth telling?

"Move forward," he heard his dad's voice again.

It was going to be like finding a proverbial needle in a haystack. He found that funny now because he had found one just before he left the barn. He couldn't miss. It stuck in his rear.

How does one find someone he has never met or even know what they look like? He hadn't seen any video or a picture of Lafil aboard the Casino. All he knew was that Lafil was human and of Babylonian origin.

And if and when he met Lafil, what would he say? *Oh, by the way, I am from the future.* On top of that, Neb thought Lafil would not believe he was from the future because no one can time travel to the future. *He will either think I am totally nuts or else he'll believe me, I suppose.*

He pulled over his Roman knapsack, as he now called it, and took out a very large red apple. He'd been able to pick a few from a tree a few miles back. He bit into the apple. It was crisp and juicy and not too soft, just the way he liked his apples.

"Two-thousand-year-old apples still taste like apples," he laughed. Finishing it, he sat back with his feet still in the water and wondered what Kel was doing and what she would think of this perplexity.

"Nebula? Neb? Can you hear me?" As he thought of her, he thought he could hear Kel's voice as if she were right beside him.

"Nebula? Neb? Are you there?" Neb heard again and jumped up. He looked all around but saw no one.

"Neb, can you hear me?" Kel asked once again.

"Maybe he can't hear us." He now heard Tict's voice.

"Hello? Is someone there?" Neb whispered, still looking all around.

"Is that you, dear boy?" Tict said happily.

"Tict? Kel? Where are you?"

"The question is, where are you and why?" Kel answered.

"I can hear you but I cannot see you," Neb replied.

"Of course you can't see us. We're on the Casino. Did you bump your head again?" Tict chuckled.

Neb felt stupid as he pulled the oval buckle from beneath his tunic.

"Damn! The buckle," he said, as he looked at it. "I forgot." He had completely forgotten about the built-in homing beacon and communication module.

"Oh, man, it's so nice to hear your voices. Can you get me out of here?

"At the moment, we only have this communication open and we are not sure how long it will last. We are also working on how it is that you're alive," Tict answered before Kel had a chance to respond.

"Yeah, that would be kind of good to know. Or is it just on pause?" Neb replied.

"Neb, you must get to Ostia as soon as you can" Kel relayed. "There you will find Lafil. We have tracked your present location.

You're six miles northeast of Ostia. Find the Imperial Villa. That is where Marcus and Lafil will meet for the first time."

"How did you know that I would be looking for Lafil? Neb asked.

"Elementary, my dear Watson," Kel replied.

"Very good, Kel. I see you have been brushing up on Earth's literature."

"Knowing that you knew, as we knew, the plan, and knowing that you knew that to thwart Marcus, you needed to locate Lafil first," Kel remarked.

"Well, Marcus did give away a lot of his detailed plans. Why do villains always do that?" Neb added.

"By the way, how are you feeling?" Tict asked.

"Besides not being dead, and the possibility that two oversized brutes may be looking for me, and presently being in the past, I would say 'OK'."

"Did you say two brutes?" asked Tict.

"Yes, big ones too!"

"Oh, dear! Can you then verify that Marcus is alive and has amnesia?"

"Oh yes, he is very much alive and the last time I saw him, he didn't know who I was or where he was, but the situation could change rather quickly if and when he remembers. If I can get to Lafil before Marcus regains his memory, we might have a chance. If he doesn't regain his memory, we still might have a chance. Any odds, Kel, on what the outcome might be? Wait, don't answer that. I would rather have hope on my side than odds. On the other hand, if he regains his memory before I find Lafil, we could be as my father once said to me."

"What is that, Neb?" asked Kel.

"What would you be if you were attached to another object by an inclined plane wrapped helically around an axis?"

There was a brief pause at the other end.

"Screwed!" answered Kel.

"Correct!" Neb said.

"Neb, I am feeling much better now, knowing you are not dead. I kind of feel responsible for you, you know, and when we couldn't find you on the Casino, well ..." Tict stopped.

"I am glad I'm not dead too, Archibald," said Neb, welling up.

"There is one more thing I would like to ask before ..."

Tict's voice trailed off into static, ending the communication.

"Hello? Hello? Hello?" Neb shook the buckle. *Before what?* He continued shaking it but to no avail. All he got was static and then that also faded away.

Neb stood with the buckle in his hand, shaking his head. He decided the best place for the buckle would be back on his belt in case the communication link was again established.

At least they knew he was alive and vice versa. And that the Casino hadn't imploded, yet. *Good to know that someone has my back up there.* He peered up into the sky. He slipped back into his sandals, hoisted his toga knapsack over his shoulder and headed northeast.

It's now or never, he thought. *Go bust or go home broke. Ostia, here I come.*

Neb figured it might take him another two or three hours to reach Ostia on foot. He made his way back up the embankment, slipping and sliding as he did, with more of those irritating little rocks finding their way in between his toes.

"Man, I can't catch a break!" he said as he finally got himself back up on the dirt road. He looked down, noticing horse hoof prints and droppings stretching up the trail. He could tell by the way the prints were placed that they must have been in a hurry.

Wish I had a horse. He sighed and continued on to Ostia.

19

Augustus and Livia settled into the Imperial Villa at Ostia. It was enough for Livia and it made her husband happy for the time being. It wasn't the vacation Caesar envisioned, though he thanked his wife for at least getting out of the city, even if they were only 12 or so miles away from Rome. Tonight they would have a light meal, enjoy some family time and entertain assorted guests, one in particular.

"Have you been able to get hold of that Babylonian astrologer?" Augustus asked his wife.

"We met yesterday. It was odd, as though he had been waiting for me to find him." Livia answered.

"Well, he is a fortuneteller of sorts, isn't he? Perhaps he saw you in his tea leaves," Augustus laughed.

"Yes he is an astrologer, but not a witch," Livia protested. "That may be, but did you tell him about the two falling stars we saw the other evening?"

"I did. He said he would look into the matter immediately. Without charge, mind you."

"Without charge? What kind of astrologer is he? Everyone charges."

"He said that being in our presence was enough payment."

"I wish everyone was so generous with their words. What sort of fellow is this Lafil?" Augustus asked. "Are you sure my dear, that he is what he says he is and not some assassin waiting to cut our throats at the first chance he gets?"

"Oh, we don't have to worry about that. I have thoroughly made sure of his credentials. He comes very highly recommended from Herod himself." She was, of course, lying.

"Well, if he's good enough for Herod," Augustus smiled at his wife.

Livia picked at her food, thinking about the things Lafil had told her about her past and present, proving that he indeed was a seer worth knowing. She wasn't easily fooled and having someone with such knowledge was worth keeping a close guard on. Knowing and using secrets was one of Livia's specialties and not many had any on her.

Never tell anyone what you're thinking, her mother had once told her, *not even those you love and trust.*

Augustus strolled out onto the terrace eating a freshly- picked pear from his own garden.

"Is everything alright, my dear?" he asked.

"Fine. Everything is perfectly fine." Her thoughts came back to the present. "I was just about to go through some of these scrolls." She lifted up a medium-sized basket full of the scrolls that sat at her feet. Augustus sat down beside her.

"Livia. Do I have to?" Caesar moaned. "I am on vacation!"

"If we get it over now, we can enjoy the rest of our little holiday." She kissed him on the forehead and handed him the basket.

"Very well." He took the basket from her hand. Augustus pulled out the first scroll and opened it. "Not again!" He shoved the scroll in her face. "It's that damn Marcus Apitippius."

"Why don't you just give him what he wants and be done with him!" Livia shot back.

"Give him what he wants! Do you know what he wants!?" "No, dear. What does Marcus Apitippius want now?"

"Here, you read it?" The scroll fell from his hands to the ground. He bent down and picked it up, handing it to Livia. Livia began to read the petition.

"Hmmm, that's interesting. Possibilities." Livia quickly eyed the petition.

"What do you mean, possibilities?" Caesar grabbed the scroll back out of her hands.

"I will say one thing. The little twerp has aspirations."

"Aspirations? He wants to start up a gladiatorial league across the Empire, build a forum in every city and, instead of fighting to the death, award each gladiatorial team with points and then have a league championship ender, with the losing team hacked to death and the victors set free."

"Don't fuss, my dear. I said it has possibilities, but who in their right mind would want such a waste of time. A gladiatorial league! Really. Besides, Marcus Apitippius will be coming later on this evening to inquire of Caesar. It would be so much better to let him down in person, don't you think?" Livia softly chided her husband.

"Of course. You're right once again, my love." He took her hand and kissed it. "I will give Marcus Apitippius one thing. He is always coming up with new ideas."

"Yes, too many for my liking. Makes you wonder what's going on in that head of his. What will this be, the fourth time you will have to turn him down?" Livia asked.

"Yes, but it will be the first time in person," Caesar answered.

"We should, for the fun of it, tell him we like his new venture, watch his face light up and then tell him otherwise. Bring him back down to earth."

"Livia!" Caesar protested. "That's not very kind at all. We must project sincere interest when dealing with these petitions, though we don't have to like it."

"Of course. You're right, my dear." Livia smiled mischievously.

***

"What happened?" Tict's happy demeanor turned gloomy.

"More time static interference. Rerouting the spatial signal," said PIC-501.

"Engaging amplification timbre," PIC-500 relayed.

"Well, at least we know he's alive and well," TeeceeFore assured Tict.

"Yes, but for how long?"

"I think it would be advantageous to remain positive, Mr. Tict. We are all concerned for the state Nebula finds himself in and we should be equally concerned about our own state and that of the Casino and all aboard.

He was so worried about Neb. He felt that it was his fault.

"Our outer shields are down 20 per cent. The comet cloak shell will eventually lose its hull integrity, exposing us to Earth's radar seconds before we implode. Earth's defence system will only detect an explosion in space, ruling out any sort of extraterrestrial presence," Kel mentioned to Tict and TeeceeFore, thinking that perhaps changing the subject would ease their worries for Neb. "It may seem to them as if an asteroid collided with another."

"Well, that's great news!" Tict exclaimed sarcastically.

Mission accomplished, Kel thought to herself assuredly.

PIC-500 and PIC-501 continued to clean up the time static and to monitor all of Earth's transmissions as requested. Nothing was out of the ordinary thus far. That was a good sign. It told them that Neb had yet to confront the situation at hand and that a positive outcome could still be reached.

The Casino shook for the ninth time and more forcefully than the last. Within minutes, incoming damage reports trickled in. The main hangar bay, every game room and the Green Room reported power fluctuations.

TeeceeFore and Tict worried about how long it would be before a major disruption ensued. Amazingly, through all of these disturbances, not one guest complained. In fact, a new game called 'casino-quake' had started and bets were being placed on when the next one would take place. No one was panicking and that panicked Tict to some degree. Kel also found it somewhat strange, not the casino-quake part, but everyone's easygoing attitude.

The last jolt caused the Casino to slow down its speed by 000000000000000000.5 per cent. Only an android could feel the change beneath the plates.

Kel informed Tict and TeeceeFore of the change. However, she didn't know if she should tell them that, after the impending implosion, the Casino would slip from a blue, shift to a red, and then slip back again and, depending on how the implosion reacted, it might take the form of a black hole. But then, would it really matter? She decided to wait.

"I cannot and will not believe we are destined for such an end!" TeeceeFore broke down. "The Triopelians would never let this happen. Never! There must be a failsafe."

Tict had never seen TeeceeFore like this in all the 228 years he had known her.

"All that I am saying is the Triopelians would have covered all bases, all situations, no matter how big or small, wouldn't they? They would not have given us the gift of Vegastriopelia if they hadn't. There must be a way out. Oh, how I hate Marcus Apitippius," she cried and fell into Tict's arms.

Well! Tict thought as he held her. This was something new. They both knew how fragile the universe could be, with beings like Marcus Apitippius cropping up every now and then, defying logic. Membob Kopp tried and failed, though look where Membob ended up. Could or would the same be said for Marcus?

***

Lafil took his time walking to the villa. He breathed in the late afternoon fresh air. The day was warm and he was sweating. He wasn't used to that after all those years aboard the Casino. It had been 75 years since his last visit, a long time. He had missed home, Earth. At times like these, he thought about giving it all up on the Casino and returning for good.

His birth home of Babylon was long ago. So many deities, rules and regulations. Rome wasn't much different in that respect, but Rome had indoor plumbing. *It's the little things in life that make us happy, isn't it?* He laughed to himself.

He had met Livia twice before on past visits. She would never remember, of course. One needed to observe the time stream. It was one thing to meet historical figures. It was another to interfere. He always, always, needed to be on his toes so as not to change one thing, however minute. One word, one wrong move, and POW, there goes the time space neighbourhood. It was almost a game for Lafil. He knew so much about Livia. He loved to tease her with tidbits, though never altering history. He also knew that she could be very dangerous. One word, one move, and POOF, Lafil was gone from the time space neighbourhood.

He had never visited the Imperial Villa at Ostia, so this was a whole new adventure. He had first met Livia 300 years ago, just before she wed Augustus, and then 75 years ago on his last trip to Earth, years after the death of Augustus. Now were the middle years, so to speak, before Augustus would die at her hands. It was his very own trilogy on the life of Livia, one of the most powerful women that Rome had ever seen and would ever see again. This, however, would be his first time meeting the Augustus One.

Lafil gave great thought to what he would say to them on the subject of the two falling stars they said they had both witnessed. Lafil had not seen the stars and neither had the Casino's sensors picked them up. According to the control room's data astro-emitter, nothing had been detected in the atmosphere at the time Augustus and Livia saw whatever they saw. Perhaps they had both had too much to drink and saw only what they wanted to see. Who knew?

He had to remember that, like in his own time period, gods, superstitions and omens ruled Rome; thus, he had to tread lightly, without sounding like an idiot. Livia could smell a rat and catch it from miles away, literally and figuratively.

Lafil had his beacon and communication module embedded into his wrist band on this trip instead of on his belt. He found it fitted much better. His wrist band hummed. He looked around to make sure that no one was watching him. Livia's spies could be anywhere. Sure that no one was looking, he lifted up his left arm and spoke into his wrist band.

"Yes? What is it?"

"We've picked up a low subspace frequency bouncing and fluctuating in and around your location." Said the voice at the other end.

"Interesting," Lafil responded. "How far?"

"Twenty kilometres or less. Hard to pinpoint at this juncture. It fazes in, then fazes out as quickly as we can detect it," answered the voice.

"Keep me informed". Lafil out."

Lafil thought for a moment about the odd transmission he had received earlier in the day. He had asked control to keep an eye out in case any unusual readings should arise. What was it? Knobby? Nubby? Nebular? Neb? Something to that effect. If he didn't know better, he'd think gremlins from Seaus 4 were the culprits. He soon forgot about it and let his thoughts return to Livia and Augustus and what grand explanation he would espouse.

20

Marcus Apitippius had slept the whole day. He opened his eyes and found himself staring up at the ceiling, not quite sure where he was. He looked about the room. It felt familiar and yet it was unfamiliar at the same time. Off to one side of the room were a couple of chairs and a table. On the other side of the room was a wash basin. He thought he saw a black and purple checkered door. He closed his eyes and rubbed them and, when he opened them again, there was nothing there but a wall.

His head ached.

An older man appeared in the doorway. "Master, I see you have awoken. I have brought you some of the medicine you asked for before you fell asleep."

Marcus eyed the old man suspiciously. "And you are?" he asked. It was Galen, Marcus's caretaker of his villa and slave. Galen's five-foot, eighty-year-old, stocky, bald frame handed Marcus a cup of hot steaming tea.

"I brought the tea," Galen said.

"Tea?" Marcus smelled it. "You're not trying to kill me, are you? What's in it?"

Galen protested. "I have served your house and your father's faithfully for over 50 years. If I wanted to kill anyone, I would have done it long ago. The tea has a blend of silphium for the pain and fennel for the nerves and a touch of sage," Galen answered backing a few feet away from Marcus.

Marcus studied Galen and the cup of tea. As much as he had been a kind of father figure to Marcus all these years, he was still a slave and knew his place. It didn't stop him from speaking his mind from time to time.

Marcus gulped the tea down in one shot.

"The medicine should ease your headache quickly enough for you to attend your engagement at the Imperial Villa this evening."

"Imperial Villa? What are you talking about, Galen?"

"Your petition, Master. The Emperor wishes to speak with you directly, don't you recall?"

"Petition! I can't even recall what happened yesterday or last evening." He rose slowly from his bed. His head felt better as the medicine was taking affect. Galen quickly brought him a toga to cover his bedding tunic.

"Thank you," said Marcus, as Galen helped him.

Galen could hardly believe that Marcus had said 'thank you'. He couldn't remember the last time he had heard it from him. *Old age will do that to you*, he thought. Maybe he was just playing a trick on him.

What happened to him last evening? When Rufus and Germanus showed up with him, he was so disheveled that Galen could hardly believe it. Never had he seen his master in such a state. It was so unlike him. Marcus Apitippius was always in control but, then again, too much wine will sometimes have that effect. If this was the new Marcus -- kind and thankful to Rufus and Germanus, asking them back, offering to pay them for their help in finding some red thief – well, so be it, Galen thought.

"I find myself thirsty and hungry, Galen. Could you please go…"

Before he could finish, Galen interrupted, "Yes, yes, of course, master, at once." He rushed off.

Marcus's head was feeling light due to the medicine in the tea. He needed to splash some cold water on his face. He walked over to the water basin, bent his head down and cupped his hands with water. The cold water felt good on his face. He did it several times until he felt somewhat better. He was also starting to feel the full effects of the drugs. With his head still bent down, the reflection of his face bounced up at him from the basin. He froze like a stone pillar and started to have strange visions. There was darkness and then light. Oddly shaped figures, not of Earth, phased in and out, stars, planets, moons flashed and a large ship, not sailing on water but on air. Voices called out his name, faces young and old, male and female, laughed at him.

Galen soon returned, bringing with him a tray of food and a fresh, clean set of clothing for Marcus. He set the food tray down on the table beside Marcus's bed where he lay his clothing.

"Would you like me to draw you a warm bath, master, after you have eaten?" he asked. "Master?" Galen asked again.

With his back turned to Galen, Marcus said nothing.

"Master?" Galen called out once more and still no answer. *That's odd*, he thought. Perhaps he gave him too much medicine. He walked up beside him. Marcus was still looking down. Galen waved his hand in front of his face. He didn't move.

"Master?" This time Galen lightly shook him.

Marcus reacted to Galen's touch. He lifted his head and looked around the room and back at Galen, but he wasn't seeing the room or Galen. His blue eyes were glazed over and had a yellow-green tinge. Galen took a step back, frightened. Marcus opened his mouth but nothing came out.

"What is it, Master?" Galen asked.

Again, Marcus's lips moved silently and then he whispered.

"Master?" Galen moved forward.

Then, loud and clear, it came out, "NEBULA YORKER."

"Nebula Yorker. Nebula Yorker. Nebula Yorker." Marcus said three more times.

"What's a Nebula Yorker?" Galen asked.

Marcus began to wobble; Galen moved forward and caught him before he fell.

"Master," Galen voiced with a hint of concern, "perhaps it would be prudent to lie back down." Galen led him back to his bed.

"My head," Marcus whimpered.

Galen had never seen Marcus so off guard and defenceless. It wasn't like him at all. Either he had really had too much to drink or this was an entirely different Marcus Apitippius.

"What are you doing?" Marcus flung Galen's hands away from him. "I told you never to touch me!"

OK. This is the real Marcus Apitippius, Galen thought.

"I was only trying to help, Master. I was afraid you were going to fall."

Marcus now sat on the corner of his bed. "Bring the food tray over here," he said, "along with the petition. Then go and draw me a bath and bring me some more of that medicine."

"At once, Master." Galen rushed over to fetch the tray and petition.

Perhaps I should have killed him when I had the chance, Galen thought, seeing how Marcus's old self seemed to have returned.

Galen brought over the food tray. It was only a few feet away from where his master sat.

"I almost forgot." Galen pulled out a copy of the petition from beneath his toga. "For your meeting with Caesar." He handed it to Marcus.

"Yes, yes." Marcus waved Galen away.

Before he left, Galen reminded Marcus that Rufus and Germanus would be returning later in the day.

"Rufus and Germanus?" Marcus shrugged his shoulders and nibbled at the food tray.

***

Now just outside of Ostia, Neb had walked all afternoon in the late October heat. All he needed was to find Lafil.

He thought, *how hard can it be to find a 2,000-year-old Babylonian concierge?* He had met a few folks on the road. His Latin was quite passable and he asked directions of those he met along the way. He wanted to be sure he was on the right path to Ostia and he was. So far, time was on his side. Lafil had to be somewhere close by, he assumed. There was only one way to the Imperial Villa and he was bound to run into him, he thought.

He had always wondered why his parents would teach him an old fading language like Latin. He wondered a lot about what his adoptive parents had taught him. Never had he thought that his knowledge of Latin would come in handy like it had now.

His father told him that he was a natural and he was. Most of what they taught him, from mathematics to languages, came in very handy when he needed it most. Could that be a coincidence? Not only did Neb become fluent in Latin, but also in Greek, Spanish, Arabic and French, and even a few other languages he had never heard of.

It started on the day he was rescued from the orphanage, when his life with the Yorkers began. First a bath was in order, then a change of new clothes, a cheese sandwich and a cup of hot chocolate, then straight into home schooling. He remembered it as if it were yesterday. His three-foot frame would look up to see this huge black chalkboard detailing the planets in the solar system. He was immediately hooked on learning and he soaked it up like a proverbial sponge. Not every lesson was taught by the Yorkers with paper, pencil or books. Often they used sight, sound, touch, taste, smell, observations of animals (mammals, vertebrates, fish, fowl), nature (plants, flowers, fauna) and, of course, Homo sapiens, male and female. All the bases were covered – religions, cultures, races, geography, history, oceanography, agriculture, sociology, psychology and astronomy, and much more.

They would take trips around the country and the world visiting numerous sites and museums: the British Museum in London, the Louvre in Paris, the Pergamon in East Berlin, the Guggenheim in New York City, the Royal Ontario in Toronto, the Galleria dell Accademia in Florence, and countless others. The list could go on and on. Bancroft and Victoria Yorker had endless energy.

Once a year in the middle of August, Bancroft and Victoria would leave for two weeks for a private vacation. Colleagues of theirs would take turns watching over Neb. They always went to the Amazon. During their last trip, communication had ended abruptly, without any warning. It was as though they had vanished into thin air.

Neb wondered if anyone missed him back home, two thousand years from now or two days ago or was it now three. It was all so confusing.

Oddly enough, this was not the first time he had been to Ostia. In the autumn of 1970, at the age of 10, he and his parents had toured the whole of Italy. In 12 BCE, the town's name was Ostia Antica. They had visited the tourist sites, the ruins of the Roman Theatre, the Baths of Neptune, the Collegiate Temple, and the Forum of the Corporations. Perhaps, if he had time, he would revisit them in their present glory. Oh, to have a camera!

Neb looked about the tranquil Roman countryside from where he now sat below a small grove of pine trees that were just a couple of feet taller than his five-foot-nine frame. He welcomed the shade as he took a break and looked at the road ahead. Neb reached over for the rolled-up toga knapsack and pulled out the last two apples. He munched slowly on a large red crunchy apple. When it got down to the core, he took out the seeds and planted them in the ground. Perhaps when this was all over, he would come back in his own time and see if any apple trees had grown. That is, when it was all over, and assuming that he succeeded. Even though he thought there was always the possibility that he could disintegrate at any moment, he tried to stay positive.

He continued pressing the comm button on his buckle in hopes that a signal would reconnect with the Casino. All he would get were short bursts of static and a low hiss.

Neb tried to take the whole situation in his stride. On the one hand, he had time travelled to Rome, which was freaking cool in itself. On the other hand, the consequences would be devastating if he didn't meet up with Lafil. The thought of getting stranded crossed his mind a few times. Maybe it wouldn't be so bad, stay out of King Marcus's (or whatever he may call himself) way and get as far from Rome as possible and live a quiet life. Then again, might history have already changed?

When Tict had explained to him for the first time how time travel worked, he couldn't fathom it. One can only travel back in time, not forward, Tict had said. Time travelling to the future was impossible. So, if and when he met up with Lafil, how would he explain that he was from the future? How was that going to go over? At least he could reason with him, knowing what he knows about the Casino and the history of the Vegastriopelia. That would be a great plus in reasoning with him, wouldn't it?

Neb pressed his belt buckle again, more static. Well, that was better than no sound at all, he thought. He closed his eyes and took a deep breath. Then he heard, "Are you there?" It was an unfamiliar voice. Neb opened his eyes and grabbed his comm.

"Yes, I am here! Who is this?" he said excitedly.

"Lafil, are you there? Please respond." *Lafil?* Neb shrugged.

"No, this is Neb. Who's speaking, please?" Neb paused and then heard, "Lafil here. Go ahead."

"My apologies, sir," the unfamiliar voice said, "but we have been picking up some rather peculiar transmission emissions again, very close to your present location. It is a ticking sound, from a location not far from where you are."

"Ticking?" Lafil asked.

"Yes, ticking or tapping, as though someone or something were repeating a signal without a concrete connection. It keeps bouncing off our link back towards the planet and now back to your direct vicinity. We thought at first it might have been your communication module, but it's a totally different set of module timbre.

Neb listened to the conversation with keen interest and then it dawned on him. He tapped at the buckle again.

"Sir, we're picking it up again," the voice sounded alarmed.

Wow! That was quick. He must be talking about my comm link, Neb thought. He began to press his belt over and over.

"Sir! We're receiving a high number of repeated beats. It sounds like a type of code."

"That's right!" Neb shouted. "Morse code, man!"

"Are you able to read it?" Lafil asked.

"We are imputing it through the computer now." Lafil waited then… "We have it, sir. It reads as follows: NEB IS SEEKING LAFIL. LOOK FOR THREE PINES.

Lafil's eyes widened. "Neb is seeking Lafil? Look for three pines? Can you pinpoint the message location?"

"Yes, sir, it is one kilometre east of your present location."

Lafil looked around the area. He couldn't see anything from where he was. He scurried up the steep incline of the dirt road he was walking on. When he reached the top, panting, out of breath, he could see three pine trees.

"I think I have found the source," said Lafil.

"Please approach with caution," the voice responded.

"Always. Stand by," Lafil answered.

Lafil saw Neb jumping up and down and waving wildly. "Over here! Over here!"

Just then, two men riding horses sped by, almost knocking Lafil over. Dirt and dust filled the air, causing Lafil and Neb to lose sight of each other.

"Where did he go?" The swirl of dust engulfed Lafil like a mini tornado, leaving Neb's view distorted. Then, out of the dust storm emerged the two riders on their horses. He watched as they came closer and closer.

"Oh shit!" Neb gasped. It was Rufus and Germanus.

Neb hit the ground behind the trees, hoping and praying they hadn't seen him. The mini dust storm left in the horses' wake finally settled. Lafil brushed the dirt from his face and his clothes. He looked out towards where Neb had been but saw nothing but the two riders coming to a stop at the trees. Lafil made a beeline for the trees.

21

"I thought I saw someone jumping up and down," Germanus said to his brother.

"Well, I don't see anyone," Rufus replied, wiping the sweat from his forehead. "Maybe it was a mirage or something."

"I swear I saw someone. It was like they were calling for help."

Rufus could now see Lafil heading their way. "Let's wait for that guy that we almost ran over. Maybe he saw something." They both laughed as Lafil slowly made his way toward them.

Neb pulled his body back along the ground, slinking behind the low-hanging thick branches of the pines. He looked out as Lafil reached the brothers.

"Good day, friend," Rufus said, sitting high on his horse.

"Greetings," Lafil bowed. "How may I be of assistance?"

"Your accent. You're not Roman."

"No. Babylonian, good sir," Lafil answered.

"Did you happen to notice anyone suspicious looking?"

"How do you mean, suspicious looking?" Lafil replied.

"We're looking for a man dressed in red. We think he may be a thief."

"Oh my!" Lafil replied. In red, you say?"

“Yes. Marcus Apitippius was assaulted by him very early this morning. Also, our mother’s washing was stolen, we think by the same thief.” Rufus pulled the piece of red cloth out from under his belt. “Here.” He handed it to Lafil. “What do you make of it?”

Lafil knew within seconds from the feel of the material. “Hmm, feels like, perhaps, Egyptian.” He handed it back, slyly looking around to see if he could spot Neb.

“Isn’t that what I said?” Germanus said to his brother, smirking.

“Look at you,” Rufus laughed out loud, “the Egyptian expert!”

“I am afraid, good men, that I have not seen anyone on my travels dressed in red. It’s not something one would miss,” Lafil politely said.

“Not now, anyhow,” Rufus remarked. “We believe he’s wearing the stolen clothes to hide his identity.”

“Stolen clothes?” Lafil asked.

“Yes, the clothes he stole from our mother’s washing line.” Germanus spat, almost hitting Lafil’s feet.

How rude, Lafil thought. Then he said “I see. And what will you do to this thief if you apprehend him?”

“Firstly, when – and it’s not a matter of if – when we apprehend him, we have orders to bring him before Marcus Apitippius. After that, whatever is left of him is ours,” Rufus chuckled.

“Where may you be found should I see this red thief?” Lafil said, spotting Neb’s left foot sticking out from under a bush.

"One foot in, one left foot out, eh?" Lafil laughed.

"What is that supposed to mean?" Germanus asked.

Neb caught Lafil's meaning, pulling his left foot in.

"Well, you know how sly footed these thieves are, one slip and they're caught and done with," Lafil splurted out.

"I guess," Germanus replied, still not getting it but pretending he did.

Lafil smiled. "So, again I ask, should I see or hear of such a thief, where might I find you good men to inform you?"

"We are going to be in Ostia for the next few days, Germanus said. "The Bath of Neptune would be a good start to find us or to ask for us."

"Let's go, brother." Rufus tugged on his horse's bridle. They both nodded to Lafil and sped off down the dirt road that led to Ostia. Lafil waved good bye.

He waited until the brothers were at a good enough distance away before he turned his attention to the brush.

"It's OK. You can come out. They're gone," said Lafil.

Neb emerged from his hiding place He stepped out from behind the pines until he was in full view of Lafil.

"Thank you for not giving me away," Neb held out his hand to shake Lafil's.

"Hold it right there," Lafil raised his hand to stop Neb. He eyed him up and down. "You're human," he remarked. "I don't know you, do I?"

"First of all, yes, I am human, like you. And, no, we don't know each other but I know who you are."

Lafil took a step back. “Then you have me at a disadvantage, sir. How is it that you know who I am?”

“Tict told me about you.”
“Tict? Who is that?”

“Of course. You haven’t met him yet, Neb replied. “How can I explain this to you in a way that you won’t think I’m crazy?” He scratched the top of his head.

“Haven’t met who yet? And are you crazy?” Lafil stepped back a few feet.

“OK,” Neb started, you were born in Babylon over two thousand years ago and I will be born two thousand years from now, give or take.”

“Come again?” Lafil looked at Neb in disbelief. “Just who are you? Perhaps I should call back those two brutes.”

“Please don’t. I don’t think you want that either. Otherwise, you would not have saved me with that left foot comment. Look, I’m going to come right out and tell you and let the chips fall where they may. My name is Nebula Yorker and it’s a very long story of how I got here but, three days ago, I was just minding my own business when this floating ball of light appeared and changed everything I knew.” Neb paused. “About everything. Now, hold on to your toga. You see, this is the tricky part that you may find hard to believe. Are you ready?”

“There is nothing that you say that will shock me. Please continue,” Lafil replied.

“I am from the year 1986. There I said it! I AM FROM THE FUTURE,” Neb let out a long sigh.

Lafil also paused. He eyed Neb and turned to walk away, then turned back.

"From the future, eh?" Lafil scoffed. "Who put you up to this? You're not even human, I bet. You're one of those new XXL androids, aren't you? Who set this up?"

"I can assure you that I am not an android. Look at all the scrapes and scratches on my legs, the dry blood, and the smelly sweat under my armpits." He lifted up his arm and waved it towards Lafil's face.

Lafil could now smell the pungent pit odour. "Step back, man!" he protested. "OK, you're not an android.

"You see?" Neb continued. "The current concierge, that is, from 1986, is a man named Archibald Tict, born in 1707 AD, whom you will meet up with in 1758 AD, just before your death."

"My death!" Lafil replied out loud.

"Yes, your death. Your assistant murdered you or will murder you or he may not, depending on how this day ends or if it ever ends."

"My assistant?" Lafil laughed out loud. Now I know you're lying. I don't have an assistant at the moment."

"That's correct, not at the moment, but today is your lucky day or, perhaps, your unlucky day. This is the exact day you meet him at the Imperial Villa."

"How do you know I am going to the Imperial Villa?"

"Man, I told you. I'm from the future. I know these things," Neb said, a little frustrated.

"Yes, you did say, didn't you?" Lafil was starting to wonder about this Nebula Yorker.

"In any event, the future is going to change. How much depends on this very moment," Neb tried to convince Lafil. "Look, I know you're the concierge of the Casino. I know about the Casino posing as a giant gas ball picking up endless guests through the cosmos. And I know this all sounds impossible, implausible and, frankly, downright unbelievable, but it's the truth. And, yes, I know about the Vegastriopelia."

Lafil paused again, mulling over in his mind what Neb had just said. *He does look and act very human; he seems to know a lot about the Casino, my job as the concierge, the Vegastriopelia, that I am from Babylon,* Lafil thought deeply. *I know he's probably a hologram.* Lafil pushed at Neb knocking him off his feet to the ground. *OK, he's not a hologram*, Lafil mused, helping Neb up.

"Sorry about that," said Lafil. "I had to make sure."

"Sure of what?" Neb asked a little perturbed.

"That you weren't a hologram. But, never mind, I believe you're human now."

"Are you totally sure?"

"Yes, 100 per cent positive. If I may ask, what is your role in all of this?"

"My role? Well, if I accept, which I have not yet done, you're looking at the new assistant concierge. You know those two brutish guys on horseback? They mentioned a Marcus Apitippius."

"Yes, what of it? Lafil asked.

"Well, he's about to become your new assistant and he kind of murders you in the future."

"Can you be more specific?" Lafil asked.

"Well, OK. He definitely murders you, not kind of," Neb said, matter-of-factly. "You see, Marcus pushes you backwards onto the transport platform. The year is 1758 AD. That is when you meet Mr. Tict, the present or, should I say, the 1986 concierge whose life you save, by the way, before you die. But before you die, you ask Tict to find the culprit who pushed you backwards. You gave, or will give, Tict your belt, thus giving Tict a way out of the predicament he found himself in."

"Which was?" Lafil asked.

"He was also about to be arrested or perhaps even killed by soldiers. He pressed the buckle and, poof, he found himself on the Casino.

"And were you also being hounded by soldiers when you, as you say, found yourself on the Casino?"

"No, I was waiting for Halley's Comet to arrive but found out that it wasn't really a comet, but an intergalactic casino.

"Halley's?" Lafil enquired.

"Yes, that is what it's called these days, Halley's Casino."

Lafil paced back and forth after listening to Neb. It was difficult to refute anything that he said. His knowledge of the Casino, the Vegastriopelia, and himself was enough for Lafil to begin to believe the young man.

"One thing I do not understand, Nebula Yorker. If you're from the 20th Century, how is it that you're here? That should be impossible or is there something new I should know about?"

"To be honest, Lafil, I do not know why. By all accounts, I should be dead. For all I know, I just may be."

"You say that this Marcus Apitippius is or was going to be my assistant. Doesn't that mean that the Vegastriopelia chose him? Why would Marcus want to kill me?"

“It would seem so but I personally doubt the Vegastriopelia chose him,” Neb said. “You see, it’s not too long after Marcus becomes your assistant that he begins to plot to take over the Casino with some inside help.

“You must be joking,” Lafil expressed utter surprise and disbelief. “How can you say that the Vegastriopelia did not choose this Marcus? Some may think that is sacrilegious, bordering on blasphemous contempt.”

“Do you?” Neb asked.

“As you know, the Babylon of my time had well over 600 deities, none of which I believed in. I have always believed that the universe must have some kind of structure to it, though why all the gods and beliefs? Why must that be the definite answer to all questions asked? No, Nebula. To answer your question, I do not believe it blasphemous. There are still mysteries of the universe that we may never have answers to and the Vegastriopelia is one of them. And I find it utterly fascinating that you think the Vegastriopelia did not choose this Marcus. Indeed, perhaps it did not even choose you or me. Please go on.”

“As I was saying, Marcus’s end game was to go back to Rome, this Rome, change Earth’s history, for starters, and then the whole of time and space. With the Vegastriopelia at his disposal, he figured nothing could stop him. But something did stop him. You did! Along with Tict.” Neb rested his hand on Lafil’s shoulder, smiling.

“If we stopped him, then what’s all the fuss about?” Lafil asked, then said, “We stopped him but it didn’t end there, did it?”

“Good deduction, Lafil. Marcus was arrested and imprisoned in his quarters for 228 years. Then recently, like yesterday, he broke out, again with inside help.”

"You say, again. Wasn't the inside help arrested as well in the first place?"

"No, he wasn't found out until the second time around."

"Why would this inside help do this?" Lafil asked, dismayed.

"Marcus can be quite the talker. He made Eno (his name) feel that his place was by his side. Eno felt slighted that he was never chosen to be the assistant concierge. He thought for sure his time had come through Marcus's plan."

"I can't for the life of me understand why Eno follows Marcus. He treats him like a dog. Neb shook his head in dismay.

"So now that he, Marcus that is, is back here in Rome, he plans to use this first meeting to do away with you, thus changing the timeline of history and crowning himself Emperor, not just of Rome but of the whole world. Though this time around, he's not interested in ruling the universe but, perhaps, owning it and leasing it out, so to speak. He's quite the villain," Neb finished.

Lafil was astounded at what he had just heard. It was too farfetched a story not to give it some wholehearted consideration.

"Let's say for a moment that you're telling the truth," Lafil began, "and you're from the future, which, as you know, I find hard to believe, although I am starting to. Why should I trust and believe you?"

"There is no reason why you should," Neb replied, "but I think I have intrigued you enough to know that what I am saying is true. May I ask you a question, Lafil?"

"Please," Lafil replied.

"Why are you posing as an astrologer to Livia?"

"Why, it's my cover."

"Yes, I know, but you're dealing with future events posing as an astrologer, are you not?"

"To some degree, yes."

"I see," Neb smiled. "So can one really predict the future before it happens unless they already know?"

"What are you getting at?"

"What year is it?" Neb asked.

"Why, it is 12 BCE," he answered.

"No, I mean, what year is the Casino in orbit right now?"

"1066 AD."

"I see," Neb replied. "1066 AD. That's interesting. So, to the inhabitants of Earth of this time era, Rome 12 BCE, you're from the future, are you not?" Neb smirked.

"Your logic is irrefutable, Nebula Yorker," Lafil finally acquiesced. "It still doesn't explain why you're alive."

"No, it doesn't. Though I am sure we will find out one way or another if we both make it out alive," Neb replied.

"Let's stay positive, Neb. On that note, perhaps I should contact the Casino. They may want to know about those signal pings that led me to you."

"It might be wise not to at this point. If they contact you, tell them it was some burning crystals interfering with a metric pattern that sent out a low tumbler permanent wave."

"Good one, Nebula," Lafil replied.

"By the way, you can call me Neb. All my friends do. Shall we then head out for Ostia?"

"Do you actually know where you're going, Neb?"

"Quite. I have been here before. Or, rather, I will be here in 1970 AD."

"That's reassuring," said Lafil. "How about I lead since I have been here a few more times than you and know the road very well. Is that fine with you?"

"Lead the way, my good man." Neb extended his hand out to his new friend.

"By the way, may I enquire how that very oversized man got his hand on that piece of your suit pocket?"

"Let's say I had a rather fiery descent where I met a couple of snooty cows and a sharp-clawed cat."

"What?" Lafil asked perplexed.

Neb laughed. "I'll tell you all about it on the way."

Neb and Lafil walked on the dirt road. They both looked down at the hoof prints on the dry ground.

"I hope they are far enough away and that they don't decide to turn around," Neb said, his toga knapsack slung over his shoulder.

"Perhaps you should ditch the toga somewhere and we can come back for it later," Lafil replied.

"I kind of got used to it, you know, like it's a part of me."

"Yes, but if Rufus and Germanus do happen to turn back, you're on your own. Just kidding." Lafil patted Neb on the back. "So really, how long have you been with the Casino, Neb?"

"Three days, could be four by now, I think."

"THREE DAYS!" Lafil spat out alarmingly, almost choking on his words. What have you gotten yourself into, young Neb?"

"I wish I knew. I was just minding my own business when this jellyfish-type orb appeared and bounced over me."

"Yeah, tell me about it," Lafil snickered.

22

The Vegastriopelia emitted a low subspace frequency signal outward. It never seemed to get very far, bouncing back every five minutes. PIC-500 had discovered the timbre while trying to readjust the comm link with Neb.

"What do you think it's trying to do?" asked Tict.

"Perhaps it is trying to contact its maker, the Triopelians, "TeeceeFore replied.

Tict and TeeceeFore had returned to Tict's office a few hours earlier. There was nothing more they could do but let Kel, PIC-500 and PIC-501 continue their work. Besides, no one was panicking. The guests were still enjoying themselves and still taking bets on the casino quakes that they all thought was just a new game. That light orangey aroma now permeated the entire Casino from top to bottom. It could have been worse. The smell, that is, Tict reckoned.

Some Council members thought it would be a good idea to inform the guests about their impending doom; others worried that it might cause a riot. They hoped that, given time, everything would just return to normal. They decided to take a vote. For the first time in history, it was a tie vote. It reminded TeeceeFore of the question Neb had asked earlier regarding this precise situation. Coincidence, she wondered?

In the end, they took another vote resulting in a decision to let everyone enjoy themselves. If this was to be everyone's last hurrah, they might as well go out with a bang, so to speak. Death by implosion would be quick. It would happen before they knew what hit them, as it were.

Tict and TeeceeFore snuggled together on the sofa in his office. A quarter-empty bottle of vintage brandy from 1758 sat on the table. They sipped their glasses slowly, enjoying every mouthful.

"Any regrets, Archibald?" TeeceeFore asked.

"Regrets? Maybe a few," Tict replied. "I wish I could have known my mother. I did meet her once, though, you know. I actually jumped in her womb at hearing my own voice. And it would have been nice to know who my father was. I may have been born from nobility. That was the gossip I heard growing up. I also often wonder what happened to those French prisoners before I came here 228 years ago. Did they have to pay with their lives because I gave them a warm happy Christmas meal?"

"You could have visited them, you know," TeeceeFore swirled her glass.

Tict said nothing. His eyes saddened, thinking about them.

"And there's..." He hesitated. "Neb. He's such an interesting young man. I can see why the Vegastriopelia chose him. Bright, eager, funny, very intelligent, though he doesn't let on."

"Let me tell you something about our young Nebula Yorker," TeeceeFore said.

"What's that?" Tict asked.

She leaned in to Tict and whispered. His eyes widened and he almost spilled his brandy onto his lap.

"Do you think?" he replied to TeeceeFore.

"It's quite possible." She finished her glass and reached for the bottle. They both sat silent for a few minutes, thinking it over.

Then Tict asked, "What about you, TC, any regrets?"

"I think with any of us, there will always be regrets, Archibald. I regret that it took an event such as this for us to find ourselves where we are now. Could you ever love someone like me in my true form? Could it be even possible?" She tugged at his bow tie.

Tict took another swallow of his brandy, looking deeply into TeeceeFore's dark blue eyes. He didn't see any hideous creature. He kissed her and she kissed him back.

The Casino shook again, causing them to spill their drinks on each other. They both laughed.

"I guess now we'll have to get out of these wet clothes." TeeceeFore giggled like a young teenager.

"Beep. Beep." Tict's comm sounded. He activated his belt comm so he wouldn't have to get up and go to his desk.

"You have reached the host with the most," he said. Tict and TeeceeFore both snickered.

"What?" It was Kel on the other end. "Kel here, sir." Now she had dropped her call letters without realizing it.

"Have you been able to re-establish a link with Neb?"

"Negative, Mr. Tict, though we may have a bigger problem on our hands."

"Oh?" Tict and TeeceeFore sat up. "What is it?"

"The service droids from the Green Room are reporting that all the guests, including Sy Dyloup, have fallen asleep. And more reports are trickling in as we speak that the entire Casino's complement of guests are experiencing the same effect, except the androids."

"Fallen asleep?" Tict replied bewildered.

“Not just fallen asleep, Mr. Tict. To clarify, they are now in a state of suspended animation. We believe it has to do with the orangey vapour. Mr. Tict? Mr. Tict, are you there?” Kel waited for a response. No response came.

Tict and TeeceeFore fell silently into each other’s arms.

“I have completed analyzing the orange odour as requested, Kel,” said PIC-500, now also dropping her call numbers. “Your suspicions have been verified. Vilit induced Tracfive Lerxstian Sodium Thiopental is causing the deep space cryosleep.”

“Interesting,” Kel remarked.

“Indeed!” replied PIC-500.

“Part of Marcus Apitippius’s plan?” PIC-501 enquired.

“I don’t think it was,” Kel answered. “Why would he induce cryosleep? It doesn’t make sense. With the transfiguror filters offline, it would be only a matter of time before every guest’s humanoid form would transition back to the original, thus adding to the cause of the implosion. With the guests now in cryosleep, technically speaking, they should hold their present forms, thus avoiding any impending implosion. I don’t think Marcus had that in mind.”

“Could it be possible that the Vegastriopelia has initiated a fail-safe that neither we nor Marcus was aware of?” PIC-500 asked.

Kel mulled over PIC -500‘s question. “Very possible,” Kel answered. “Mr. Tict had alluded that the Vegastriopelia would not go down without a fight.”

“Go down without a fight, Kel?” enquired PIC-501.

“A human idiom meaning to continue the struggle until defeated.”

"I see. Then, shall we also not go down without a fight?" PIC-501 asked.

"That is affirmative, Pic-One," Kel answered. "From this time onward, until further notified, PIC-500, you shall be known as just Pic. PIC-501, you are now Pic-One. No more call numbers."

Both Pic and Pic-One responded with a simultaneous rhythmic low hum which Kel took as a happy emotional response.

"Let us resume our duties. I believe that Mr. Tict would wish us to do so." Kel nodded.

Pic continued monitoring the Vegastriopelia subspace frequency. "Its signal must be bouncing back for a reason that we are not detecting momentarily. Pic-One, resume work on resolving our time static problem. We must get through to Nebula."

"I find it very interesting that we can read Nebula Yorker's bio signature from the past with great clarity, yet have such a difficult time with connecting through the time static barrier," Pic-one said to Kel.

"That's interesting." Kel paused. "Please proceed."

"I have not finished my synopsis," Pic-One answered.

"You have answered correctly, Pic-One, please proceed with your equations. I have faith in your ability to find the solution."

"Faith?" Pic-One enquired.

"A human term, Pic-One. It means I have confidence in your abilities and in you as an individual."

"It has nothing to do with faith; it's merely a matter of mathematics," Pic-One dryly commented to his counterpart, Pic. Pic just smiled, shrugged his shoulders and continued his work.

***

Neb and Lafil walked together on the narrow dirt road leading to the Imperial Villa.

"When we get to the Villa, Neb, let me do all the talking. They are only expecting me. I will explain that you're my nephew and new assistant in training. It is very important that you not speak unless first spoken to. Follow my lead and everything should go fine," Lafil explained.

"No problem, Kreskin," Neb replied.

"Kreskin? Oh, never mind." Lafil gave Neb a look. "So, any ideas where I meet up with this Marcus?"

"Sorry, I don't. All I know is this is where it all begins."

"Too bad your communication with the future is down. I still can't get over that you're from the future or one possible future, depending on what transpires today."

"Time static interference, I am afraid. I know they're working on it. Not sure how they're going to get me back to 1986 if they can't fix the comm link, though I suppose I could always go back with you, right?" Neb replied.

Lafil gave Neb that look again. "For the time being, let us focus on Marcus and not worry about where you might end up later. Pear?" Lafil pulled a couple out of his satchel, handing one to Neb.

"So, getting back to business. Let me get this right. Marcus Apitippius murders me in 1758 AD and now wants to kill me again. Wasn't once enough?"

They both laughed. They discussed Lafil's life as concierge, how when he first arrived on the Casino, he thought for sure that the gods he didn't believe existed were getting back at him.

Neb related that, on a trip to East Berlin, Germany, he had visited the Pergamon Museum and saw the Ishtar Gate.

"Yeah, that was fun to work on," Lafil treated Neb with a few stories about the Gate.

Lafil envisioned one day retiring in Rome of this era, perhaps finding a quiet spot in the country and living out his natural life on Earth. Returning to Earth permanently after thousands of years on the Casino would have its effects. It was quite possible that Lafil could live another 300 years or more due to the slowing down of his cellular structure on the Casino. One of the perks, you could say.

Neb told Lafil of Marcus's amnesia on arriving and that he didn't know if he had recovered or not. This was a factor they needed to consider. Not only did they have to coordinate a plan to thwart Marcus, they also had to take away any technology he might have stolen.

Lafil studied the situation. "So, let's get this straight. With Marcus's present amnesia, he doesn't know what I look like or that we're to meet, and neither does he even know of the Casino's existence, so that's a plus. On the other hand, he knows what you look like, though he doesn't know anything about you except that he thinks you're a thief. We may be able to use that to our advantage. On the other hand, if he's regained his memory in the interval, that may pose a different set of problems.

"I'll say!" said Neb. "I rather prefer the first scenario."

"We also have to be on the lookout for Rufus and Germanus as they are on the hunt for you. They told me where they could be found in Ostia. Let's give them what they want."

"What?" Neb yelped.

"You!" Lafil concluded.

“What! Are you kidding me, Lafil?” Neb was dead set against the idea.

“Why not? It would give us the upper hand. We find him. He finds you and he finds me. We take back what he stole. He’s none the wiser and we pop back up to the Casino and figure how to get you back to 1986.

“You’re forgetting one thing, Lafil. What if he’s his old self again? Won’t that kind of defeat this whole plan? And where would that leave us? I will tell you where that will leave us. Screwed!”

“Screwed? Do you think he would torture us first? I would prefer that he just kill us there on the spot, forget torture.” Lafil pondered being tortured. He didn’t like the thought of it.

“No, no. It means we would be put in a hopeless situation.”

“But the screwed thing could still mean being tortured, right?” Lafil asked. “With Marcus, anything is possible and he might delight in that.”

“For now, let’s just see what happens here first.” Neb rested his hand gently on Lafil’s shoulder. “Let’s keep offering ourselves or myself to Rufus and Germanus as Plan B or C or D.

With the Imperial Villa now coming into focus, Lafil reminded Neb to follow his lead. “Keep your mouth shut and, whatever you do, do not speak unless you are first spoken to. It’s extremely important, Neb. Do you understand? These people might seem very cordial, likeable, and normal, if you will, but they are also distrustful, two-faced, superstitious and deadly. One slip and it will be them torturing us, not Marcus Apitippius. I think it would be a good idea to ditch your toga roll now.” Lafil pointed. “Over there by that bush near the large boulder. If your suit and shoes are found there, it won’t be a big deal. But if they’re found in your possession, that is a different story altogether.”

Neb tucked the rolled up toga underneath the big rock. He stomped on it to make sure it stuck under the rock. Then he broke a few branches and laid them around the rock's edge.

Soon, Neb and Lafil were back on their way. The dirt road turned into a tree-lined cobblestone way with the Imperial Villa in full view.

"Outstanding!" Neb gasped. "The last time I saw this Villa, in 1970, it was in ruins. I guess a couple of thousand years will do that. It was barely standing, a few pieces here and there. Some of this era's Roman architecture is still standing and preserved in 1986, much like Egypt's pyramids. They are now tourist attractions."

"Tourist attractions!" Lafil mused at Neb`s description of the future.

"So how did you and Livia come to meet?"

"To be honest, I kind of found her. This is my third trip to Rome, though at different time intervals, mind you. I have met her twice before. She is an interesting woman."

"Yes, and dangerous from what I have read," Neb added.

"I know, I know, but there's something that draws me to her. Don't worry, I am very careful. I mean, that's the fun of time travel, you know. You can keep going back, though not at the same instant or you might bump into yourself."

"Is that even possible?" Neb asked.

"You see, once you insert yourself into a timeframe, if you find yourself stranded for more than 72 hours, you might meet yourself, though chances are low. From what I have read and been told, that is. I have never stayed more than 70 hours at a time.

"So you're saying if I or we were to get stranded here, there is a possibility that we could meet ourselves?" Neb sounded alarmed.

"It may be possible," said Lafil.

"What would happen if we did meet ourselves then?"

"Past, present and future would collide, blotting one out of existence, I suppose."

"You suppose? But you don't know for sure."

"No, not for sure. I did do some reading on it in the Casino`s archives, but I never finished the article, I'm afraid. Don't worry, my comm beacon will alert us when it gets to 70 hours," Lafil assured Neb, lifting up his arm and tapping his wrist band. "Besides, you've never been here in this time era before, have you?"

"Not that I know of," Neb shrugged his shoulders. "Like I said, it was back in 1970 with my parents."

"I wouldn't worry about it, Neb. What are the odds? Look, if it makes you feel any better, if I meet you before I met you, as in earlier this afternoon, I'll just ignore you."

"Yeah, but how will you know that you've met me?"

"I don't know," answered Lafil. "I guess we'll just have to go straight into Plan B."

Neb's face squinted. "I don't think I like that idea, then or now."

There is something peculiar about this likeable fellow, Lafil thought to himself.

"One more question," Neb asked, "if I may enquire of you, what's Plan A?"

23

Three pairs of Praetorian Guards stood at attention. They could see the two men walking up to their station before the Imperial Villa's entrance. Each guard held a javelin. A sword and a dagger hung at their sides. The red festoon attached to their bronze helmets blew lightly in the early evening breeze. Their shoulder plates and body armour stuck out, giving them a fierce, yet regal, appearance. They were aware that two visitors would be arriving, Lafil and Marcus Apitippius, but did not expect them at the same time. The head Praetorian, standing at the front, turned to the others without saying a word. They all understood. Be on your guard.

Neb and Lafil came closer to the large estate of Augustus and Livia. They could see the guards standing stoic at the entrance.

"Remember, stay quiet. Let me do all the talking," Lafil reminded Neb.

"Greetings!" Lafil approached the two outer guards.

The guards swiftly positioned their javelins crosswise, and then struck the hard steel into the ground with a loud thump. It made Neb a tiny bit nervous.

"We are here at the invitation of Caesar and Lady Livia. I am Lafil of Babylon whom Caesar awaits and this is my assistant Nebula of Achaea," Lafil presented himself clearly and concisely.

The guards, tall in stature, looked down at Lafil and Neb.

"Wait here," one growled.

The guard in charge turned to the other and sent him up to the Villa. Twenty minutes later, he returned and spoke to the one in charge who then told Lafil and Neb to proceed to the Villa's entrance.

Now within the confines of the Villa, Neb admired the surroundings. He noticed a group of slaves, men, women and children, attending the well-kept grounds. Two medium-sized fountains lay on either side of the stairs leading up to the main atrium of the Villa. One fountain had a huge marble lion head spitting water from its mouth into a pool below. The other fountain had two dancing cherubs holding jars in their hands, the water spilling out and down. Hibiscus plants, to the east side, some still flowering, were being pruned. Gigantic ten-foot tall sunflowers stood leaning over, with a few birds having a late day feast.

When Lafil and Neb reached the top of the stairs, they were met by two young girls, Ethiopian slaves. They escorted them through the main atrium, the most important part of the house, where guests were usually greeted. Augustus's own atrium contained a statue of Apollo. There were also many Lares, the household gods, throughout the Villa.

One couldn't have enough gods, Neb thought.

Lafil and Neb were led from the atrium through a separate passageway to another part of the Villa. Neb was in total amazement at the splendid state of the Imperial Villa as it had not totally survived through all the years and had largely disappeared from history. How Neb wished he had a camera.

Neb and Lafil walked past several different parts of the villa. Finally one of the slaves stopped and motioned for them to enter a room. She smiled and bowed and then left without saying a word.

Stepping into the room, they were greeted by a wall painting that engulfed three-quarters of the room. It was a depiction of a garden. There were birds of every sort, some perched on tree branches and others flying about. An eagle was sitting atop a wall that gave the impression of a marble fence surrounding the garden.

Irises, roses and poppies were strewn among the various trees, big and small. Oak, Italian cypress, oleander and palm trees gave the illusion that the branches were bending in the wind. A vast blue sky encompassed the entire landscape. On closer observation, one would discover much more hidden. Neb aptly christened the wall mural 'The Sweet Garden of Livia'.

On the one wall that was not part of the mural was a fresco of five cherubs dancing around a large puffy white cloud and playing flutes and harps. And if that weren't enough, there was a lavish picturistic mosaic floor depicting wild horses running towards the sea, with a lone charioteer chasing behind.

Neb was in awe. It was all so magnificent. He had never seen anything like it. He knew that no one in his future would ever see it, as time would ravage the Villa.

Various candles in holders lit up the windowless room, giving it an early morning or late day vibe. The furniture in the room was centred and consisted of three couches large enough for one or two to sit or lie on, and a large oval table in the middle. A group of eight slaves, male and female, of different shapes, colours and sizes, stood at attention around the room. There was another doorway that was hard to notice. Neb wasn't sure at first whether it was part of the painting or not. Lafil also stood amazed.

A middle-aged man seemed to come out of the painting, followed by three women bearing trays and plates of food and wine. It now became apparent that the doorway was indeed real. They lay the food and wine on the table and quickly left.

Within minutes, Livia appeared through the garden entrance, followed by Augustus. Talk about meeting celebrities. Neb was as much in awe as he was in fear. He was surprised by Augustus's appearance. He was unusually handsome. He was short in stature but this was not noticed in comparison to his fine symmetry. His walk was as graceful as his personality, which was easy to see. He had bright blue eyes and his hair was lightly curled and golden for his age. He wore a white and red toga with purple fringes. In another two years, he would be dead and Tiberius, Livia's son, would be emperor.

Livia carried herself in a queenly manner. Her golden dress and red cape flowed behind her as if she was one of the birds flying on the wall. Her died ash-brown hair was done up high with a see-through white veil hung over it. Long golden earrings hung from her earlobes; a necklace made of black and white pearls loosely swung about her neck.

Livia, of course, recognized Lafil immediately, but her left eye cocked up on seeing Neb standing beside him. Both Augustus and Livia sat on the couch opposite Lafil and Neb, who stood silent. Neb wanted to burst out saying how grateful he was to meet both of them and he was about to do so when Lafil gave him a little nudge, reminding him to stay quiet.

Livia clapped her hands and one of the slaves came and filled her's and Caesar's wine glasses. She lifted her glass, slowly taking a sip and eyeing Neb suspiciously. She didn't like surprises. She, on the other hand, loved giving others surprises of many different kinds.

Finally she broke the awkward silence. "It is good to see you, Lafil, though I am not familiar with your companion"

"Your Majesty," Lafil said, bowing. "I ask pardon, my good lady," he said, his head down. "This is my nephew who has just come to Rome from Achaea."

"A Greek!" Livia questioned. "I thought you told the guard that he was your assistant."

"He is," Lafil answered.

"Well, which is it?" Augustus asked half-jokingly.

"I am both," Neb spoke. "My mother, Lafil's sister married a Greek. My father recently died and my dear uncle graciously offered to train me in the arts. I arrived today and, surprisingly, met my uncle without warning while we were travelling on the same road. I now find myself honoured to be in your presence."

Augustus and Livia paused. They looked at each other and back to Lafil. Lafil gave Neb a very stern look that said, *I told you to not speak until spoken to.*

"Very well," said Livia. "I'll let it pass just this once. You are a very well mannered young man and well spoken. What is your name?"

"Nebula," he answered, his head down.

"A Greek and a Babylonian. Is that even allowed?"

"The best of both worlds, eh?" Caesar took a gulp of his wine. "Please sit." He waved his hand towards the couch opposite them. Lafil's heart rate settled down as they both sat.

"Have some wine and food, if you wish," their hosts offered.

As soon as Neb heard, "have some," he dug into the food tray on the table. Bread, cheese, vegetables and fruits were spread out. He made sure to taste each one. As Neb indulged, Lafil couldn't believe what he was seeing.

"OK, Neb, don't make a pig of yourself," he whispered.

"Whoops," said Neb under his breath. He hadn't eaten anything except the apples and the one pear all day. The last full meal he remembered eating was in the Green Room. He looked up and saw that Caesar and Livia were somewhat humoured by Neb's hunger.

"Do they not have any food in Achaea?" Livia mused to her husband.

"Apparently not, by the looks of this young fellow," he replied.

"I trust the food is to your liking?" Livia remarked with a sarcastic whim.

"More than enough, good lady." Lafil elbowed Neb to stop. Neb quickly finished pouring a cup of wine and sat back contented and loudly burped. Lafil was not amused.

"Lafil, I hope that your young assistant here will be just as fine a seer as you are. If not, we could always use a new food taster. They seem to come and go quite quickly, you know." She smiled wickedly at Neb.

Livia soon got to the point of the visit. "So? What have you for us, Lafil? Come on, tell us. We didn't invite you and your family here for supper." Livia's demeanor changed. "What is the significance of the falling stars we witnessed?" Livia and Augustus leaned in to hear Lafil's answer. Lafil stood.

"First of all, these falling stars that you saw mean that there is chemistry between you, solid and true, that no one can break. Your witnessing this event shows this great bond. The gods have blessed you by allowing you to see their work at play and it was for you alone that this took place, as there is no record of it and no one else has come forth as having witnessed it.

"Did you hear that, dear? We are blessed." Livia smiled at Augustus. "See, haven't I always told you?"

"On the other hand, the one star breaking apart and creating two could mean that a life or life path is coming to its completion or to a new beginning, Lafil continued.

"I don't like the sound of that," Augustus quipped. "You're not pregnant, are you?"

"Don't be a fool. Do I look like I am young enough to bear a child?"

Lafil continued. "Two falling stars, one after the other in the manner you have seen, could also be directly linked to the gods descending and maybe walking among us, perhaps cloaked among us in human flesh and frailty, testing whether we are worthy."

Augustus excitedly stood. "That's what I was talking about. The gods themselves have become mortal. I knew it! We must prepare for their arrival."

"And what makes you think they're coming here?" Livia remarked with cynicism.

"Why, where else would they go?" Caesar blared.

The slaves all shook with terror on hearing that the gods had become mortal. Had they also come to judge them?

Caesar was quite beside himself with joy.

Livia, having noticed the slaves' trepidation, dismissed them all, leaving only Caesar, herself, Lafil and Neb in the room.

"Is that all, Lafil? Is there no more that you have discerned?" Livia smartly changed the subject, looking for a new answer that would please her or her husband more than the last.

Augustus seemed satisfied, unsurprisingly, but Livia always needed more. *How much more does she want?* Lafil thought, and worried about what he should say next. He really had thought the answer he gave was his best bet in trying to explain the stars. It had seemed to work on Caesar. It was while he was thinking about Marcus and Neb that he got the idea. They had been the shooting stars. They certainly weren't gods, but it was as plausible an explanation as he could come up with to answer Livia and Augustus's query. He wasn't too far from the truth. Livia, though, was not easily swayed. Caesar found the answer to his liking; she, on the other hand, wanted something more to her liking, as usual.

Lafil froze. He turned to Neb. Neb could see the fear in Lafil's eyes. It was now or never, he thought.

"Well, come out with it." Livia waited.

"The great Oracle has at times been revealed though the Sibylline," Neb began and immediately caught Livia's attention. *Now this is what Livia wanted to hear*, he thought.

"Was it not foretold in years past that one who is low would be brought up on high where the mighty eagle sits? That out of confusion, peace would ensue?"

Livia thought about her grandson, Claudius, how when he was a child the Sibylline had prophesized that one day he would rule all of Rome. Not again! She always felt that Claudius was not what he appeared to be. Could he be playing the fool so perfectly that no one even bothered to take a second look? For now, though, no one but her son Tiberius would rule after Augustus. Livia continued listening to Neb.

"Two stars have fallen, one after the other. As one power falls another rises. From father to son," Neb continued. Like Lafil, he worked the room to his liking, using his knowledge of the future without giving it all away. He molded Livia's thoughts with his words.

Tiberius! Livia thought. *Of course he will follow Augustus when he dies, if I have anything to do with it.* She soon forgot about poor, poor Claudius.

"You see, husband, there is always more than one meaning." She turned to Caesar, but he had quietly left the room, enthralled with his own answer.

Neb finished with a poem.

"*I have wished for many wishes*

None have come true

I have wished upon the first evening star

What is mortal man to do?

I have seen it out of reach and oh so far

Seasons come and go

And we are still where we are

Waiting for our dreams to come true"

Livia was barely breathing. Neb had mesmerized her. Lafil was also surprised.

"I knew it! I knew it!" Livia gasped. "You are truly one of a kind. And here I thought your uncle was the greater seer! I can see the Greek in you now. I didn't see it at first. I rather trust a Greek, if it be known. Other than yourself, of course," Livia said to Lafil.

"Your words are gracious, as is your wisdom, good lady," Neb nodded.

Lafil stared at Neb with a totally different view of his new friend.

"There is no need to butter me up, young man," said Livia. "Your insight is far above anything I have heard in a very long time. On the other hand, though, whether or not the gods have become mortal and are walking among us is left to be seen. Caesar is quite content with your uncle's explanation and I am with yours. And your poem was magnificent! I do so love wishes. Sometimes you have to give them a little push in the right direction." Livia gave Neb a knowing look that made the hair stick up on the back of his neck.

"Please stay. I will return shortly." Livia rose and left the room.

As soon as she was out of sight, Lafil reached for the wine, filling his cup and Neb's.

Neb, where did all of that come from? That was exceptional! Brilliant! Livia has really taken a shine to you."

"I just said what I thought she might like to hear and she did. This is all so fascinating." He took a sip of the wine. "WOW!" he blurted out, "I have just met Caesar Augustus and Livia! My Mom and Dad would have freaked out!"

"You mean like you're doing right now?" Lafil clinked their cups in a toast.

Later, Augustus and Livia returned together and, by that time, Lafil and Neb had had a little too much wine.

"I must say I have very much enjoyed our meeting. It is not every day that I am so well pleased with men of your occupation," said Augustus. "Livia and I thank you. Now, I have other duties to perform – listen to and turn down daft petitions and the like." Caesar had Marcus in mind. "What do you think, gentleman? Should Caesar have to decline these petitioners in person?"

The question caught the men off guard. What was he up to?

"If I've told you once, I've told you a million times, husband, having you speak with them personally is worth more than the frustration of their ideas not seeing the light of day," said Livia. "They can go home and tell their families and friends that they were in the presence of the Augustus One." Livia took his hand and said in a kind, tender and loving voice, "What more does one want?"

"What would I do without you?" Augustus replied and kissed her lightly on the lips.

"I am sure Marcus Apitippius could not ask for more," added Livia.

Lafil and Neb looked at each other and silently mouthed, *Marcus Apitippius?*

Turning again back to Lafil and Neb, Augustus asked, "What do you think? Should every town, city or dustbowl have its very own forum? What's wrong with the Circus Maximus?"

"To what extent?" replied Lafil.

"To the extent that this fool wants to own and run all of the gladiatorial games throughout the empire. Have you ever heard such a thing?"

"Sounds like he wants your job," Neb said aloud, thinking he was just thinking it. *Damn!* He thought.

"What did you say?" Caesar rose in a fury. "Have you seen something else in the stars that you are not telling me?" Augustus glared at Neb.

"Please forgive my nephew," Lafil begged. "He's young and the wine is affecting him."

"Is it?" Livia asked.

"I think there is more to this young man than he lets on," Caesar said.

"Husband, please," Livia intervened. "Young man, I want you to accompany us in the presence of Marcus Apitippius. You too can come," she said to Lafil. "If you are the seer I think you are, your reading of this man would be of great service to your emperor."

Before Neb could a say word, Livia commanded, "Case closed!"

Caesar and Livia stood. "Follow us, Livia ordered.

"Now?" Neb and Lafil said simultaneously.

"No, next week," Livia rolled her eyes. "Of course, now. Marcus Apitippius should be here very soon. The guards informed us that they saw him on the road heading this way not more than 30 minutes ago. He was with two other very large fellows."

"Two other large fellows?" Neb gulped. *Rufus and Germanus!*

"What was that?" Livia asked.

"Oh, nothing. Just clearing my throat," said Neb.

Lafil looked at Neb. "Now what?" he whispered.

"I don't know," Neb whispered back, shrugging. "I guess, when in doubt, go with the flow."

"Go with the flow? What kind of answer is that? Really, that's all you have?" Lafil slapped Neb lightly on the head.

"What do you want me to say?" Neb brushed off Lafil's hand.

"Is everything alright between you two?" Livia turned and asked.

"Yes, yes, all is well. Just discussing family matters," Lafil replied.

They followed slowly behind Augustus and Livia, passing through the garden paintings exit (or entrance. Neb wasn't sure; everyone and everything was so surreal.) The exit turned into a small cramped tunnel that opened up into another of the many atriums that the villa seemed to have.

What was it with these atriums? Neb wondered to himself taking mental notes as he did.

Augustus and Livia remained reserved. They stopped before a statue of Juno. She was sitting with a peacock at her side, armed and wearing a cloak. Hand in hand, Caesar and his wife bowed their heads in silent prayer before the protector of the state. Neb did likewise. He thought it wouldn't hurt to have some protection on their side as well. Lafil did likewise, even though it went against all that he believed.

24

Marcus, Rufus and Germanus rode their horses towards the Imperial Villa. The brothers had returned to the villa as guns for hire to find Neb. Marcus was only too happy to hire them. It would be one less thing for him to worry about if they could nab Mr. Yorker and deal with him after he had dealt with Augustus and Lafil.

“I need to take a piss!” Germanus suddenly stopped and got off his horse.

“Why don’t you tell the whole world?” Marcus said, annoyed.

“I need to take a piss!” Germanus belted out loudly. Rufus laughed along with his brother.

“The things I have to put up with,” Marcus said, shaking his head.

Germanus walked over to the bush beside a huge rock. As he was relieving himself, he looked down and saw a shred of something red sticking out from beneath the rock.

“Hey, what’s this?” He bent down and tugged at the cloth.

“What do you have there?” Rufus said as he watched his brother pull out a toga. Germanus fell backwards, hitting the ground hard, as the rock let go of its grip on the toga. Marcus eyed the red pant leg of Neb’s suit. He quickly hopped off his horse, followed by Rufus. Marcus leaned down and unraveled the toga to find the entire red suit, black shoes and white turtleneck. He noticed there was no belt. Rufus pulled out his piece of red cloth and matched it to the rip on the breast pocket.

“I think we may have found our red thief,” he said, looking up at Marcus.

Germanus picked up one of the shoes and examined it.

“What type of sandal is this?” He smelled it. “Fine leather,” he said.

“Take a piss anytime you want,” Marcus remarked. He mischievously looked at Germanus with a wide grin.

“Where could he be?” Rufus asked. “There was no one on the road except those soldiers we met.”

“I have a good idea where they are,” Marcus said as he turned back to his horse.

“They?” Germanus asked.

“A figure of speech. You know, ‘we’, ‘us’, ‘them’.”

“Who are them?” Germanus asked again.

Not as stupid as he looks, Marcus thought.

“Both of you stay here and wait for me. If that thief should come back for his clothes, hold him until I return.” Marcus jumped back on his horse and headed for the Villa. Rufus and Germanus watched as Marcus galloped away.

“I get the feeling that Marcus Apitippius is hiding something from us,” Rufus said to his brother.

Marcus’s horse trotted onto the cobblestone path and the Villa was now in full view. All was going to plan except for a few minor bumps. There were always bumps.

With most of his memory back, he surmised that Nebula Yorker had somehow managed to meet up with Lafil and perhaps had filled him in.

Nonetheless, Lafil would face his demise today and not in 1758. Augustus and Livia would also soon find themselves meeting the same fate. And Nebula Yorker? Well, he had something special in store for him. That is, if all went according to plan this time.

Caesar would turn down his petition. He would graciously accept. Then, they would introduce Lafil, who was watching in the wings. This time, he would get rid of Caesar, along with Livia, and then kill Lafil, cry havoc and let slip the dogs of war!

The only fly in the ointment was Nebula Yorker. How did he survive the time jump? What part would he play in all of this? Perhaps Mr. Yorker's presence would somehow turn out to be a bonus that he could sway to his advantage? Marcus's mind was working so fast that he was not paying attention to his riding and he almost ran over the guards at the Villa entrance.

"HALT!" the guards shouted.

Marcus pulled back on the horse's bridle, stopping it. The Praetorians stood in formation, pissed that they were just about run over. This time six guards were blocking the entrance. Marcus dismounted his horse. He had great admiration for the Praetorian order and thought that soon they would be at his command.

"I am here at the request of Caesar!" Marcus announced proudly, holding his head up high as if he were Caesar himself.

"Name?" the head Praetorian barked. He wasn't about to let this snooty aristocrat take charge.

"Marcus Apitippius. House of Quinctilia."

The guard nodded to another who returned the nod and disappeared behind the wall.

"Wait here," the guard said to Marcus.

Well, so far, everything seems to be going the same as the last time, Marcus thought as he paced back and forth with his arms behind his back.

Five minutes later, the guard returned and handed his superior a note. He read it quickly.

"This way," the guard ordered Marcus. One of the guards stepped out of line and took Marcus's horse aside as two other guards, one on each side of Marcus, escorted him up to the Villa.

OK. This isn't the way it went before, Marcus thought as he eyed the guards at his side. They walked through the garden and up the stairs leading to the atrium. No words were spoken between them. Marcus clutched at his belt beneath his toga. He was glad that the guards hadn't searched him.

Augustus and Livia waited, seated in their private receiving room. It was an attached room outside the many atriums that acted as a maze of sort, Neb reckoned. It was a large enough room, somewhat bigger than the Sweet Garden of Livia. They sat seven steps up on an oval platform looking down on those privileged to be accepted into their presence.

Wafting purple curtains hung behind the dais. A breeze that swooped down from a window high up in the room caused the curtains to appear like flags. The face of an eagle loomed large on the tiled floor, looking up.

Neb and Lafil sat up in a squat balcony looking down on their hosts. It seemed as though they were sitting in a jury box awaiting a trial. In some ways, they were. Neb looked around the room. There were four columns, one in each corner. He had thought there was only one window but noticed another small one high up near the ceiling. *Inaccessible and useless*, he thought, *unless you were a bird.*

What was Livia up to? From what he'd read about her in history, she never did anything that wasn't aimed at achieving a broader goal. Did she really think Marcus wanted to be Caesar? Of course, Neb knew he did. It was just a slip of the tongue, a wine-fueled tongue. He should not have had that last glass of wine, but it was so real, so good! How many times had he blurted his thoughts out loud? It was part of who he was and it was not the first time and would likely not be the last. He didn't even need any wine for it to happen, though in this case it didn't help very much. Maybe he should go back to smoking pot. At least then he just had visions. He wondered if the Romans smoked pot.

"What was that about a pot?" Livia glanced up at Neb.

"Nothing," Neb replied sheepishly. He had done it again. Livia continued to keep count of Neb's actions.

"What are you talking about?" Lafil nudged Neb. "Marcus will be here any second."

Four Praetorian guards entered the room. They bowed before their emperor and turned. Each walked over to one of the four columns and stood at attention. Marcus soon followed them into the room. He walked with a swagger towards a chair that was placed below the dais.

Augustus pretended to read the scroll with Marcus's petition. He did this in silence for ten minutes. Marcus sat waiting, knowing that Augustus and Livia were just toying with him. He relished the moments to come.

Caesar handed the scroll to his wife, who waved it like a fan in front of her face. She eyed Marcus with keen suspicion, like a snake watching its prey. Finally, Caesar spoke up.

"Marcus Apitippius, I have never in all my days read such a request. Do you really think building a gladiatorial forum in each city is a good thing? What about the Circus Maximus here in Rome? Why, all the people love coming to Rome to watch the games. If we were to have Circus Maximus in each town, what fun would that be? Are there not enough gladiatorial training schools? What are you proposing?" Augustus stirringly asked.

Now here it comes, Marcus thought as he watched Caesar. He knew what his next word would be. A flat out NO!

Instead, Livia spoke up. Marcus did a double take. This isn't how it went.

"Marcus Apitippius, have you other ideas beside this petition?" She let the scroll drop from her hand to the floor. "What do you really have in mind?"

"How do you mean, good lady?" Marcus wondered what she was getting at. "I have many ideas. This is one of many proposals. I would like to think that all of my petitions have great benefit."

"Benefit to whom?" Livia asked.

Marcus was caught off guard. What was she thinking?

"Why, benefit to the empire, of course," he answered. He turned to Caesar hoping for some relief from his wife's grilling. He didn't get it. Caesar sat mindfully.

"Don't look at me!" Caesar mocked. "She asked you the question."

"You mean benefit to you, don't you, Marcus? Livia gave a hint of that devilish smile that so many had come to know.

"My lady, any shrewd businessman expects to make a profit. Why bother to go into business of any sort if it is not to make money. I, the seller, have come to you, the buyer. If the trade is fair, is it not of benefit to us both? One hand washes the other."

"I am still not convinced," Livia said to Marcus. Then, looking up to the balcony, she said, "What do you think?" Caesar also looked up.

"What?" Marcus murmured, turning to see where Livia had directed her question. Looking up, he saw two hooded figures, their faces hidden deep in their hoods. He thought at first they were shadows. Were they real or was Livia playing a game of her own?

"Livia, I need to go and relieve myself," Caesar suddenly proclaimed and stood up, virtually throwing everyone off. "Whatever you're doing, wife, do it quickly and get on with it!" Augustus remarked, inching his way down the seven steps of the dais. Two of his Praetorian guards moved forward to escort him to the lavatory.

"Will you be back, my love?" Livia sweetly asked.

"Yes, of course I will."

"Should I wait then for your decree on Marcus Apitippius' petition or should I go ahead without you?"

"Do as you wish. You always do," Augustus said.

The room went silent. Livia now cautiously approached Marcus, her eyes darting back and forth, her mind working, as always.

"Let me be very plain, Marcus. I have known men like you all my life, always trying to climb the ladder to the top. Unfortunately, for most, it's a long fall to the bottom. Your family house is known, for the most part, for its loyalty, Marcus. Why try to rise above it when you will only fall. So, I ask you, Marcus Apitippius, what is your place?"

"My place is to serve Rome and Caesar!" Marcus replied. "Where else should it be? My father died an honourable senator. He upheld the law. All the days of his life, he never asked for anything from Caesar nor took anything that was not his."

"It is true that your father was loyal and knew his place. But you, Marcus Apitippius," Livia paused. "I know nothing of your loyalty, only your schemes."

"You should know about schemes," Marcus muttered.

"Hold your tongue!" Livia spat out. "Fine, you want to play? Let's be plain, shall we. You will never be more than you are. Why continue to bang your head against the wall, Marcus? Is it not clear enough that the wall will last longer than your thick head? There is no defeat in Caesar turning down your petition. You should take it with gratefulness and honour that your Emperor even receives you in person. How many can say that? Yet I see in you something more, more than meets the eye. As you know, I am a very good judge of character and I have eyes and spies everywhere. They keep me well informed. And once in a while, something else, something new comes along that attracts my attention. Shall I tell you, Marcus?" Livia almost salivated with delight.

"Please do, good lady," answered Marcus. He so loved Livia's way of dealing with people and things, how people could easily disappear, or appear for that matter, with just one word from her mouth. She was an eel swimming upstream, a snake slithering, and a lion ready to pounce. He admired all of her attributes; he adored them. Too bad she had to die. He smiled to himself as he listened to her drawl on.

Livia gazed back up to the balcony and Marcus followed her gaze.

"Are you going to introduce me to your phantoms?" he asked.

Livia nodded, motioning for her two new friends to come down. Neb could feel the pit of his stomach turning. This was it, the unveiling of all that was to be unveiled, the past, present and future all rolled into one. They made their way down to the floor.

Lafil looked at Neb. "Are you OK? You look kind of pale."

"I'll be fine. Just a little digestive trouble." Neb held his hand to his stomach. "Give me a few seconds, Lafil." Neb heavily panted. "Let me catch my breath. You go ahead. I'll be right behind you."

"Are you sure?" Lafil asked with a concerned tone.

"Yeah, yeah, I'll be fine. I'm starting to feel better already."

"Hurry, before Livia starts to panic, or Marcus, for that matter."

Neb smiled and rested his hand on Lafil's shoulder with assurance. "Everything will be alright."

Lafil pulled back the hood from his cape, straightened his toga and tunic, and walked out onto the floor.

"My good lady," Lafil bowed. "Good sir," he faced Marcus, nodding.

"Let me introduce …" Marcus cut Livia off.

"Yes the Babylonian astrologer. Lafil, is it?"

"Do you know this man, Lafil?" Livia asked, quite surprised.

"I've never met this man until this moment," Lafil truthfully replied.

"Come now, Lafil. Don't you remember me?" Marcus grinned. Oh, that's right. We have met but haven't met and now have met. Isn't time a funny thing? Where's your partner in crime?"

Livia watched baffled. "What's going on here? Is this some kind of conspiracy? Guards!" she called out.

Marcus pulled out a concealed phaser, stunning the guards. Then he pressed a button on his wrist ban, activating a force field through the room.

“Guards! Guards!” Livia shouted fearfully, watching the guards fall to the floor as the blue pulse of light hit them. Chaos was ensuing.

Lafil grabbed on to Neb. “Let’s get out of here.”

“Not so fast, you two.” Marcus pointed his phaser at them. Lafil tried to activate his wrist comm. Marcus noticed and fired a pulse at Lafil. It hit his wrist comm and then went straight through his flesh. Lafil fell to his knees writhing in pain. Neb bent down to help his friend.

“I know this might be a stupid question, but are you alright?”

“I’ll be fine Neb, though I may not be here with you much longer. As soon as the Casino locks onto my bio readings, they will automatically pull me out. Pain and distress kind of have that effect with the bio metre. Don’t worry, Neb, I will do everything I can to help you get back ....” Before Lafil could finish, the Casino locked onto him and he was gone.

“Why can’t people ever end a sentence around here before they’re whisked away or the communications fail?” Neb shook his head.

“Damn!” Marcus shouted on seeing Lafil disappear.

Neb looked back up to find Marcus now pointing his weapon at him.

“Not so fast, Mr. Yorker. I still have plans for you. Move now! Over to the dais. Sit!” Marcus barked. Neb sat on the lower dais steps.

Marcus turned his attention back to Livia, whose whole body was trembling uncontrollably.

"I really do like you, Livia. Perhaps, in another time, we two could have had a great partnership." Marcus held his arm steady, pointing the phaser at Livia's head. "Your best works are behind you, except for when you kill your dear husband two years from now, though I'm afraid that won't happen now. Tiberius will have to settle for whatever I have him do. That is, if I decide to keep him around, though I highly doubt it. Caligula, on the other hand... What do you think about that, Livia dear?" asked Marcus, grinning.

Livia was speechless.

Neb began to feel queasy. He could feel a cold surge of energy filtering through his entire body. He looked down at his hands. His fingertips were turning reddish yellow. Small micro-currents of electricity penetrated his cells. A ghostly voice came out of nowhere.

"Neb, are you there?" It was Kel.

"I am trying to boost the signal," said Pic. "There seems to be something blocking the transmission link. I am getting a force field reading."

"A force field?" Kel remarked.

"Yes, it seems to be interfering with the link," Pic-One replied. "I believe our link at present is one-way. I am positive that Neb can hear us."

Pic-One was correct. Neb, Marcus and Livia could hear what was going on.

"The gods have come down! The gods have come down!" Livia cried out. "Lafil was right!" She looked at Neb in utter confusion.

Where is Augustus, Neb thought between thoughts?

"Oh, shut up," Marcus aimed at Livia, stunning her. Livia's eyes rolled as she fell limp to the floor. "That's more like it."

"Nebula Yorker, if you are hearing us, which I believe you can as the transmission is presently one way, our sensors are indicating a strong presence of a Vlata force field. Did you bring a Vlata force field module with you?" asked Pic-One.

Neb's whole body was now humming uncontrollably. *What the hell is going on*, he thought. He could feel a slight tingle shoot from his toes up to his head.

"Nebula, if you are presently feeling any sort of discomfort, we apologize," Kel said.

"What's going on with him?" Marcus shouted.

"Pic and Pic-One came up with an ingenious procedure by fusing Neb's bio scanner to the subspace network time stream, theorizing it would connect through the electric impulses in his body and, presto, it worked!" Kel happily stated. "By the way, with whom am I speaking? Lafil?"

Maybe I won't have to kill him, Marcus thought, as he watched Neb writhing in pain.

The currents racing through Neb's body unexpectedly began to heighten his synapses. Everything was becoming so clear to him, it was a revelation. He saw people he had never met and places he had never been to. He could now see his father standing and looking towards him. He was saying, "MOVE FORWARD, NEB. MOVE FORWARD."

Marcus fired his phaser at Neb, the blue pulse bounced off him. He fired three more times with the same result. Nothing. The plan was not working. Everything was falling apart. Again! There was no Eno to blame this time. Marcus wracked his brain for a way out. He looked up and directed his phaser at the ceiling, firing off five pulses. Large chunks of concrete began falling, narrowly missing Neb and Livia. The stunned guards were not so lucky. Unknown to Marcus, the blast deactivated the force field. He made a beeline for the exit. He was met by Rufus and Germanus blocking the way out.

"What are you doing here!?" Marcus screamed. "Get out of the way!"

Rufus and Germanus pulled Marcus back into the room. "Not so fast, Apitippius." Rufus grabbed Marcus by the collar.

"Let go of me!" Marcus held up his hand to fire at the brothers, but saw that he no longer had the phaser.

"Looking for this?" Marcus turned and saw Neb hovering in mid-air, holding his phaser. Rufus and Germanus hadn't noticed Neb at first. They were too busy with Marcus. Only now when they gazed up at the wide open gap in the ceiling did they take full notice of him.

25

"Look!" Pic-One said, looking down at his console, "the force field has dropped."

"Neb. Neb. The force field has gone down," said Kel.

"What's he doing up there?" Germanus observed Neb.

"Where are those voices coming from? Don't you hear those voices?" Rufus asked.

"I don't see any strings," Germanus said as he scratched his head. "You hear those voices, too? I always thought it was just me," Germanus added.

"What?" Rufus said. "You always hear voices?"

"We have some good news and some bad news to report, Neb," said Kel.

"What's better, the good or the bad news?" Neb replied.

"The good news is we have not imploded yet and the bad news is that we are about to. The Vegastriopelia, unknown to us, had a failsafe guard that has protected everyone on board. Everyone is in suspended animation. We thought it would protect the whole vessel, though the outside cloaking shield is slowly disintegrating, making us vulnerable to Earth's radar. We are trying to compensate, though we are…" The comm link broke off the connection. It also broke the bio connection with Neb, causing him to fall. Germanus ran over and caught him before he hit the floor.

"Thank you," said Neb, sitting in Germanus' arms. Neb looked heavenward through the hole in the ceiling and saw Halley's fading out of sight. Germanus let Neb down.

Marcus came running towards Neb. He jumped on him, knocking him backwards and then, sitting on top of him, started choking him. Neb reached for a hand-sized piece of the fallen concrete and hit Marcus on the side of his head. Marcus fell over unconscious.

Neb got up on his knees, out of breath. "How many times does this guy need to be knocked out before he gets it?"

Rufus started piecing it together. "You're the red thief!" He now took his turn lifting Neb off his feet.

"Man! I can't catch a break," Neb muttered.

"Put him down!" Livia called out. Rufus swung around to see Livia descending the dais. He let go and, once again, Neb found himself on the floor.

"Rufus Titus Maxis and Germanus Jove Maxis, better known as the Juggernaut Brothers, let that man be!"

Rufus and Germanus now grovelled on their knees.

"Lady Livia," they both said, heads down.

"What business do you two have here and with this man?" She pointed at Marcus, out cold. "Never mind, I don't want to know." Livia walked over to Neb and helped him up. "Oh, how will I explain this one to Augustus?" She looked around at all the debris.

"You two," she addressed the brothers, "I want you to take hold of Marcus Apitippius and do not let him out of your sight or you will be back in the arena as quick as you can fart!"

"Yes, good lady." They bowed and gathered up Marcus and took him outside the doorway.

"Are you injured?" Livia asked Neb with concern.

Am I dreaming? Neb thought as he looked up into Livia's motherly face. *Livia, wife of the Emperor of Rome, is asking how I am. Who would believe me?*

"I should be asking how you are," Neb replied.

"Just a few more battle scars and bumps to add to this old collection, said Livia. "Who exactly are you or, should I ask, what are you?"

Without warning, a blue pulse hit Livia, stunning her yet again. Marcus emerged through the door, phaser in hand, and without Rufus and Germanus. Neb knew that they were dead just by the look on Marcus's face. The phaser was now pointed directly at him.

"You know, Marcus, I am really tired and fed up with you. Why don't you just pull the trigger and get it over with," Neb said as he sat exhausted beside a numb Livia. "For someone bent on world domination, you sure are a moron," Neb laughed. "Can't you see, Marcus, time and history have changed? Lafil's gone. Contact with his Casino and ours is gone. It's quite possible your wish has come true and the Casino has imploded. I am not supposed to be here, but I am, and now stranded, by the looks of it. This is your Rome, your original timeframe. Perhaps it's time to give it all up, Marcus. Run away while you can before Augustus returns and finds all of this mess.

"Do you hear yourself?" Marcus replied. "Give it all up? No, no, dear boy. This is way better than I could have planned! Of course, I would have loved to kill Lafil personally but I guess you will have to do it instead."

"How is this way better than what you planned?" Neb echoed Marcus.

"Can't you see," Marcus began, "with the Casino now out of the way, and with the stolen technology, I have Rome of 12 BCE, soon to be Rome of the 25th century. I figure it will take a few years to complete, maybe two. My body won't start to resort to its normal cell structure for at least two, three hundred years and, by then, I should have come up with the formula for everlasting life or perhaps clone myself and just transfer my consciousness from one clone to another. Mind you, this is all in its early stages."

"What technology do you have that is so powerful? Did you steal a piece of the Vegastriopelia?" Neb let out a little snicker.

"Why, yes," Marcus grinned back. "And all thanks to you, by the way." Marcus reached into his toga and pulled out the metallic case that Eno had dropped and that Neb had tried to return. "Inside this case is a micro-sliver of the Vegastriopelia. It will aid me greatly in building my own Marcustriopelia."

"Marcustriopelia? Now I know you've lost your mind. It will never work," Neb retorted.

"I have had a lot of time to delve into its matrix, thank you very much, Mr. Yorker. I've had over 2,000 years, during my time as a free man and then while I was locked up. I may have failed the first time and, if it weren't for Tict, we wouldn't have had to go through all of this again. What's that old saying? Practice makes perfect. How long have you spent on the Casino? Two days? I hardly think you're in a position to tell me what I know and what I don't know.

"Do you?" Neb confidently replied.

"What gives you such smugness, Nebula Yorker?" Marcus growled.

"If there is one thing that my parents taught me, Marcus, it is to always be aware of the people you associate with and to keep in mind one's surroundings." Neb inched closer to Marcus without him knowing it. He stood three feet away from him before Marcus realized he had somehow snuck up.

“That’s far enough.” Marcus aimed his weapon at Neb’s face.

Neb lifted up his right hand, palm open, so Marcus could see.

“What are you doing?” Marcus watched. The metallic case in Marcus’s hand became so cold that he could no longer hold it. He dropped the case and was left with an imprint of it on his left palm. The case was now open on the floor and the familiar yellowish green glow of the Vegastriopelia emitted from it. Like a fine mist, it swirled upwards and danced in front of Marcus’s face. Marcus was mesmerized as he looked into it. He saw his whole life played out before him, from birth up until now. Marcus stood, unable to move. He watched the yellowish green vapour coil like a snake and empty into Neb’s palm. The case then melted into the floor as Marcus remained paralyzed.

Seeing that Marcus was going nowhere, Neb walked over to Livia, sprawled out on the floor. He felt sad for her.

He bent down and whispered, “I am sorry.” He reached for her wrist to check if she had a pulse. Livia was still alive even after two stuns from the phaser. Neb was relieved. She groaned, opening her eyes. She tried to speak. Her mouth moved, but nothing came out. She looked so harmless and hapless, lying on the cold floor. But this was Livia Drusilla, wife of Caesar Augustus, Emperor of Rome, a formidable foe and now friend. What would she do once she regained her facilities? She’d seen and heard a lot of things she shouldn’t have. What impact would that now have on history? Neb wondered.

Livia grasped Neb’s hand. It took a few moments for Neb to register this as he was going over the consequences of the day in his mind. Neb peered at Livia with relief. He could feel her grip tightening.

“Nebula,” she muttered, in a low mousy voice, “I am not sure who or what you are. The things I have witnessed this day are truly unexplainable and I am sure that no one would believe me if I were to speak of it."

It was hard for Neb to separate the Livia he had read about from the Livia who lay so helpless before him. He helped her up onto one of the dais chairs.

"Thank you," she said and lightly patted his hand. "I have done many things in my life, Nebula, which some would consider evil, but I have always had my family's best interests at heart." She sighed heavily and asked, "What will history think of me?"

Neb reflected for a moment. "History will remember you, Livia Drusilla. Books will be written, good and bad, true and false, but without a doubt I can assure you that you will be remembered."

Livia smiled. "Thank you. Hurry and go before Caesar returns."

"What will you tell him?" Neb asked.

"Nothing," Livia replied.

"Nothing?" Neb replied.

"Well, not nothing," she let out a little chuckle. "I suppose I will have to tell him about how that hole in our ceiling happened, and about the two dead Praetorian guards. But, don't you worry, Nebula, I will come up with something. I always do. Will I ever see you again, Nebula, my favourite seer?"

"Your favourite? Really?" Neb blushed. "What about Lafil?"

"Oh, he's my second favourite," Livia said.

Neb smiled. "I can't say if we will ever meet again, my good lady. I'm not sure where I'm going next." Neb gazed over at Marcus.

"I can take care of him, if you like," Livia said as she watched Neb looking at Marcus.

"That won't be necessary," a familiar voice spoke up.

They turned to see Lafil, all decked out in his black tuxedo, a white rose sticking out of his lapel, and those damn blinding red shoes. Next to him stood Tict, in hologram form. He wore a red suit, white turtleneck and shiny black polished shoes.

Marcus stared at Lafil. You could see the wheels in his head turning. *What the hell just happened and is happening!*

"One to transport to med bay," Lafil barked into his wrist comm, "and be sure to have a heavy security detail on hand, priority X." With that, Marcus leered Neb's way and was transported out of sight.

Neb was as overwhelmed with joy as he was confused to see Lafil and Tict. Livia was just plain confused.

"Sorry it's taken us 920 years to get back, Neb, though I guess to you it has only been 15 minutes or so? I would not have missed this for all the world. And it's thanks to you!" Lafil said.

"920 years?" Neb asked, dumbfounded. *Why is Tict dressed as the assistant?* Neb thought. His head was full of fog, though it was slowly clearing.

"It is so nice to finally meet you. I feel like I have known you all my life," Tict said happily.

"So nice to finally meet?" Neb was taken aback by Tict's comment.

"Put it together, dude!" Lafil egged Neb on. They could see Neb was starting to get the picture.

"You see, Neb, after the med-bay read my bio readings and returned me safely to the Casino, we found ourselves unexpectedly jumping out of Earth's orbit and resuming our normal course. By that time, we were too far out of reach to get a lock on you and bring you aboard." Lafil explained.

"Why 920 years? Couldn't you have just come 75 years later?" Neb asked.

"We could have but the Council decided after all that you told me about what happened in the future regarding Marcus and Tict, they did not want to upset the time line any more than it had been altered. We waited patiently until 1758, picked up Mr. Tict and explained everything to him. It wasn't easy though, was it, Tict?" Lafil turned to Tict.

"No, it wasn't," Tict shook his head. "In fact, I was caught red-handed feeding and drinking with all the French prisoners, having a merry old Christmas. I was about to be executed when Lafil here showed up," Tict replied. "I think every guard crapped their pants that night!"

"And, if I recall correctly, you did also, Tict," Lafil matter-of-factly said.

"Did you have to tell him that?" Tict's face blushed.

"Regardless, my dear boy, we are here to save you!"

"Well, better late than never." Neb walked over to Lafil and gave him a big hug.

"Amazing!" Livia breathed out. "Are you really the gods?" To Livia, it indeed appeared as though they were the gods.

"What are we going to do about her? She's seen so much," Neb whispered in Lafil's ear.

"No need to worry. That will be taken care of soon enough."

"You're not going to kill her, are you?" Neb asked with some trepidation.

"Don't be daft, Nebula Yorker!" Lafil remarked. "This time sequence will soon be wiped out of existence. Livia and Augustus will remember nothing and everything will resume as normal. That is, except for a few things which we will get to later. Are you ready then?"

Neb looked around one last time. He saw Livia with tears rolling down her face. Neb waved good-bye.

"Let's go," Neb said to Lafil. "I'm ready."

Hologram Tict faded as Lafil and Neb prepared to be transported up to the Casino.

"Funny, eh," Neb grinned.

"What's funny?" Lafil asked.

"I came to Rome falling through a hole in a roof and now I am leaving Rome going back up through a hole in a roof."

"You should know by now there are no coincidences," Lafil winked.

"Ready to transport," Lafil spoke into his wrist comm.

Livia stood and watched in awe as a yellowish green aura wrapped about their bodies. They gradually shrank in size, finally forming two flying jellyfish orbs that swung once around the room and then straight up through the ceiling into the evening sky. Livia gazed upwards as they cleared the ceiling. Halley's was in full view, sweeping across the clear, bright night sky. Livia didn't know whether to scream or faint. She did neither.

Soon after, Augustus walked into the room with his two bodyguards at his side. His eyes widened at the room's destruction. He spotted Livia and ran to her.

"What in Jove's name happened here?"

"You wouldn't believe it. The ceiling came crashing down. Those poor guards." Augustus could see feet and hands sticking out from beneath the large chunks of concrete.

"Guards, he called out, "quickly go and get some help and a doctor." The guards hurried at their emperor's orders.

Soon after, more guards arrived. They lifted the heavy debris off their fallen comrades.

"Where's the bloody doctor?" Caesar demanded of the guards.

"Coming, my emperor," one of the guards replied.

"Livia, what of our guests? "They're not buried under this mess, are they?"

"No, my dear." Caesar sighed with relief. It was enough that two of his Praetorian guards were dead.

"I gave the bad news to Marcus Apitippius. He wasn't overjoyed, as is the case when most petitions are turned down. He said he would try again at another time and hoped it would be more favourable. He said to thank you, my dear, and left. Lafil and Nebula left soon afterwards. They also wanted me to thank you for your hospitality. I sat alone for a few minutes and then heard this loud cracking sound. The next thing I knew, the ceiling was collapsing. Those guards didn't have a chance. I thought I was going to die as well."

"The gods must have been protecting you!" Augustus hugged and comforted his wife.

"You don't know how true that is." Livia held on tightly to her husband and proceeded to faint. Augustus held her.

26

Neb sat up in a bed in med-bay. Beside him in the next bed was a sedated Marcus, drooling as he sipped water through a straw. He was speaking gibberish, like a baby trying to talk. The med-bay visit was a precaution in Neb's case, and to clean up all his scrapes and bruises. An android medic came in through the med-bay door with a chart in his hands.

"You're good to go, Mr. Yorker," the medic said.

"What about him?" Neb pointed to Marcus.

"Regression memory therapy," the medic replied.

"Regression memory therapy?"

"We are reprogramming him for his return to his century. I overheard Lafil say that he is too much of a danger to have him locked up here again, though I don't remember ever seeing him before. You would have to clarify that with Lafil, I suppose, if you want more information."

Just then, Lafil and Tict came into the med-bay.

"That will be all. Doc-One." Lafil took the chart from him. Doc-One nodded and left the room.

"How's our wittle baby boy today?" Lafil softy patted Marcus on the head. Marcus squirmed and giggled.

"What's this all about?" Neb was getting changed into his jeans and t-shirt that were left for him beside the bed.

"It's a new procedure. Marcus is the first to be tested with it." Lafil tugged on Marcus's cheek. "That's a good boy and now it's time to go to sleep." Marcus obeyed and closed his eyes and soon was fast asleep.

"Wow! How did you do that?" Neb marvelled.

"It's all part of the procedure. You see, by regressing Marcus back to childhood, we've wiped out his entire memory and can now start over with new ones."

"Interesting. Why not just lock him up again?" Neb said, putting on his sneakers.

"He's far too dangerous for that."

"That's what the medic said."

Lafil turned to Tict. "Tict, remind me before I go to do something about some of those gossipy androids. It's very unbecoming of them."

"Will do, sir," Tict said, making a mental note.

"As I was saying, Neb," Lafil continued, "Marcus is far too dangerous to have around twice. He's tried to kill anyone who got in his way. What's to say if we lock him up he won't try again? No, this is a much better way to deal with him. This way, we can train him to be a productive member of society and my assistant. It should only take a few more days of treatment to get him up to speed."

"Your assistant!" Neb blurted out. "After all he's done to you! To everyone on the Casino and almost to Earth!"

"Now, now, take it easy, Nebula," Tict assured Neb. "It's not what you think."

"I will explain everything to you tonight in the Green Room," Lafil added. "Now, I think you and Tict need some time alone to get reacquainted. I'll see you both later, say around twenty hundred hours?"

"That will be fine, Lafil. Until then," Tict replied.

Neb and Tict exited the med-bay, leaving Lafil to continue his treatments with Marcus.

"Is he for real, Tict? Having Marcus become his assistant again?"

"I know it's hard to fathom at the moment, dear boy, but let's just wait until this evening. Cheer up. We're having a party in your honour. The entire Council of U will be there. And John Lennon, too!"

"What time is it now, Tict?"

"Thirteen hundred hours," Tict replied.

"I could really do with a shower about now," Neb said as he yawned, "and maybe a short nap."

"Of course, Neb. I'll show you to your quarters. Afterwards, when you're feeling refreshed and invigorated, you can come to my office and we'll talk.

They walked down the hallway. Tict chatted briefly about the new modifications to the Casino's cloaking shell and *Star Trek*. "I am a big fan!" Tict expressed excitedly.

Neb chuckled, patting him on the shoulder.

"Beam me up, Scotty!" Tict said.

"You know, Tict, neither Captain Kirk nor anyone else ever quoted that line."

"Oh dear! Are you sure?" Tict asked, a bit deflated.

Neb noticed his disappointment and said, "Wait, I think you're right. He did say 'Beam me up, Scotty'. It's been a very long week, years, decades, centuries or whatever. It will be nice to get in the shower and clean up." Neb smiled

"Ah, here we are," Tict said. They stopped as a door swished open. "Your quarters," he motioned to Neb. Pop around about seventeen hundred hours and we'll have that chat and a drink."

"Will do," said Neb. "Oh, and by the way, you look better in black than you do in red. Somehow, it's just not your colour." Neb winked as he entered his quarters, leaving Tict happily walking down the hall.

After his shower, Neb lay in his bed, wrapping his head around all that had happened. He had asked Interface to awaken him at sixteen hundred hours. It was now 13:30. He closed his eyes and took a few deep breaths. Before he knew it, the Interface was waking him up.

It is now sixteen hundred hours, as requested," the Interface said. "Is there anything else I can assist you with?"

"A cup of coffee would be nice, said Neb, yawning. Within seconds, the doors to his quarters swooshed open and there was Kel, rolling a cart holding a small pot of steaming fresh coffee.

"Kel!" Neb excitedly shouted. "How are you? It's great to see you again!" Kel poured Neb a cup of coffee and handed it to him. She then backed away a few steps, staring at him blank-faced.

"I have no current data to suggest that we have met. Perhaps you have mistaken me for another Kel model?" she stated impassively.

Neb was confused. "Are you not KEL-345?"

"I am, though we dropped our call numbers centuries ago."

That's interesting, Neb thought.

"Why, of course!" He blurted out.

"Of course what? I don't understand?" Kel enquired.

"Don't you see, Kel? Time and history didn't just change during my stay on Earth, minute as it was. It must also have changed here on the Casino. But how much is the question. Let's see, with no Marcus to interfere, Lafil remained the concierge, picked up Tict in 1758 who became his assistant. Hmmm?" Neb rubbed his chin. "What happened to Eno?"

"Are you speaking about President Eno of Repooc Ecila 6?" Kel asked.

President! OK. Let that settle in for a moment, Neb thought.

"Yes, Repooc Ecila 6 is actually being sworn into Council membership this evening," Kel added.

"This evening, you say? I wonder what else has changed. Interface," Neb called out, "please upload and direct all information on the Casino's history for the last 920 years to my personal console."

"Working," replied the Interface.

Neb took a sip of his coffee. A few seconds later, the Interface completed its task.

"Will there be anything else?" Kel asked.

"Call me Neb, please."

"Will there be anything else, Neb, please?" Kel answered.

Neb had to laugh. There was a very unusual symmetry taking place. "Neb would be fine. Kel."

"Very well, Neb. Will there be anything else I can do to assist you?"

"Well, my jeans and T-shirt seem to be missing. Might you know where they are?"

"Perhaps they are located within your wardrobe," Kel pointed.

"Yes, of course," Neb slapped his head with his hand. "Should have had a V8!"

Kel nodded her head in a robotic fashion and said, "How would an Earth V8 engine assist you in finding clothes? Unless you had...." Kel was about to go on when Neb interrupted her thought process.

"Plus ça change, plus c'est la même chose." He smiled, then burst out laughing.

"Language, French, Earth," Kel began. Neb couldn't stop her so he let her go on. Before he knew it, it was 16:40 hours.

Kel left, promising to meet up with him soon and get reacquainted, as Neb suggested. However, she was puzzled with the thought of getting reacquainted with someone she had never met before.

Neb headed for the wardrobe. "Open," he said. The wardrobe opened. He looked for his jeans, t-shirt and sneakers, but all he found were three red suits, three white turtlenecks, three pairs of black shoes, three pairs of white socks, one black belt with an oval belt buckle and a wrist watch. Upon inspection, though, he saw that it wasn't really a watch but an updated wrist comm made to resemble a watch. Neb didn't know what to make of it.

"Interface," Neb called out, "connect me with Mr. Tict's office, please."

"Connecting, said the Interface.

Neb poked his head into the wardrobe again, hoping that by chance he might find his jeans.

"Connection to Mr. Tict's office open," said the Interface.

"Neb!" Tict responded, "I was just about to a call you. Great timing. Look, I won't be able to make our 17:00 hours meeting. Something came up with President Eno's pre- reception signing that needs my expert attention. Sorry for the short notice, but I will catch up with you later in The Green Room tonight. Hope all is well. Tootles." Tict out.

Neb couldn't even get a word in. *Tootles?* He thought. *What's happened to the people around here?* Neb had to laugh to himself. *Tootles. Well, I guess I don't have much of a choice.* He reached into the wardrobe and pulled out a red suit, turtleneck, shoes, belt and the watch, which he thought was very cool. Soon, he was dressed and admiring himself in the wardrobe mirror. He figured he would now have time to go over the Casino's last 920 years of Earth's historical records seeing as his meeting with Tict had been abruptly cancelled.

He sat down at the console, adjusted the monitor and began going through all the requested data. As he pored over the information, there was something bothering him. He wasn't a hundred per cent sure what it was. It egged him on as he scrolled through pages and pages of documents of the Casino's last 920 years.

OK, now this might prove what I have been wondering about. Neb thought, as he came to the Casino's Earth index:

1066 AD, Lafil returns from Earth, Rome, 12 BCE

1145, no change

1222, no change

1301, no change

1378, no change

1456, no change

1531, no change

1607, no change

1682, no change

1758, Lafil visits Earth, encounters Archibald Tict

1835, Lafil visits Sardegna 2 BCE and Rome 12 BCE

1910, cosmic anomaly detected: low to no risk reported

1986, ongoing data compiling

1835 and 1910 caught Neb's eye and piqued his interest. Before he was able to make a more thorough search, he remembered what it was that he had forgotten to do.

27

The Green Room was filled to capacity, as usual. Guests mingled with members of the Council of U, laughing, shaking hands, and toasting one another. The delegation from Repooc Ecila 6, along with President Eno, basked in the attention.

Though Repooc Ecila 6 and President Eno would not be part of the 15-member Council Guild, they would now be part of the larger spectrum of planets and worlds united, tied together as one, where every voice counted. The Earth, unfortunately, was still far from that day when they too would have a voice.

In the meantime, tonight's induction celebration would be broadcast Casino-wide and to all the Council worlds. Each table was lavishly set, with a centrepiece of illuminated Rainbow Darby fish from Lanoishull Prime, a rare breed of singing fish. Each table would of course be equipped with earphones for each guest's listening pleasure.

A banquet of food from all Council worlds was spread out around the room and was being enjoyed by all. Surprisingly, the one food item that everyone was raving about was from the one non-Council world, brought in from Earth and personally prepared by John Lennon. Fish and Chips! To everyone's delight, John assured the guests that no Rainbow Darby fish were involved and that the Atlantic Codfish he used were no relation to the Rainbow Darby. "They can't even play guitar!" he was quoted as saying.

Sy Dyloup was seen scurrying on and behind the stage, preparing for the evening's main musical event.

"It's going to be smashing, dashing, bashing, clashing, crashing, flashing, dancing. With lots and lots of prancing!" Sy Dyloup dropped hints to anyone that would listen.

"Really?" He had cornered President Eno's wife Salasibar. Sy loved the attention!

Tict stuck his head out from behind the stage curtain, followed by Lafil's head and then Sy's. Three talking heads lined up in a row.

"Good crowd," said Tict.

"How come no one's eating at the salad bar?" quipped Lafil, sarcastically.

"Oh, how I love a parade!" Sy giggled.

"What parade? Tict asked. "You didn't say anything about there being a parade tonight."

"There isn't. I just love parades." Sy watched the crowd.

"I love parades. Those upside down clowns are a hoot," replied Lafil.

"OK, OK, I love parades too." Tict gave in.

Tict's head disappeared behind the curtain, as did Lafil's. Then a long cane wrapped around Sy's neck and pulled him back as well.

***

TeeceeFore could be seen dressed in a sparkling blue gown. Rings of gold adorned her beehive hairstyle. She glided as always across the floor and then she made her way up the spiral staircase to the Green Room's VIP balcony where other members of the Council Guild were gathering.

The air was festive, not only in the Green Room, but all around the Casino. Council worlds from across the vast deepness of space engaged in their own festivities leading up to the swearing in ceremony and they were also glued to their home viewing screens. It almost felt like when the Casino was first launched on Lerxst so many millenniums ago. The only thing missing were the Triopelians.

It was getting close to 20:00 hours.

"Has anyone seen our dear Nebula Yorker?" TeeceeFore asked about.

"Oh, he'll be around shortly, I reckon," said John Lennon, shuffling up beside TeeceeFore unexpectedly, like a shadow hiding from itself in the dark.

"You know I hate it when you do that, John!" TeeceeFore held her breath.

***

Neb crept along the Casino's hallways, making sure no one saw him or was following. He was wearing a long grey cloak with a hood covering his entire body and face. The only thing visible were his black shoes. Most of the guests were either enjoying themselves in the games room or inside their guest quarters viewing all of the celebrations. A few service androids Neb encountered paid no heed to him. He made his way past the employees-only section beyond the games rooms and hangar bays. His destination was the main control room that housed the Vegastriopelia.

Kel was busy working with Pic and Pic-One as Neb inched his way slowly into the room. Kel caught a very small, but precise, glimpse of Neb out of the corner of her eye as he slipped in through the swooshing door. She made a mental androidian note of it. The room was bright white, but soon was enveloped in pitch blackness. Gradually, the light began to trickle in and eventually filled the room. Once illuminated, the yellowish green glow of the Vegastriopelia filled the space.

The circular orb within a box within a triangle within a circle hovered and rotated before Neb. He pulled back the hood that covered his head and face. Closing his eyes, he began to meditate.

Kel was now watching this all unfold on her security monitor, along with Pic and Pic-One. After a few moments, Neb opened his eyes and smiled. He raised his right hand. His hand glowed as a swirling mass of yellowish green light wisped out of it. It then formed around Neb's body, the aura so blinding that it blanked out Kel's monitor. Pic and Pic-One sighed sadly.

With no one now watching, Neb and the Vegastriopelia merged. It absorbed all that Neb had to offer as, indeed, Marcus did manage to steal a very, very, very light particle of the Vegastriopelia. Neb fell to his knees.

The Vegastriopelia began to sing. Its musical vibrations echoed through the entire Casino and were felt in all Council worlds, even on Earth. It tingled every living being that was. For mere seconds, a joyous sensation was felt by all. Even the androids could sense the notes and keys.

Many years into the future, some believed this was when the New Age movement began on Earth, though the jury is still out on that one.

"Thank you," spoke the Vegastriopelia to Neb.

"You're very welcome!" Neb bowed.

The room again slowly faded to black, and then returned to its normal hue of white. Kel's security monitor flickered back on. The room was back to normal, minus one Nebula Yorker.

"What happened? Where did he go?" Pic and Pic-One asked Kel, quiet confused. Kel stood up from her console, walked across the Vegastriopelia room. There was, indeed, no one. On the floor was a grey hooded cloak.

***

"Attention. Attention. May we have your attention, please?" a voice blared out from the overhead Green Room speakers. "We shall begin the swearing-in ceremony in five minutes. That's five minutes people, get it together."

Everyone nonchalantly began to return to their assigned seats, as requested. One or two guests were heard asking where that overhead voice was coming from. "Newbies!" others laughed.

The Council of U Guild members were all seated up in the balcony. Four chairs remained empty, three for Lafil, Tict and Neb, and one for any Triopelians that might show up, though they never did. It had always been symbolic to have one empty chair at all Council Guild meetings and celebrations to represent the founding members of the Council. It reminded them of where they had come from and where they were now as a united people.

"Where has that Nebula gotten to? He's going to be late and miss the swearing-in ceremony." TeeceeFore stood at the edge of the balcony looking down to see if she could spot Neb.

"Don't get your knickers in a twist, love. He'll be here soon," John Lennon once again snuck up on her.

"John!" TeeceeFore said, exasperated and shaking her head. "You really need to stop that. I bet you were a handful for your Aunt!"

"I was, but she loved me, yeah, yeah, yeah." John batted his eyes at her.

TeeceeFore couldn't resist. She gently patted the side of his face and smiled. "Now, go and sit down," she said with a motherly tone.

A drum roll sounded. She took one last glance around without seeing Neb and sat down.

Neb was standing below, in the balcony's blind spot, looking straight out at the stage. The black stage curtain gradually inched open, revealing a single desk and chair. On top of the desk was an open book. To the right of the book was a multi-coloured six-inch feathered pen sitting in an inkwell. A fanfare of music progressively built up until the sounds of crashing cymbals splashed across the room, ending the interlude.

The room went black. A lone spotlight shone on the desk. Another spotlight appeared, following President Eno of Repooc Ecila 6 as he walked ever so presidential-like across the stage until he sat at the desk. He pulled the pen from its inkwell and began signing. After he completed his signature, he placed the pen back into the inkwell. He rose from the desk, stood in front of it and bowed. The curtain closed.

Repooc Ecila 6 was now part of the larger collective.

The house lights were turned up and all returned to normal, as though nothing had happened. *Well, that was quick and to the point*, Neb thought. He was about to make his way up to the balcony when Lafil came walking out on the stage. He could tell by the reaction in the room that it wasn't something planned. A hushed tone swept over everyone in attendance.

"Dear friends," Lafil began, "thousands of years ago, I found myself thinking about all that there was and all that would never be. I lived in a culture where many deities were worshipped, none of whom were real. I wondered who these would-be gods made of stones and wood were and whether they really had any bearing on my life. If I chose not to bow down and pray to them, would lightening rip down from the sky and strike me? No. Instead, one evening a long, long time ago, I was visited by my past, present and future. 'Ah, you say, 'how can one know or go to the future? That's impossible.' A friend showed me that all things are possible if you have an open mind and reasonable logic to back it up."

Lafil looked out, trying to find Neb. Neb waved in Lafil's direction but didn't know if he saw him.

"Tonight," Lafil continued and paused. "Tonight, I am happy to tell you all that I am retiring from my entire concierge duties and have passed them along with consent and blessing from the Council to our one and only Mr. Archibald Tict, also known to all of you as Mr. Tict."

Tict then walked out, all decked out in his black tuxedo, just as Neb remembered him. There was a standing ovation for both of them. Lafil and Tict hugged one another and walked off stage shoulder to shoulder, waving to everyone.

Neb soon rushed up to the balcony and was greeted by a sour-looking TeeceeFore.

"Mr. Yorker, you're late!" she said, with crossed arms and a stomping foot.

"No, he isn't." Lafil and Tict appeared from behind Neb. TeeceeFore did a double take.

"Have you men been taking lessons from John Lennon's bag of tricks?" TeeceeFore asked.

Tict gave her a warm hug and a kiss that she returned. Neb was delightfully shocked at seeing their affection for one another.

"That's new! When did that happen?"

"About a hundred years ago." Lafil slapped Neb on the back. "Come, we have much to talk about!"

But, before they could, the stage curtains once again opened. Sy Dyloup stood there, his back to the room. Dry ice seeped over the stage, then rose and hovered over the room.

Turning, he addressed the crowd in a teasing voice. "You didn't think this party was over, did you?" He hovered over to the balcony, a spotlight following him. "Well, as you know, we can't have a concierge without an assistant!"

"May I?" Sy asked Tict. Tict nodded.

"Ladies and gentlemen here, there and everywhere, I give you Mr. Nebula Yorker!" A spotlight shone on Neb. The room went dead silent. One person clapped and another yelled out, "WHO'S THAT?" which caused an uproar of laughter.

Soon Sy was zipping back down onto the stage. "Tonight, we have a super-duper band of lads to entertain and thrill you."

"I know who that is," Neb said to Tict.

"Really? He wouldn't even tell me," Tict replied.

"Hold on to your seats!" Sy excitedly screamed.

"The Rolling Stones!" Neb said out loud.

"Who?" Tict asked.

"Ladies and Gentlemen, and you know who you are," Sy giggled, "I give you QUEEN!"

"What!" Neb muttered.

The stage exploded into a sea of high octane music and flash bombs. Freddie Mercury came running out, shaking his butt and teasing the crowd. Brian May blazed out the riffs on his guitar. John Deacon jumped up and down with his bass like he was on a trampoline, while Roger Taylor pounded the drums like there was no tomorrow.

"TIE YOUR MOTHER DOWN. TIE YOUR MOTHER DOWN," they sang.

Lafil asked, "Whose mother and why would you tie her down?"

They were on for two hours straight. The Green Room loved it, as did all those viewing it from all around the Casino and everywhere, except Earth, of course. For the last song of the night, Freddie came out wearing his long red cape, trimmed with fur, and a crown.

"Thank you, all you good people, for showing up tonight. I am having such a wonderful time, I don't even know where we are," he laughed. "This is a new song from our latest album. We hope you love it. It's called 'Who Wants to Live Forever'."

There was not a dry eye in the whole Green Room when they finished the song. Lafil was most touched by it.

Sy Dyloup came out after the boys from Queen took their bows. They watched Sy as he hovered around the Green Room.

"Do you see any strings? I can't see any strings," Brian asked Freddie. "How about you guys? You see any strings?"

John and Roger both shook their heads. "I don't see anything, do you?"

Sy touched down back on the stage, beside Freddie.

"That's a great trick. How do you do that?" Brian waved his hand in front of and behind Sy.

"Most importantly," Freddy turned to Sy, "when do we get paid?"

Sy Dyloup looked to his stagehand standing in the wings. "Now would be a good time!" he shouted out to him.

"Gotcha!" The stagehand replied. Soon, the curtain closed. Freddie was still hounding Sy when the band faded out.

The next morning, Freddie called up Brian. Brian was half asleep when he picked up the phone.

"That was a fantastic show last night!" Freddie said.

"What show are you talking about?" Brian answered.

28

With the Green Room now all but emptied and the video feeds shut down, the service androids were busy cleaning up. The only remaining occupants of the Green Room were the Council Guild, high up in the balcony.

“What a most enjoyable evening!” said Notlen Hoj, Duke of Landanphishfri. “I can’t for the life of me remember such an evening.”

“So unforgettable!” TeeceeFore agreed with the Duke.

“Is that so?” Tict poked her on the shoulder. “What about our wedding night?”

Everyone at the table laughed as TeeceeFore's face turned red.

“So Neb, what can you tell us about *Star Trek*?” asked Mleh Novel. The table went silent at his question. All eyes focused on Neb.

Neb dropped his head down. *Not again!* This time, he kept his thoughts to himself.

“That is a very important question, Mleh Novel, but I believe there is a more burning question for our young friend here, “Lafil interrupted.

“Oh?” Mleh Novel cocked an eyebrow.

“Yes. Nebula, how did you survive the time jump into Rome 12 BCE?” The entire Council Guild nodded their heads in agreement to the question. There was a long pause. Neb had just opened his mouth to speak when John Lennon interrupted.

"Isn't it obvious? He's a Triopelian!"

Neb lifted a finger to his nose, tapped it three times and then pointed at John Lennon. "Give that man a cigar!" Neb said, trying his best W.C. Fields impersonation.

A hush presided over the table. After some silence, they all began to laugh, except TeeceeFore, Tict and Lafil.

"I knew it!" TeeceeFore rose up. "I had a feeling!" As TeeceeFore stood, the laughter stopped. "I had a feeling!" she repeated.

"Have you always known?" Tict asked.

"No," Neb answered.

"That still doesn't explain how you survived the time jump and if you are indeed a Triopelian," Tict said. "How is it that you were able to time travel so far back? We have always been led to believe that time travel was only accessible to one's own home world and based on one's age."

"This is true," began Neb. "I wasn't born on Earth. I was, though, conceived on Earth."

TeeceeFore's mouth gaped open. Slowly, she sat back down.

"Waiter!" she yelled out. "I think we're going to need more drinks over here!"

"Please go on. This is fascinating!" said Lafil. "When did you first know?"

"When Tict first introduced me to the Vegastriopelia, it spoke to me, not verbally but internally. I didn't really know it at the time. It gave me frames of memory. Not the whole memory, only frames. As time went on, those frames began to fall into order but only my subconscious mind was aware of what was taking place. The next time I came in contact with the Vegastriopelia was when Marcus stole a micro-fraction of it.

Actually, come to think of it, it was Eno who stole it. At Marcus's bidding, of course."

"You don't mean President Eno, do you?" Tict asked.

"I thought you filled everyone in," Neb said to Lafil.

"I must have forgotten," said Lafil. "It's OK, everyone. That was in the old time frame," he assured the table.

"Is there anything else you forgot to tell us, Lafil?" TeeceeFore enquired.

"Let's hear Neb out. Maybe I have," Lafil answered.

"Indeed," she remarked.

"As I was saying," Neb continued, "the second contact happened before we time-jumped to Rome. I thought for sure I was a goner. However, before the third contact, Pic and Pic-One had found a way to communicate with me – while in Rome, that is – engineering and filtering my bio readings into my communication module in my belt through the time stream plugging into the electrical currents in my body. It caused my subconscious to release those memory frames. It was as though I was watching a movie about my life and my parents' life. This led to my third contact with the Vegastriopelia. It released itself from the case, where Marcus had hidden it. It then entered into me and I became fully aware of everything. Now, how I was able to survive the time-jump gets a little tricky at this point. You see, my parents, my real parents are Ruban and Blulay."

"What?" the whole table gasped.

"Yes. Ruban and Blulay had conceived me while on Earth, before Earth was Earth, during one of their many explorations. So that explains why I survived the time-jump. I wasn't born on Earth, though. I was born on their ship in deep space while en route back to the Plexus Rim."

"Just how old are you?" Luapyentraccm, Viceroy of Dregonion, asked in awe.

"Again, that's kind of tricky. You see, after I was born, my parents' vessel encountered a Cosmic Shift, forwarding them into the future. Before they knew it, they were back on Earth, but in the year 1910 AD. I was nowhere to be found. They, of course, were in total shock, as any parents would be. Their vessel had landed deep in the Amazon rainforest. They were able to locate my Triopelian bio readings, but we were not in the same timeframe. I had jumped forward to 1960 AD. They pinpointed my exact location to the western seaboard of North America outside San Jose, California, USA, and a couple of miles east of Woodside, California. They thought a rescue was at hand when Halley's Casino or Comet became visible a few months later but they had no way to communicate. The only thing they could do was wait it out until it was 1960 AD. It then took them another six years to find me. Over the course of time, their outward appearance changed, corresponding to the Earth's gravitational pull and its rotation. However, their minds or internal Triopelian philosophy remained the same. So, when we finally met up again, they resembled 66-year-old humans."

"Why didn't your outward physical appearance also change?" asked Tict.

"Well, you have to remember, I was only days old before this all transpired and, having been conceived on Earth, I inherited its DNA."

"So, you're like Mr. Spock, half human, half Vulcan, except in your case, part human, part Triopelian," said Tict.

Neb let out a huge belly laugh, almost falling over in his chair.

"Not quite, Tict, not even close. Gee, what is it with you people and *Star Trek*? Anyhow, as I was saying, I inherited a strain of human DNA which kept me physically adapted to Earth's growth cycle. I am 26 years old and at the same time, millenniums in age. Ruban and Blulay adopted the personas of Bancroft and Victoria Yorker and decided to raise me as a human. I never knew any different, though I always felt there was something off about my parents. I chalked it up to eccentricity. Then, two years ago, they disappeared into the Amazon. I have a good idea where they went and where they are now. So, in a nutshell, I survived the time-jump into Rome of 12 BCE because I can. I suppose, technically, I could venture back to anywhere in Earth's past, if I wanted."

Neb grabbed his glass of wine and sipped it coolly. The entire Council Guild sat absorbing the whole truth they had just heard. No one spoke a word for some time.

"An honest to goodness, real live Triopelian! I'll be dammed." Tict slapped his knee. "Will more of you be coming?"

"Whoa there, Tickety-boo. I have only just found out my true heritage. I have no idea where the rest of my people are, let alone if any more are coming this way," Neb cautioned Tict and everyone else. "For the time being, I'm afraid I am it."

"Should we not share this extraordinary news with everyone?" Jonibleeuw, the Samrajni of Ekaveo, joyfully sang out. A debate ensued among the Guild members, resulting in an immediate vote taking place to determine if they should share this extraordinary news. In the end, the vote on whether to share the news was a tie. They all turned to Neb for the tie- breaking vote.

"Nebula," TeeceeFore began, "It would seem that, as the lone Triopelian and fifteenth member of the Guild, it lies in your hands to decide whether to divulge this information to the Council worlds. Neb had to laugh to himself as he remembered asking TeeceeFore in the other time frame what would happen in the case of a tie. He'd had no idea that it would ever fall on him.

"One moment, please, if I may?" Snilloc Lihp, Fifth Master from Oootopopah, spoke up. "I do not wish to be ungrateful or to come across as opposed to your revelation, Nebula. I must ask, though, for as they say on Earth, 'talk is cheap', what proof can you give, if any, that you are truly who you say you are?"

"Wait for it," John Lennon interrupted Snilloc Lihp.

As soon as John Lennon spoke, the balcony's comm system rang out. *Beep. Beep. Beep.*

TeeceeFore walked over to the comm panel on the wall and pressed the button.

"TeeceeFore here. Go ahead."

"Sorry to interrupt, Madame Prime Minister, but I think there is something you should all see." The voice on the other end of the comm was Kel. "I am patching the video feed through now."

The balcony's view screen activated. Pic and Pic-One, along with Kel, had managed to decrypt the missing security index video link of Neb while he was with the Vegastriopelia after it had shorted out. In reality, though, the Vegastriopelia had allowed it for just this very purpose. The feed would later be forever deleted. At least, that is what the Vegastriopelia wanted them to believe. Nothing, in fact, was ever lost or deleted from the Vegastriopelia.

With proof finally shown and the vote decided, the Guild parted ways for the night. Lafil, Tict and Neb stayed behind.

So?" Neb said to Lafil. "What are your retirement plans?"

"Why do I have the feeling you already know the answer?" Lafil smirked.

"Honestly, I don't," replied Neb. "Though I was researching the Casino's historical records and came across an entry that you had visited Sardegna in 2 BCE and Rome 12 BCE."

"Well, if you must know, I have not only decided to give up the conciergeship but to return home to Earth. I actually purchased a vineyard. Thus, my trip back to 2 BCE. I think I am going to give up fortune telling and just enjoy life as long as I can. One truly misses the open blue sky and fresh air."

"Amen to that!" Tict agreed.

"What about Marcus?" Neb asked.

"As I told you," Lafil said, "he's going to be my assistant. You see, Neb, there is a spark of good in all beings. One just has to know how to ignite it and keep the fire burning, so to speak. Marcus has such a spark. On the other hand, you lit a spark in Livia but her spark didn't last long. She did go on to murder Augustus and place her son Tiberius on the throne. She died alone a broken woman."

"So she kept her word regarding our episode?" Neb asked sadly.

"She did, though some years later, hundreds of years actually, some documents were unearthed that were attributed to Claudius, her grandson, who went on to become Emperor, as you know. One document was entitled *Livia's Dream*. The scroll was very parched and torn and not much was deciphered apart from the title. My second stop to Rome 12 BCE was done as a favour to you."

"To me? Whatever for?" Neb asked.

"I know how you felt about stealing or, should I say, borrowing those clothes from Rufus' and Germanus' mother's clothesline. I made restitution on your behalf and also saved Rufus and Germanus from certain death at the hands of Marcus." It was Lafil's turn to sit back and enjoy his glass of wine.

"You changed history?" Tict gasped.

"Just a wee bit," Lafil held up his thumb and finger, winking at both Neb and Tict.

"What did you do?" Neb leaned forward on his chair.

"You know that Rufus and Germanus set out to find you at Marcus's request for help. Well, something got in their way and they didn't quite make it to Marcus nor did they care about the stolen clothes or the red thief."

"What? What?" Tict and Neb both said at the same time.

"They kind of found a huge pot of gold on the way."

They all erupted into laughter. Then, they filled their wine glasses and toasted Rufus and Germanus. They sat back quietly, enjoying the moment.

"When do you leave, Lafil?" Neb asked.

"In a day or two," he replied. "Marcus's regression process is coming along fine. I want to make sure that when we leave, his new memory is intact. The last thing we need, or he needs, is to become his old self again."

"Is there any chance of that happening? Regaining his old memory?" Tict asked, with concern.

"There is always a slight possibility but it's a chance I am willing to take and, should it happen, we'll cross that bridge when we come to it."

"You're a brave man, Lafil," Neb nodded his head and lifted his glass in a toast.

"What about you, Neb?" Tict asked. "What's in store for you now that you know you're a Triopelian? Have you given any thought to finding your people?"

"Perhaps one day. Perhaps they will find me first. Who knows?"

"Well, since your tie-breaking vote vetoed releasing your true identity for the foreseeable future, it may be a while," Lafil remarked.

"Yeah, but something tells me they know already. We'll wait and see." Neb got up from his chair. He stretched out his arms high above his head and gave a long yawn. "Now, gentlemen, if you'll excuse me, there is a little matter I must attend to." Neb reached for his glass and gulped down the last mouthful of wine. "I bid you good evening." He bowed and left the Green Room.

29

Tict and TeeceeFore were lying in their bed, talking about the evening's events – President Eno of Repooc Ecila 6, Lafil's retirement, Tict's promotion, the musical entertainment and, of course, the one and only Nebula Yorker.

"I don't know if I will ever live to see another night of such excitement and revelation," TeeceeFore said as she snuggled with her husband.

"Nor I." Tict held her.

"It makes one wonder what else is going on in the universe that we don't know about," TeeceeFore mused.

Beep. Beep. Beep. The comm sounded. Tict pressed the comm panel on the desk beside the bed.

"Tict here."

"Incoming message for Madame TeeceeFore," said the controller.

"On speakers, please," TeeceeFore asked.

She sat up excited when she heard the voice. "Hello cousin. How are you?"

"LeBeau!" TeeceeFore happily answered. "How are you? It's been ages since we last talked!"

LeBeau was a very distant relative on her father's side. Or was it her mother's side? She could never get it straight. LeBeau was also humanoid in appearance, very human in fact.

"You're not in any sort of trouble, are you?" she asked.

Loud laughter shot out of the comm speakers.

"No, not yet anyway," LeBeau replied. "I was watching the celebrations tonight and spotted you in the crowd with your husband. By the way, hello Tict."

"Hello LeBeau," answered Tict. "It's so nice to hear your voice again. I do hope to meet you one day in person. TeeceeFore has told me so much about you."

"Everything, TeeceeFore?" LeBeau jested, "I hope not! Anyhow, as I was saying, I saw you two and just had to let you know that I am on my way to Marine. You remember Marine, don't you?"

"How could I forget?" TeeceeFore replied. She rolled her eyes at Tict, putting her fingers to her lips to shush him.

"Is there anything you would like me to bring back for you?"

"How about yourself? Safe and sound," she answered.

"OK, I think that's doable. The transport freighter is just about to leave for Marine. I'll send you a holocard as soon as I can."

"Be careful, LeBeau," TeeceeFore added.

"You know me," he replied.

"I do. That's the problem." They both laughed.

"Alright then, LeBeau out." The comm went silent.

"What do you think he's up to?" Tict asked.

"I have a feeling we're going to find out sooner rather than later."

Oh my! Tict thought to himself.

"Interface," Tict called out, "please deactivate the wakeup call."

"Deactivated," the Interface answered.

"Turn the lights out, dear. I am tired," said TeeceeFore, as she rolled over on her pillow.

***

Neb handed Mot Yttep, the chief transport Transfiguror officer, a white Green Room embroidered napkin with coordinates printed on it.

"Tell no one," he charged Mot Yttep.

"Of course, sir," he acknowledged. Mot Yttep took the folded napkin from Neb. He opened it and read:

Wednesday July 9th, 1966, 10:00 AM
San Jose, California, USA
Blue Heron Diner

Mot Yttep folded the napkin, nodded and handed it back to Neb. He then imputed the information into the computer.

"It will only take a moment or two, sir, to transfigure the Transfiguror."

"Great!" a nervous Neb replied. He stepped into the circular glass Transfiguror tube and, within seconds, he was gone.

***

Victoria and Bancroft Yorker were eating their breakfast at the Blue Heron Diner. Every Wednesday morning for the last fifteen years, at 8:45, they would show up for their two eggs, sunny side up, three strips of bacon, two slices of whole wheat toast, lightly buttered, two slices of fresh tomato, and coffee. Sometimes they ate alone; sometimes they were joined by their colleagues and sometimes by strangers who would soon be called friends. This morning, a couple in their mid- forties, who had been strangers three years earlier, joined them. The Yorkers treated them to breakfast.

As usual, they all enjoyed a very long, stimulating and enjoyable discussion. When they were finished, the couple thanked the Yorkers for their wonderful hospitality and their company. As they were leaving the Blue Heron Diner, they brushed by Neb. Neb looked back at the couple, thinking there was something oddly familiar about them, but he let it pass. He had more important things on his mind than recognizing a familiar face or two.

He stood in the doorway of the diner. The morning sun reflected off the glass-plated window and he lifted his hand to shield his eyes. The glow of the sunshine made Neb's entrance look spectacular. He walked slowly over to the booth were his mother and father sat. Their faces beamed as he approached the table.

"It's about time, son," his father said.

"Would you like some coffee, dear?" His mother asked calmly, as if nothing had happened. His father called to the waiter, "Another round of coffee, please."

"About time?" Neb sat opposite his parents in the booth, stone-faced.

The waiter soon returned with three cups of coffee. "So, when were you going to tell me?"

"Never," his father said, taking a sip of his coffee.

"Never? Really?"

"Nebula," his mother took him by the hand, "after we first lost you in 1910, we didn't know what to do. Our ship was in dire need of repair. We were very fortunate that, before all of the ship's power drained, we were able to locate you here in 1966. We waited patiently to catch up to you and, along the way, we fell in love with the Earth. We knew that, when we finally found you, we wanted you to have the best upbringing any Triopelian ever had. We Triopelians think we're too clever for our own good, that we know everything about everything, which is true, but to have hands-on knowledge of this world and its potential firsthand was too easy not to pass up. We wanted you to experience the Earth in all its wonderful marvels, to have you see and feel it with your own eyes and with your mind and not through any preconceived database. We knew that one day you would find out about your heritage and that, when you did, all this vast knowledge of Earth in all its glory and in all its not-so-glorious past would make you a better being. We knew that the knowledge you gained of all the worlds, races and societies you came in contact with, and will come in contact with in the future, would give you empathy that no other Triopelian has. You would be one of a kind in that respect, Nebula."

His mother smiled and, as she let go of his hand, a slight yellowish green current flowed from their fingertips.

"On our last annual visit to the Amazon back in 1984 – or ahead, you might say – we were astonished to find the ship systems all restored," Neb's father said. All this time, the ship's organic matrix was soaking in the rich Amazon environment, rejuvenating itself. When we entered the ship, it automatically read our bio scans and thought we were ready to launch out into deep space. It only forgot one thing."

"What was that?" Neb asked.

"You! Without you, the ship would not launch. It was waiting for you. We found ourselves trapped in the ship as it tried to detect you, which it did two years later but, by then, you were on your way up to Halley's. The ship then put us into cryo status and the next thing we knew, we awakened and it was 1910 all over again. A time shift had taken place. How, when and why, we have no idea. We had no choice but to wait and live it all over again, which was interesting in itself although we had to be very cautious not to change anything that would disrupt the timeline and history. So, tomorrow morning, we get to meet you again and start all over. It's been quite the adventure, Nebula." Victoria smiled.

"Tell me about it!" Neb rolled his eyes and paused. "That would explain the 1910 cosmic anomaly."

"What's that, Neb?" His father leaned in. "A cosmic anomaly, you say."

"It's a long story," Neb said. "Let's say history hit a Roman road bump."

"Roman road bump, Nebula?"

"Yeah, I kind of time travelled back to Rome of 12 BCE."

"You kind of time travelled back to 12 BCE Rome?" Bancroft asked, alarmed.

"Like I said, it's a long story," Neb responded, "but I assure you, Earth's history has stayed intact, I think."

"You think!" Neb's mother let out.

"Now, now, Mother," Neb replied, patting her hand. "Just to change the topic for a moment, and before I fill you all in on my adventure, who was that couple exiting as I came into the diner? My Triopelian spider-sense was tingling as they brushed past me."

"You mean Gene and Majel?"

"As in Gene and Majel Roddenberry?" Neb loudly replied.

"Shhh," Victoria said, popping her head up and looking around the diner.

"Yes," both Neb's parents smirked.

"What have you been telling them? Do they know who you are?"

"Firstly, no, they do not know we are Triopelian, if that is your worry, and secondly, we have been giving them encouragement and maybe a little input on creative writing. That's all, dear," Victoria replied.

"That's all! Do you know how much grief I have taken from the Council of U on this? They have actually set up a committee to get to the bottom of how a television show like *Star Trek* from an underdeveloped non-guild planet like Earth got it so right."

Neb's parents reached out and each took one of his hands, forming a Triopelian triangle. Neb could feel himself absorbing their energy and they felt his greater pulse infuse them – past, present and future entwined, the three of them living and experiencing each other's lives in a matter of seconds. As they let go their hands, a yellow greenish wisp of energy zapped from their fingertips.

"HOLY SHIT!" said Neb, "that was incredible!"

"I told you he smoked pot," Victoria said to Bancroft.

"Never mind that, dear. Our son is the assistant concierge of Halley's Casino," he said with pride. "Who would have thought? It's almost like coming full circle."

"How so, Dad?"

"When we constructed the Casino, we never thought of running it ourselves. It was a gift for the rest of the universe to enjoy in peace and unity," replied his father.

I wonder if there is something else at play here, Bancroft thought, but he kept it to himself. "Let's take a step back here for a second," Neb laughed, "I am only the assistant concierge. I really don't have any plans on being the head concierge any time soon."

"Of course not, son," Victoria said. "So ancient Rome, eh! Just think, Neb, you could go anywhere in Earth's history if you wanted to!"

"Yeah, but I think I'll settle for the present if that's OK, with both of you in it. That is, when we, or I, get back there."

"Well, we get another 20 years with you starting tomorrow. So, I think we will be fine until then."

Neb's wrist comm sounded. "Neb here. Go ahead." He held his wrist up to speak.

"Ready when you are, sir," Mot Yttep replied.

"OK. Give me a few more minutes. Neb out."

"Standing by, sir," Mot Yttep echoed.

"'Sir!' You have come a long way, Nebula," his mother and father gushed.

"Can I ask a question, Dad?"

"Sure, Neb. You know you can ask me anything."

"How many times have we done this before? You know, met here in 1966. And how many times will this happen again?"

"As far as I know, this is the first time."

"Yeah, but how would we know if this was the first time or the hundredth time? From what I have gleaned about time loops, it may be virtually impossible to distinguish one moment from the next when they occur. Unless?" Neb rubbed his chin and thought.

"Unless what?" Neb's mother asked.

"Forget about it. It's too far-fetched to even fathom."

"What, Neb? Nothing is too far-fetched. You should know that by now," Bancroft said.

"What if time itself is unaware that it is caught in a time loop?" Neb asked. "How would it know and how would it reverse the loop or stop it from ever occurring?"

"Neb," his father replied, "time cannot change itself on its own. It has to be manipulated through action and reaction, cause and effect initiated by a deliberate, controlled circumstance. For example, we have already – once, to our knowledge – picked you up at the orphanage. That is fact and we know it because we remember doing so. If we were locked in a time loop, that memory would be erased and we would have no recollection of it. But, since we know, time is not locked or looping. If time itself were unaware that it was locked in a time loop, it would only exist with a parallel conundrum and I see no evidence of that."

"A parallel conundrum?" Neb asked.

"Yes, a parallel conundrum, where not just one instance of time has changed, but all of history. Remember the *Star Trek* episode, 'Mirror, Mirror', your favourite, I believe. A parallel conundrum is something very similar, except it's contained to the planet where time has been manipulated. It's not a parallel universe but a parallel world, though if it were to extend beyond the region of its own orbit, it would and could contaminate the universe's time stream, blocking out the existing time stream and replacing it with the time stream of the planet of origin, where the parallel conundrum erupted." Bancroft concluded.

"Wow, like a virus," Neb said.

“Exactly,” said Victoria.

“Sounds like you guys have gone through this before, am I right?”

“Not really, but the possibility of it is not unthinkable, though highly improbable,” Bancroft exclaimed.

Neb's wrist comm once again sounded.

“Sorry to interrupt, sir.” It was Mot Yttep. “Transportation range window is closing in.”

“OK, got you, Mot.”

“Well, looks like I’d better go or I will be stuck here. I definitely want to continue this conversation.” Neb rose from the booth and gave his parents each a warm hug. “See you in 20 hours or in 20 years or in 20 seconds. Time is so linear, isn’t it?” With that, Neb left the diner to ensure that he would not cause a scene when he disappeared into a ball of light.

When Neb left, Bancroft and Victoria ordered more coffee.

“So, are you ready to do this all over again?” Bancroft asked, sipping his coffee.

“I wouldn’t have it any other way.” Victoria smiled.

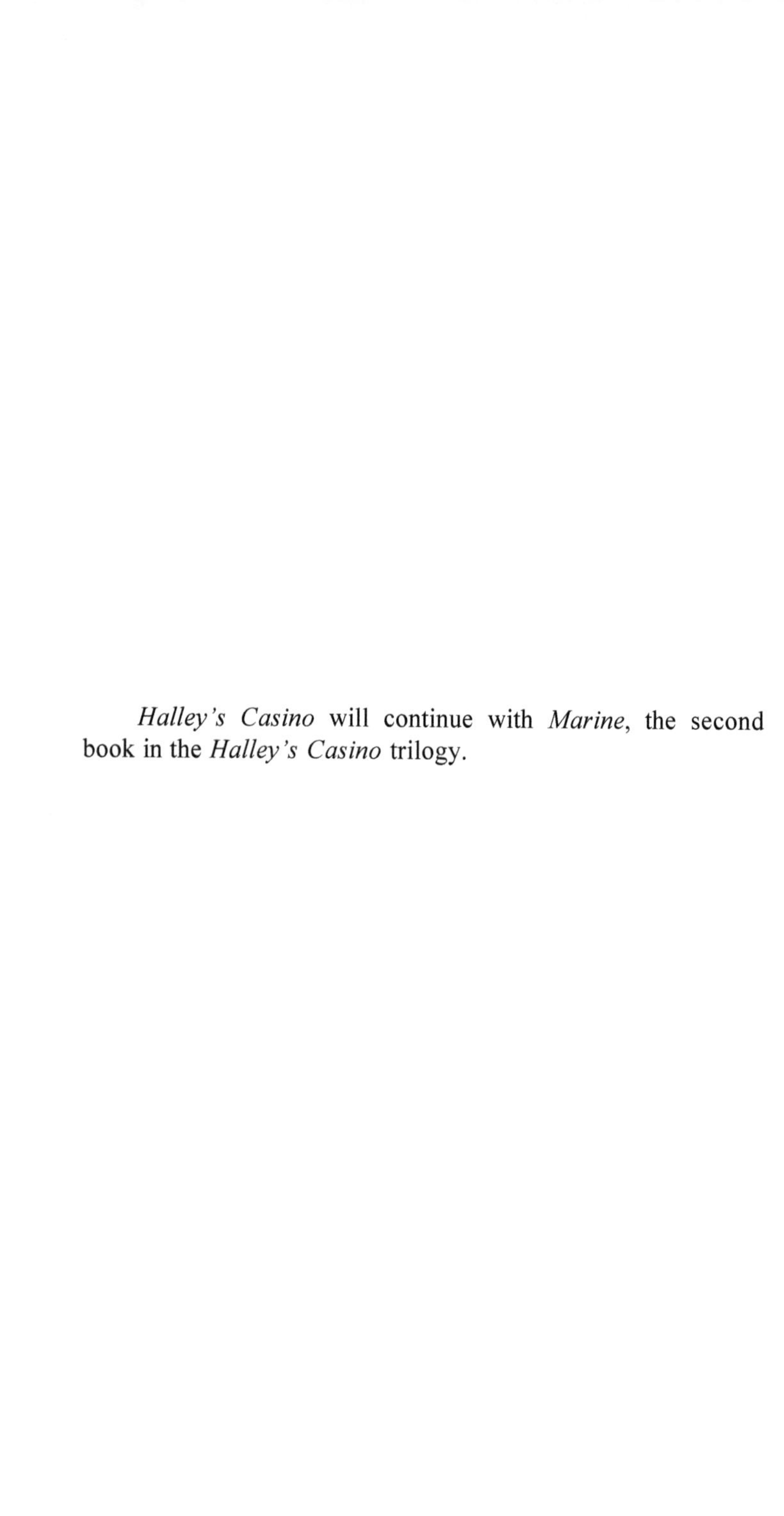

Halley's Casino will continue with *Marine*, the second book in the *Halley's Casino* trilogy.

Author's Note

This book is entirely a work of fiction. Certain historical events are here rendered, but in an entirely fictitious manner. At the same time, the real names of certain actual historical figures are used in this novel, but the characters themselves are fictional creations. In all other respects, this book is a work of fiction. Names, characters, places, dates, geographical descriptions are all either the product of the author's imagination or are used fictitiously. Any resemblance to actual persons, living or dead, or to actual events or locales is entirely coincidental.

The Wonderful Thank You List

First of all: To that which is

My Mom, Patricia Kearney Fahey. Dad: Gerald Oscar Fahey and Sister: Rosemary, we miss you both. My brothers: Bryan, Michael, William, Leo, Thomas and Kevin. Mary Taker Baskin, Lili O'Reilly and Gordon Demell, Helen Durrant, Catherine Koulik for their invaluable assistance.

To everyone at Library & Archives Canada (You know who you are.)

For music in all its forms from which I derive the most pleasure in life, from the crash of a drum to a songbird that sings...

About the Author

Mark JG Fahey is not an alien, contrary to what you may have heard, though he swears he has been to space. Mark has dabbled in various undertakings throughout his illustrious career, from on-air hosting/reporter/stand-up comic to messenger for the Prime Minister of Canada. Mark also holds a degree in Restaurant Services. His family and friends can attest to his excellent cooking skills.

Born in Ottawa, Ontario, Canada, Mark was raised and still resides in Aylmer, Quebec, Canada. *Halley's Casino* is the first book in the *Halley's Casino* trilogy.

For up-to-date information on the trilogy, find us on Twitter @jg_fahey and on Facebook www.facebook.com/*HalleysCasino*.

Website - www.markjgfahey.com

www.ingramcontent.com/pod-product-compliance
Ingram Content Group UK Ltd.
Pitfield, Milton Keynes, MK11 3LW, UK
UKHW020224250726
13967UKWH00001B/179

9 780994 891808